War on Halloween

Robbie Dorman

War on Halloween by Robbie Dorman

www.robbiedorman.com

ISBN-13: 978-1-7336388-4-5

Cover design by Bukovero

For Halloween.

1

Sarah Hamilton waited in her car. This wasn't supposed to happen. She had expected this to be a fluff piece. And now she was waiting in the dark for a shady meeting to reveal something terrible about some small-town reverend.

The park was on the outskirts of Laurel City, a small parking lot bordering a tiny swamp. She felt vulnerable in the dark, being the only car out here. She hadn't seen any traffic driving past on the highway either, but that didn't surprise her. Laurel City was quiet and buttoned up. Nobody would be coming or going this late unless they were trucking.

"I've uncovered some dirt on Laurel" were the words her informant had leaked to her. He worked at the church, but he didn't want to meet her in town. Too dangerous, he said.

When she first showed up, she wouldn't have believed in any danger. Laurel City was just a fluff piece.

Founded last century by a family of Bible thumpers, the town continued, survived, persisted until today, with the Laurels, that same family of Bible thumpers, still alive and preaching at the Laurel City Holy Church. When she had heard about the little burg and its history, she thought it'd be a quick three-day trip. She would grab some choice quotes from the family and some local yokels and then return. She'd file a piece and then move onto the next one. To get the next paycheck.

But she had found things she hadn't suspected and faced dead ends for innocuous information. None of the Laurels would talk to her. That wasn't strange, in and of itself. A lot of small-town folk didn't trust journalists, even ones who were freelancing and trying to make enough money to pay the bills this month. But she ran into the problem repeatedly, and when most people weren't willing to meet, her gut told her they were hiding something.

So she ended up staying longer than three days, though she couldn't afford it and she'd already run a credit card to the max at the cheap motel at the edge of town. She had to check out, but hopefully this would be the info that would get someone to buy the story on spec and she could afford dinner tomorrow.

Where the hell was he?

He'd said he would meet her at midnight. It was a quarter past, and still, there was nothing.

The more she dug into the history of Laurel City, and of the Laurels themselves, the less she found. For a family so integral to the founding of the town, and presumably in its ongoing leadership, she unearthed zilch in the local newspaper archives. It felt scrubbed clean. It was impossible.

And that was before she learned of the disappearances. And not just recently. Over the entire history of Laurel City, as far back as she could track, occasionally people would go missing. A farmer here, a police officer there. Sometimes she found a name, with almost no information. But for a place so small, a staggeringly high amount of folk had vanished over the years.

And so she had stuck around. And she waited. But he hadn't shown so far, and she wouldn't stay there all night. She'd give him ten more minutes.

And then she heard the noise, and her blood turned to ice.

Hrrnnnnhhhhhhhh

It was impossible.

Hrrnnnnhhhhhhhh

She looked around, hoping it was a passing truck, or maybe, just maybe, her source was here, and she had misheard the sound of his car. But no, she was still alone.

Hrrnnnnhhhhhhhh

She opened her door and got out. She slammed it behind her.

Hrrnnnnhhhhhhhh

The noise increased, and she followed it into the little swamp at the edge of town. It grew louder and louder as the ground sang under her feet, and then the smell hit her, a scent that wasn't possible, not here, not out in the middle of nowhere.

Hrrnnnnhhhhhhhh

She sat in the hospital, watching her father die. The odor

wasn't special. It smelled sterile, and sad, and fatal. Just being in the room felt oppressive, but she had to be there, because there was no one else who would stay with their dad while he died.

He mostly slept, the breathing machine pumping his lungs in and out.

Hrrnnnnhhhhhhhh
Hrrnnnnhhhhhhhh
Hrrnnnnhhhhhhhh

He'd wake up from time to time, and call for a nurse, who would bring him more painkillers, or his meal. Long enough to smile at her and then eat a few bites of something. She'd finish the food for him.

He couldn't talk anymore. He had lost his voice box last year to cancer, and he was too old and stubborn to learn sign language. When she first showed up, he had written requests for cigarettes, but she had denied him, over and over, and now he stopped asking. He still smiled at her.

But it was small solace, because he would lapse back into sleep, and the sound of the breathing machine would fill the room. No matter how many times she heard it, she couldn't get used to it. It kept her awake, on the small cot she slept on. She hated the machine, the thing that kept her father alive.

And the thought had crept into her brain. The thought of no longer waiting for her dad to die, to provide him comfort in his last few moments on Earth, even if their relationship had never been the best, even if she had resented him growing up. She had always considered herself better than that, stronger than her memories of him. She would be the only one in the family who would do the right thing and try to help this old man in his dying days.

And so the thought had crept into her mind, of not waiting for him to die, but *hoping* he would die. Praying he would pass soon, just to stop the awful noise from that horrible machine.

Hrrnnnnhhhhhhhh

The sound was impossible. She knew it was, and she pushed the memory away, forced herself back to the surface, even as her toes got wet from the swamp. She opened her eyes, and then she saw something. Something impossible.

But it was real, she realized quickly. But it was too late.

It was impossible, and it killed her before she could give it a name.

2

"Dad, look at the guts on this one!"

Mike Dawson stopped examining the severed hands to see what Marion was talking about. She stood near a large display in the Spooky Halloween store. Corpses and torsos and larger props hung in the corner. She stared at one with wonder. Mike wheeled his shopping cart over to her. Mike was just under six feet tall, dressed in jeans and a t-shirt. He considered it a second uniform. He pulled off his cap to ruffle his short brown hair before replacing it.

"This is new," she said. She held a tendril of rubber intestine in her hand, rubbing it between her fingers. She belonged in the store. Her dark clothes and long black hair didn't hurt the illusion either. She loved Halloween, just like him.

"What are you doing?" asked Mike, half laughing.

"I wanted to see if it felt real," she said.

"You know what real intestines feel like?" he asked. "I thought I knew my daughter."

"If you really knew me, you'd obviously know that the answer is yes," she said. "We need to get this."

The coil of intestines hung from a disembodied head, its spine and all its guts dangling out of it.

"It does look good," he said. "Where do you think it would go?"

"Right out front," she said. "We could hang it from the tree. Back light it at night."

"Hmm," he said. He looked at the price tag. "Oof. That's a spicy meatball."

"Come on, Dad," she said. "Halloween only comes once a year. It's an investment in our future."

"If you're going to twist my arm," he said, and grabbed one of the bundles that hung nearby, plopping it on top of a cart filled with other props.

"Gross," said Daniel, walking up to join them. Daniel was tall, taller than Mike even, and wore blue shorts and a plain white tee. His dirty blond hair was cropped close. He did not belong in Spooky.

"I know, it's great," said Marion. "It will look awesome."

"Wait, you're buying that?" he asked. "I'm going to see it every day for a month?"

"Your sister has excellent taste. It'll be a a perfect centerpiece for the front lawn," said Mike.

"I'm sure all the neighbors will love it too, Dad," said Daniel. "How much longer are we going to be?"

"I don't know," said Mike. "We still need some accents

enjoyed some of them. He had to force himself not to buy any. He needed to focus on the decorations.

They had always decorated their house in Plinkett, and it had gotten a bunch of attention before everything went to shit. The Dawson Halloween party had always been the biggest in town, among the adults at least. He regularly drew a lot of trick or treaters, who wanted the whole candy bars he gave out with abandon.

Would they have a party this year? He wasn't sure. They didn't know anyone in town, and it wouldn't be much of a party with just him and Marion. Daniel had never enjoyed Halloween as much as they both did. He had only resented it more as he grew up. Marion had always loved the holiday, had enjoyed splattering the walls with fake blood even as a little kid. As she entered her teens, she was just as obsessed as Mike was. Daniel resented that connection, Mike knew, but there wasn't much he could do about it. He had tried to connect with Daniel, but they just didn't share many hobbies.

Maybe somebody at the office would have a party. He would find one, come hell or high water. Even if he didn't, he'd make a costume, and wear it for the trick or treaters. What would it be? He didn't know yet, but he had some ideas. He still had a little bit of time. He'd let the ideas simmer in his mind, and the winner would rise to the top.

"Dad! They have a giant inflatable Audrey II from Little Shop of Horrors," she said. "It looks awesome."

She walked him over to it. It loomed over them both.

"It doesn't really go with our theme," said Mike.

"But—"

"I know, it looks great," he said. "But do you want the

head with the guts hanging off, or Audrey II?"

"I—"

"Marion?"

"The head with guts hanging off," she said finally.

"I think we have what we need," he said, looking over their cart.

"We need more skeletons," she said.

"We have five," he said. "That's enough. We can take stock after we've decorated and come back if we need to."

"I guess you're right," she said. "But remember I told you so after we're down a few skeletons."

"We should check out and find your brother," he said. "We have a long drive home."

"Why doesn't Laurel City have a Halloween store? Seems like it should."

"I don't know," said Mike. "Might be they just don't have an empty storefront big enough."

*

Mike sensed it as they decorated their front yard. Their neighborhood in Laurel City wasn't that much different from their old one, in Plinkett. Mostly single-family homes on medium-sized lots. Laurel City wasn't a huge town, just large enough to demand a mall and a few department stores like Walmart and Target. Their house was no different from most of the houses on the street. A few decades old, with a little bit of renovation done over the years. The previous owner had added a room to the back and had enclosed the lanai before selling it. He had noticed some curious neighbors when they moved in a couple of weeks ago. As a cop, he had developed a sixth sense when someone was watching him. He had dismissed it then as simple curiosity. None of them had introduced themselves and he assumed it would happen with time. But they watched again as he and Marion decorated. He felt them judging him. Cars hesitated as they drove past. He saw curtains part and eyes peer out at them from neighboring homes.

"Does this look good, Dad?" asked Marion, balanced on a ladder as she attached the head to the lowest branch, about eight feet off the ground. The spinal column, ribs, and guts hung below it, right at eye level.

"Perfect," he said. He had laid out the cemetery below the guts, a spin on the famous tombstones from The Haunted Mansion ride at Disney World. Each had a punny name on it. Some of the markers were worn, or cast askew. They had used these props for years now, and they were a Halloween institution for them. Every year they would rotate decorations around the cemetery. This year the head and guts would hang above them, and they would use chicken wire to pose their skeletons on the roof.

"Excuse me," said a voice from behind him. Mike turned to see a nebbish looking man, short and thin, wearing a polo shirt and wire-framed glasses. He extended his hand. "I'm Tim Blanton. I live across the street."

"Hi Tim," said Mike. "Mike. This is my daughter Marion. Nice to meet you." Tim's hand was a little clammy. Mike sensed a nervousness in him. Tim struggled to meet his eyes.

"Nice to meet you as well," he said. "We saw you moved in a few weeks ago. Sorry it's taken so long for me to introduce myself. And under these circumstances."

Circumstances? What circumstances?

"What do you mean?" asked Mike. He towered over Tim. Mike didn't consider himself in shape, and the perpetual spare tire around his waist didn't disagree, but the muscles he had built in high school had hung around, weathered by the occasional scrape on the job. He could be intimidating if he wanted to be.

"I mean—we—we noticed your decorations," said Tim.

"Yeah," said Mike. "What about them? Halloween is a month away. Feels like it's the perfect time to decorate. Is there some sort of homeowner's association that Bernie didn't mention?"

"Oh no, nothing like that," said Tim. "I mean, you're new in town, so I guess we shouldn't expect you to know everything right away. I wanted to tell you, before it got ugly."

"Tell me what, Tim?" asked Mike. Marion watched them, still up in the tree.

"Um—Laurel City—you see, is a Christian town," said Tim.

"And?" asked Mike. "I'm Christian."

"Oh—well—" said Tim, leaning in toward him. "However you worshiped before—you should realize."

Mike leaned in reflexively. Tim whispered to him.

"We don't celebrate Halloween in Laurel City."

3

Daniel didn't feel anxious on his first day at a new school. Instead, he felt nothing.

Plinkett hadn't been perfect, but he had liked it there. He had enjoyed his school, and his friends. He had one more year. Just one more year. He could have graduated with his friends. He could have finished off his high school career with *his* football team. But instead Dad had taken them out of state, because of work. Because of trouble he had started. He hadn't stopped to think of them. Marion had put on a brave face for him, but she was scared to death inside. He knew it. And he was here, having to finish high school, not knowing anyone.

Daniel felt eyes on him as he walked from class to class, sitting in rooms full of people who had spent years together at this point. He had gotten used to it. He had always been big. His baby fat stuck with him through elementary school, into middle school. He was always hungry, and his weight ballooned through puberty, and as he grew up, he grew out.

It changed his freshman year in Plinkett. They all went to the extracurricular fair, to try to figure out what their electives would be. He didn't want to do anything. But Coach Wayne yelled at him from the football table, called him over. Told him he could use a kid like him. That he could harden him up. Make him something.

And over a year or two, he did. Daniel got bigger and lost his baby fat. He would never be lean, not in his entire life, but he wasn't soft anymore. His back, his chest, his hips all became iron, and Coach put him on the offensive line, where he moved other guys around. He enjoyed being on the team. Of having a group he belonged in. Where he was valued. Where he was *known*.

Here, he was just a big stranger.

Classes washed over him. He had already fulfilled most of his difficult requirements at Plinkett, and the Laurel City High guidance counselor had taken pity on him and transferred all his credits over without issue.

Weightlifting was the one class he was looking forward to. He hadn't lifted at all during the long summer. He had been exiled from the high school weight room after what happened with Dad, and he missed it. He had used some dumbbells at home, but it wasn't the same as a bench, or a squat rack. The iron bars and plates comforted him. He couldn't explain it. Maybe it was just how simple they were.

Still, the anxiety that had been absent earlier was there now as he walked into the weight room, at the far end of campus, near the track and football field. It was nice inside, with newer equipment, the markings on the plates still legible. Any label on the weights at Plinkett had worn off, and they had constantly fought the onset of rust. The bars had been falling apart, the caps unscrewing at the merest touch. These looked new. The weight room wasn't full, maybe only a dozen other boys there, and a couple girls. A few of the guys already worked out, spotting each other. He hadn't been sure if they'd work out on the first day, but he'd brought his workout clothes with him just in case. He was glad he had.

Coach Hillman went over the syllabus, which was nothing much. Turns out everyone but him had been in this class last year as well. Almost no one opted for it as an elective unless they were an athlete.

"Dawson," Coach said. "Have you lifted before? Looks like you have."

"Yes, sir," said Daniel, talking to him like he talked to every coach, the cadence right there.

"Then I won't go over the safety crap, except to say to use a spotter. You all know what you're doing. Get to work." Coach disappeared into his office.

I guess that's it.

Everyone quickly found their stations and started working. Daniel was the odd man out, so he grabbed some dumbbells and exercised his arms. He didn't need a spotter for that. Some butt rock played over the speakers in the room a moment later. Chatter came from the other kids there, as they taunted and encouraged each other. The two girls worked together, and the boys formed loose pairs. All of them were big, but none as big as him, and he could feel their eyes glance to him once in a while. Daniel said nothing. He concentrated on his reps.

It felt good to work out again. The cold iron warmed between his fingers, and the familiar ache as his muscles grew taut. He had missed this. The thoughts of Plinkett and their exit from the town disappeared. Daniel counted to ten with one arm and then switched to the other. The burn in his arms took his mind off of everything. The music and the chatter vanished, and soon it was just him and the weights. He worked.

"Take it, take it!" yelled a voice near him, and it brought him back to reality.

"I'm trying, I'm trying!" yelled another. It came from two boys, occupying the bench nearest to him. One laid on the bench, a bar on his chest. A quick glance told Daniel there was over three hundred pounds on it. Heavy weight for most high schoolers. The boy tried to push it, but was failing. The spotter couldn't handle the load, his fingers between the bar and boy's chest. The cords in his arms and neck stood out as he strained, but he was smaller than the lifter, and didn't have the strength.

Daniel didn't think, he just acted. He dropped the dumbbell with a thud to the ground and moved to help. He stood beside the spotter, and climbed up on the bench, one foot on the elevated spotter's platform and one higher on the bench itself, to give him as much leverage as possible. He forced his hands under the bar and pulled up. It was a lot of weight, but Daniel was strong. It inched up and Daniel gained leverage, and he yanked it up to the set of safety racks, where it clanged and stopped.

His heart thudded inside his chest. Daniel had used

muscles that had idled for a few months, but he was glad that the strength was still there. The boy who laid on the bench breathed hard for a moment and then sat up, his hands on his knees.

"What was that?" he asked, looking at his original spotter.

"I thought I could get it," he said. "I guess—"

"I guess you were wrong," he said, with a dark glance. He looked to Daniel. "I'm lucky I didn't have to rely only on you. Dawson, right?"

"Daniel," he said. "Are you okay?"

He smiled wide, showing two rows of white teeth. "I'm good. I was trying to max out for the beginning of the year. Guess I'll have to set my sights a bit lower." He stood up and extended a hand. "Isaac."

Daniel took his hand and shook it. His grip was firm.

"Nice to meet you," said Daniel.

"Are you new?" he asked.

"Yeah," said Daniel. "First day."

"That explains a lot," said Isaac. "We could use you on the football team."

"I wasn't sure about playing this year," said Daniel. He hadn't even really considered it. He had loved playing at Plinkett, but after everything—he didn't want to go through the whole process again for a new team, for only a year.

"Are you kidding me?" asked Isaac. "A guy your size? You've played before, right? What position?"

"Offensive line. Tackle," said Daniel.

"That's exactly what we need," said Isaac, grinning. "Running behind you, no one could stop me."

"You're a back?" asked Daniel.

"Yeah," he said. "Starter."

"Wow," said Daniel. "I didn't realize."

"You should talk to Coach Holland. I can put in a good word for you. We need a big body on the line. We have practice after school—"

"I have to drive my sister home," said Daniel, even as he felt a kernel of hope inside his heart again. He could get on the team. He could get on the team.

"I'm sure she can find another way home," said Isaac. "Right?"

Isaac stared at him with hopeful eyes, silence hanging between them. Daniel could feel his chance hanging right alongside it.

"I'm sure," said Daniel.

"Great!" said Isaac. "Coach will take one look at you and go bonkers. I was about to start my set. Will you spot me?"

"Hey, man," said the other boy. "What about—"

"I think I trust Daniel more at this point, Ted," said Isaac, not making eye contact. He didn't say anything else, and Ted lingered there for a moment, and gave a quick glance to both of them, his face red. He backed away and moved to a bench of his own.

"I'd rather have someone who can handle the heavy weight," said Isaac to Daniel, his voice loud. There was no way Ted didn't hear it. Daniel smiled, but a glance at Ted told him that Ted had heard it. He looked deflated. Daniel felt a twinge of uncertainty. But he couldn't be some judge of friendships. Isaac wanted him, and he had accepted.

He needed friends.

*

"Good God in Heaven, look at the size of you," said Coach Holland.

"I told you, Coach," said Isaac.

Daniel stood in the coach's office, in the field house, next to the other offices and the locker room. It was new and beautiful, just like the weight room, which was next door. He had come over right after his last class ended. He could talk to them and then get back to Marion. He felt his phone buzz in his pocket on the walk over.

Where are you?

He didn't answer. This would only take a minute. She wouldn't understand.

"You weren't lying, Isaac," said Coach. "You said you played. For who?"

"Plinkett," said Daniel. "In Indiana."

"Haven't heard of them," said Coach.

"We weren't very good," said Daniel. "Our quarterback set the state record for interceptions in a season."

"They had you and they were passing?" asked Coach. "Don't answer that. But we aren't a passing heavy offense. Isaac here is our moneymaker, and if we add you to the line, man, we'll kill 'em out there. We need to get you some gear."

"I—I still don't know if I'm playing," said Daniel, stumbling over his words.

"Are you kidding me?" asked Coach. "You gotta play. We need you out there."

"Come on man," said Isaac. "I thought we were friends."

Daniel felt their eyes on him, and he felt the tension in his guts build. He needed to drive Marion home. She was probably waiting for him now. She had never liked taking the bus, had hated it in Plinkett, and that's when she knew people.

That's not your fault. You didn't force her to move here. Dad did.

"Alright," said Daniel, and the tension dissipated.

"Let's find you some gear, and get you to Coach Andrews. He's our line coach. He'll see what you can do."

"Don't worry about the fees or anything," said Isaac. "The Church will take care of it. Right, Coach?"

"Of course," he said. "They always support us."

"See you on the field," said Isaac, who left for the locker room.

He followed Coach Holland to the equipment room, and they got him gear. As he changed, his phone buzzed again, Marion's name popping up on the screen, calling him.

He didn't answer. He had friends now. He needed to belong.

4

Laurel City High School loomed over Marion. It stood only two stories tall, but it felt taller, a beige brick dragon that snorted and wheeled above her.

When Dad told her they were moving, she had taken the news in stride. His experience in Plinkett had nearly destroyed him. She understood why they moved, and she could rationalize it.

But she had pushed off facing what it meant. She had said her goodbyes to her few friends there. Most had abandoned her after the news about her dad broke. No great loss. But just because she only had a couple allies left to miss didn't mean moving was easy.

Marion had put off that worry for months, as they planned the move, packed, drove, and unpacked. Even as they shopped for Halloween decorations and worked on the house, she hadn't thought about going back to school. The summer had more juice in it. She could spend time with her dad and push off the inevitable return to school. The anxiety waited for her, and it had built over the last few days, as the ending of her last weekend before her return got closer and closer.

It built as she worked on Halloween decorations. It built as she arranged her belongings in her room, and it built as she played a video game, to get her mind off of things.

As she got ready that morning, it grew and grew inside her. She forced it aside, but there was no avoiding it now, the dragon looming over her.

Marion had tamed that beast already at her last school. She had broken it in, like a good pair of jeans, and she knew its secrets and habits, but this was an alien world, and she was an astronaut.

Daniel had driven them both in his old truck. She didn't have a car yet. He had worked for his, and she was glad he had it. Riding the bus would have been another layer of anxiety she didn't want.

"I'll wait out here after school," he said, and then he was gone, striding inside. For all his complaining about a new school, he went in without hesitation. A jealousy quickly rose and then disappeared again, eaten by the mass of anxiety.

Kids walked by her, flowing into the entrance of the school, moving to the other buildings that orbited the main one. She took a deep breath and walked inside before her cowardice tried to keep her outside forever.

They don't notice you. You're just another kid to them.

Marion felt their eyes on her just the same. She was a new kid, an experience she hadn't had. Even in Plinkett, she had known all her fellow freshmen. Here, as a sophomore, she knew no one, and she felt it.

Get to class and everything will take care of itself.

Marion realized she didn't know where her first class was. She had looked at the map of the school online, and had rehearsed her route mentally, but it had vacated her mind, along with all her courage. She stopped, and after a few other kids brushed past her, she ducked to the side, taking off her heavy backpack. After a minute of digging, she found the paper copy of the map she had printed out just in case. She was glad she had.

"Looks like you dropped something," said a loud voice, from across the hallway. She looked up, thinking he was talking to her, a snap self-conscious glance of her head. But it wasn't directed at her.

It came from a boy, tall and broad shouldered, his blond hair almost invisible from being cut so close to his head. He was conventionally attractive. She could recognize it. He was *big*. He loomed over everyone and his plain white t-shirt hugged his shoulders and arms. A small group of boys hovered in his orbit, all smaller than him. But he wasn't talking to them. She couldn't see who, the boy's size hiding them. Marion looked harder, craning her head.

She saw her then. The girl stood against the lockers, her big brown eyes looking down, her whole body bent, cradled against itself. Her deep chestnut hair highlighted her round face, soft and pale. She wore a black Misfits shirt and simple blue jeans that hugged her hips. She was cute, or she would be, under normal circumstances. Right now, she looked shy, nervous. As the moment stretched on, Marion realized she didn't look nervous. This girl wasn't timid.

She was afraid. She was terrified.

The girl bent down to pick up what the boy was talking about, a beat up notebook, the cover scratched and worn. She never once looked up to him, or any of the boys that flanked him and surrounded her. She picked up the journal and one of the surrounding boys quickly swiped, knocking it out of her hands and down to the ground. The girl flinched, still not making eye contact.

"Looks like you dropped something," said the large boy again. Marion could hear the smile on his face. "You should be more careful."

The girl froze.

"Are you going to pick it up or not?" asked the boy. "You shouldn't leave garbage on the floor."

Marion couldn't stop herself then. She didn't know anyone here, knew nothing about Laurel City or Laurel City High. But maybe that was what compelled her. She had nothing to lose. And the girl was cute.

"Hey asshole, I see you," she yelled. "Fuck off."

The world froze in that moment. The kids flowing by all stopped and stared, everything quiet. The large boy turned and looked at her, his face not full of anger, but of confusion. As if he had never been challenged before, not once in his entire life. His face contorted in this unfamiliar feeling. The boys flanking him turned as one, all four of them. They all stared at her.

"Who are you?" he asked, words finding their way to his mouth.

"I'm a witch," she said. She shouldered her backpack

and walked directly at him, with the darkest look she could summon on her face.

The fear that replaced the confusion on his face secretly delighted her, but she maintained the death stare as she looked not at him, but through him. He was double her size, but he backpedaled out of the way, moving into one of his cohorts, knocking him backwards. Marion bent down and grabbed the notebook, handing it to the girl, and in one swift movement, slid her arm through the arm of the girl.

"Do it again and I'll curse you all," she said, full of the confidence and courage which had vanished earlier. She let her eyes bore into the boy for a pregnant pause, and then turned, pulling the girl with her.

"Keep walking, and don't look back," said Marion quietly, after they were a few steps away. She could feel the girl's stare, but Marion looked ahead, moving briskly, leaving the group of boys behind, even as they stared at the girls as they pushed farther into the school.

"I'm Marion," she said.

"Hi, I'm—I'm Cara," said the girl, her voice warm. "That was incredible. How did you do that?"

"I-I don't know. Do you know where Mrs. Backstrom's room is?"

*

Cara showed her to Mrs. Backstrom's room and then left with a harried smile, and Marion's stomach fluttered. Mrs. Backstrom's class passed quickly, taken up with talking about syllabi and behavior. Marion tried to earmark anyone who could be a friend, but the simmering anxiety had returned. She had forgotten the foreboding witch that had briefly possessed her. No one seemed an ally here, and she found her next class by herself, her memories of the school's hallways flooding back into her mind.

Her first few classes flew by. She stayed quiet, noticing only a few people who would fit in a theoretical circle of friends. The anxiety that had loomed large that morning was still there, but Marion had fought it back. The monotony and boredom of high school helped.

Then it was time for lunch, and it surged to the surface again. In Plinkett, Marion had a group to sit with, consistent and reliable, at least until near the end, before the trouble. She sailed unknown waters as she stood in line, sandwiched between two groups of friends to buy cardboard pizza and chocolate milk.

She held her tray, and stared out into the sea of students, all finding their acquaintances, working out where they would sit for the entire semester. The look of acknowledgment, the smiles as friendships forged in freshman year or earlier paid dividends in a place to belong for the twenty-five minutes of lunch.

Marion looked for a seat to land, any isolated table where she could sit by herself, just to get her bearings, anything to ease the worry inside her. Just a chair to sit in and eat without worrying about belonging. Then she heard her name.

"Marion!" a warm voice yelled. She looked toward it, and saw the big smile of Cara, waving at her from a table a few down from the end of the cafeteria. Cara waved, beckoning her over. All the worry eating her alive inside dissipated in a flood, sluicing through the floor, and she hurried over to where Cara sat, sitting across from her.

"Hi," said Marion.

"Hi," said Cara. "I didn't know we had the same lunch schedule."

"I didn't either," said Marion. "I'm glad we do. I don't know anyone else." She sat across from Cara and she felt at home.

"I don't think any of my friends have this lunch," said Cara. "Not that you're not my friend. But you know—my friends from before. Sorry—"

"No, it's okay," said Marion. She smiled.

"Are you a new student?" asked Cara. "Did you go to Libertine?"

"Libertine?"

"It's a private school," said Cara. "Run by the church. Only goes to middle school, though, so students get dumped here after eighth grade. But I guess you didn't go there."

"No," said Marion. "We just moved here."

"You moved *to* Laurel City?" asked Cara. "Why?"

"My dad's job," said Marion. "There was a big mess where we used to live, so we moved here. Should we not have?"

"I mean, no, it's not—" said Cara, struggling, "I guess I've just lived here for my entire life, so it doesn't seem so great. Thank you, by the way."

"For what?" asked Marion.

"This morning," said Cara. "I never said thank you."

"We had to get to class," said Marion. "It happened very fast."

"But still," said Cara. "If you hadn't been there…"

The pause hung in the air. What would have happened?

"Who was that asshole?" asked Marion.

"Oh, Christ, that's right, you're new. You don't know,"

said Cara. Her voice went a little quiet, and her eyes surveyed their immediate area, and then the lunchroom as a whole. Apparently satisfied, her big eyes returned to Marion.

"Know what?" asked Marion.

"You don't know about Isaac," said Cara. "The big guy is Isaac. The *asshole* is Isaac."

"Is he always like that?" asked Marion.

"Not always," said Cara. "Only when he thinks he can get away with it. Which is still pretty often."

"Is he popular?" asked Marion. "Does he play football or something?"

"Yes," said Cara. "I mean, look at him. He's good at it. I don't go to games, but he's the running back. They made it to the playoffs last year."

Marion hadn't hated the sports teams at her old school, even if she didn't watch or cheer for them. Some of her friends did, but she mostly considered them harmless. They emboldened the occasional jock asshole, but she had no problems with them in Plinkett. All their teams were terrible, which might have had something to do with it. But it helped explain his behavior.

"He's the star, so he's an asshole?" asked Marion. "And I assume all of those friends are on the team too?"

"Actually, no," said Cara. "I don't think any of them are."

"Then who are they?" asked Marion.

"They're all part of the LYE," said Cara.

"The what? The lie?" asked Marion.

"Oh, god," said Cara. "I'm such an idiot." Cara's palm went to her face.

Marion felt lost.

"The el why ee," said Cara, spelling it out. "The Laurel Youth Experience. The youth church group."

"They're part of the church group?" asked Marion.

"Isaac is Isaac *Laurel*," said Cara.

"Isaac Laurel?" asked Marion, before it spun around in her mind. "Laurel? As in Laurel City?"

"As in Laurel City. As in the Laurel City Holy Church," said Cara. "As in Laurel City High School. He walks around like he owns the place. Because he sort of does."

*

Marion waited by the parking lot after her last class. All the kids who drove walked by, meandering to their cars, most leaving as soon as they could.

The minutes crawled by and Daniel didn't appear. She texted, and there was no answer.

What the hell?

A half hour passed, and he still wasn't there. The buses had all left by this point. She was tired, and she just wanted to go home and relax. She called him, but it went to voicemail. Soon, only a few cars remained in the parking lot.

Where the fuck are you, Daniel?

She didn't know Dad's schedule, but she needed a ride. She called him.

Forty-five minutes later he showed up.

"Still nothing?" he asked.

"No," said Marion.

"And he didn't say anything?"

"No," she said. "Not a word about anything after school. It was our first day. What could he have to do?"

5

"Do we usually get calls for this?"

"No, but the fire department is busy at the burger place on 4th. It's up to us," said Janine. Janine was Mike's partner. They had only worked together a few days now, and she was still a little cold with him. He didn't blame her. Mike was sure his reputation had preceded him. He'd have to work to earn her trust.

Mike sighed. "This isn't a joke, right? I mean, I knew Laurel City was pretty calm, but this—this seems like I'm getting trolled."

They stood in a residential neighborhood, a few miles from the main drag. It looked like perfect suburbia. White picket fences. They were next to a tree. An orange kitten stared down at them from three branches up, softly meowing once in a while. It didn't seem afraid.

"It's just one of our many official duties. And if dispatch is trolling us, they'll have to answer to me," she said with a straight face. Mike definitely didn't want to be on the wrong side of Janine. She was tall, with bronze skin, and dark curly hair, pulled back tightly. If it was a joke, she was taking it seriously.

"You'll get her down, right?" asked Laura, her cheeks still wet from her tears. She stood to the side, no older than four or five. It was *her* kitten. Her mother peeked out from behind the curtains inside the house. They had borrowed a ladder from her garage, the top platform as high as the first set of branches.

"Of course, dear," he said. "You should move back just a little bit. I don't want you getting hurt."

"Yes, sir," she said, and she backed up, taking big, dramatic steps until she was ten feet away.

"I can't go up there, Janine," he said. "I'm afraid of heights. I can barely climb on my own roof."

"You have to," she said. "I'm allergic to cats. Real bad. I puff up like a balloon. You don't happen to have an Epipen with you?"

"Fuck," he said, under his breath. "Could we just wait it out for the fire department?"

"Could be hours."

"Jesus," he said. He looked up to the cat. It peered down, rubbing its ears against the bark of the tree, oblivious to the fact it was thirty feet off the ground. The backs of his knees ached at the thought of being up so high. He could manage decorating his roof, but even that made his heart race faster than he was comfortable.

He looked over at Laura again, and she only stared up at the cat. Her small hands were clasped together, and her lips moved. He realized she was praying. *Oh Goddamnit.*

Mike unbuckled his belt and holster and laid it on the hood of their patrol car. He wanted as little extra weight as possible. He limbered up, doing some quick squats and rolling his shoulders. He sneaked a glance at Janine, and she quickly hid a smirk.

"You enjoying yourself?" he asked.

"What do you mean?" she asked with a straight face. *They're fucking trolling me. I'm literally rescuing a goddamn kitten.*

"Could you at least hold the ladder?" he asked, putting a foot up on it, testing its stability. It shook slightly, just enough for the pit of anxiety in his stomach to deepen into a well.

"Of course," she said, and grabbed it. "Holding it steady."

He climbed, one foot after the other, not looking down. He looked at the first row of branches as they got closer and closer. He slowly scaled the ladder, one step at a time. The gigantic oak dominated the yard, hanging over the street, the power and telephone lines strung through carefully pruned leaves and twigs.

Fuck fuck fuck. Mike had reached the top and climbing out onto the lowest branch was his first order of business. He always hated that moment of uncertainty, when his body wasn't firmly planted on either the ladder or the thing he was moving to. He took a deep breath and stepped over. His hands grabbed the wood above. The steps wiggled as he left them and he hurriedly hugged the trunk of the tree.

"You doing okay?" asked Janine.

"Great," he said. "Doing great."

At least he was off the ladder. He looked up. The kitten stared down at him with big eyes. It stood another fifteen feet above him, a few sets of branches jutting out between him and it. Mike didn't look down and he climbed, moving branch to branch. They were tightly clustered, and all were stable. He would be fine. Just get to the cat and climb down. He thought of little Laura praying below him, and it helped push the fear from his mind. Troll or not, he would rescue this damn kitten.

The wind blew through the tree, and the branches shook around him. He froze, and the fear he had worked so hard to dispel returned. *Move, you idiot.* He couldn't stay up there forever. The kitten mewed again, and the noise was close. Only a few more steps and he could reach it. He climbed up, twisting his body through the more closely packed wood farther up in the tree. One more step up, and the cat would be there, and he could grab it. He would button it up inside his shirt, and then he could climb down. Onto the nice firm ground.

He took the step up, the smaller branch flexing slightly, his knees aching as his feet moved. He pushed it aside and searched for the kitten. It should be easy to spot a little puff of orange amidst the brown and green of the tree. But it wasn't there. It mewed again. He followed the sound and realized it had crawled out farther away, nearer the edge.

Mike looked down to see his footing and immediately regretted it. The ground seemed a million miles below him. He refocused his eyes on the wood and saw he could move out a little more before he reckoned it would be too thin to bear his weight. He nudged himself outward, inch by inch, the kitten sitting and staring at him. It wasn't moving anymore, maybe also sensing it had reached the limits of the branch it sat on.

Mike edged closer, and the cat hissed, baring its tiny teeth.

"It's okay, little kitten," he said. "Don't you worry. We'll get you down from here."

It hissed again, and yowled, the noise seeming strange from such a small body. It wasn't happy on his intrusion into its adventure.

"Alright, you don't want to go down," he said. "I'm sorry to say, it doesn't really matter. We're going down together."

Slowly, I hope. He edged out, the cat almost in his grasp. It hissed and yowled as he got closer, but it didn't move. He inched out carefully, the branch beginning to bow beneath him, and he was within range, and he grabbed the kitten with a free hand, taking it by the scruff of the neck. It cried even louder, but he held on until he could back up to the relative stability of the trunk. Now to just slide it into his shirt—

Mike opened his collar, and as he moved the animal, it squirmed in his grasp, swung around and sunk its claws into his forearm, all four sets dug in tight. It didn't want to leave his arm.

"Fuck!" he yelled. "Goddamnit!" He hoped the kid couldn't hear him.

"You okay up there?" he heard Janine yell.

"I've got the cat!" he yelled down through gritted teeth. The little monster held on tight. He grabbed it with his palm, to help relieve some pressure, but he couldn't pry it off up here. He could live with the pain until he got safely on the ground. Now just to climb down with one hand.

The ache of the cat's claws somehow helped, because the fear of looking down wasn't nearly as bad going down as it was going up. Maybe because he was getting closer to the ground. The creature's claws didn't ease up, and he let his legs carry him down, as the branches got thicker and he felt safer standing on them. He reached the ladder, and found Janine waiting on it, her arms out to take the cat. She wore gloves. *Of course. They had gloves.*

She pulled the kitten loose from the skin of his forearm and he breathed in with pain as a couple of claws snagged on him. He felt the blood trickle down his arm. She took the cat, climbing down and handing it to the small girl, who retreated inside. Mike waited until she came back to the ladder so she could hold it as he climbed down. His knees ached again as he reached the top step, but then he was on it, off the tree, and on the ground.

"We usually try to curse a little less when there are kids around," said Janine, not trying to hide her smirk anymore.

"That's easy for you to say, you didn't have a couple dozen needles dug into your arm," said Mike, grabbing the first aid kit from the trunk and wiping his arm down. "I didn't even get a thank you. Also convenient that you remembered the gloves after I've already climbed up."

"Hey, you're the new guy," she said. "It's only fair you climb the tree."

*

"I see it only took me to be in extreme pain to crack your hard-ass exterior," said Mike. It was early afternoon, and they drove, on patrol duty.

Janine sat behind the wheel. She side-eyed him. "It was pretty funny, that tiny orange puff-ball stuck to your arm."

"I could have fallen," he said. "How would you have felt then?"

"Maybe a little guilty for laughing," she said. "And my hard-ass exterior is well earned, alright? Dudes got it easy. They're allowed to have a sense of humor. They can still be Dirty Harry when they gotta be. I can't."

"I understand," he said. "I'm totally cool with you being Dirty Harry. I just wasn't sure if my reputation had preceded me."

"Your reputation?" she asked.

"Yeah, all the shit that went down at my last gig."

"What happened at your last gig?"

"I thought you knew," he said. "I thought everyone knew. Figured the chief would fill everyone in."

"Well he didn't," she said. Silence filled the air. "So? Spill. You think I'm going to let that mystery just sit there?"

"Fine. I worked in Indiana, in a town called Plinkett. It wasn't big, but there was a huge problem with opiate addiction. We had a disproportionately high number of overdoses."

"We've mostly dodged that bullet," said Janine. "I don't know how. We're lucky."

"It was terrible," he said. "It was constant. All the time. We started carrying overdose kits with us, just to bring people back. It's—it's haunting, seeing these people dead, and then bringing them back. It was exhausting. Constantly dancing on the edge of a legion of folks living or dying, and them not caring which way they went."

"So what's the story? Why the reputation?"

"We kept trying to curtail the problem, but it wouldn't go away. We couldn't find out where the pills were coming from. It shouldn't be that hard, but we always ran into dead ends. Everyone else became apathetic toward it. I dug. And I found out why everybody was ignoring the issue."

"Why?"

"Because the chief was getting a kickback from the main pill mill in the area. And it got passed down to everyone else. Except for me, and a few others. I phoned the papers and leaked the information. Everything got taken apart, me included. Like I said, It wasn't a big town. All my friends were on the force. Well, they *were* my friends. I had called in anonymously, but it wasn't long before everyone knew I had blown the whistle."

"You shouldn't be ashamed of that," said Janine. "You did the right thing."

"It doesn't always feel like it," said Mike. "It cost me friendships. We had to move. I had to uproot the kids. I can't imagine it was easy on them either. A lot of apple carts got turned over, and everyone knew it was Mike Dawson that caused it. I was worried, coming in, that people wouldn't trust me."

"I can't speak for everyone," she said. "But if they don't trust you because you rooted out corrupt scumbags, then, excuse my French, but fuck 'em."

The radio buzzed. Janine grabbed it.

"Come in."

"We've got reports of an illegal brushfire coming from Candlewood," squawked the radio.

"Got an address?"

"Came in from 311. Smoke rising. You'll have to sort it out."

"Got it," said Janine, and slid it back into position.

"Another job for the fire department thrown to us?" asked Mike.

"Probably somebody burning leaves without a permit," she said. "Easy peasy. Candlewood is the oldest part of town. We'll go have a chat."

Janine drove there, and they could smell the smoke before they saw it, pouring into the sky from behind a cluster of big houses in a cul-de-sac. Janine looked up at the home and realized where they were.

"Oh shit," said Janine. "This will be interesting."

"What do you mean?" asked Mike.

Janine smiled. It wasn't a good smile, functioning closer to a grimace than the smirk she wore earlier.

"This is David Laurel's house," she said.

"David Laurel?" asked Mike. "Laurel? As in Laurel City?"

"The very same," said Janine. "Oldest of the living Laurels. And a descendant of the founders of the town. Current reverend at Laurel City Holy Church."

"What's the problem?" asked Mike. "You look anxious." He said anxious, but he thought scared. Janine looked scared.

"He doesn't necessarily enjoy being told what to do. And generally, no one tries. He has a lot of sway."

Mike glanced at the house. A plume of smoke rose behind it. It was an old Victorian mansion, a trim and landscaped front yard framing the home. No Halloween decorations.

"Someone called it in," he said, finally. "Even if God himself was burning leaves, we still have to take care of it."

They got out of the squad car and went to the front door. Mike rapped on it hard, three loud knocks. No answer. He pushed the doorbell twice before knocking again. They waited a few more minutes. Nothing.

"He lives alone," said Janine. "He's probably out back with the fire."

"Well, we have plenty of probable cause," said Mike. "There's a column of smoke rising from the backyard."

"You're not wrong," she said. Mike tilted his head and breathed deeply, making his way to the side of the house. He pushed open the unlocked gate. He immediately saw the massive trees that overhung the backyard, which would shed an enormous amount of leaves as the season changed. Janine followed him in. The sound of the fire got louder and louder as they came around to the back.

Mike saw David Laurel for the first time. He was tall, 6'3 or 6'4, and mostly bald. There was a thin horseshoe of white hair that still clung to his head. He had a mustache, also white, but no beard. He was staring at the fire he stood next to, poking it with a burnt wooden axe handle, the metal head gone. He wore a long-sleeved flannel shirt, jeans, and boots. His face was red, from the work or the smoke, Mike didn't know. A massive pile of leaves smoked into the sky. It seemed in control, but one errant breeze could knock it into an adjoining house.

"Excuse me? Reverend Laurel?" asked Mike, finally. The Reverend whipped his head, shocked to see someone in his backyard.

"Hello, officers. I didn't give you permission to come onto my property," he said. He reacted quickly, and his grip on the long axe handle shifted into a defensive position, intentional or not.

"We got a call, sir," said Mike, still walking to him. "About the fire. It's illegal to burn leaves without a permit. We could see the smoke from the road. We have probable cause."

Mike's words washed over him, and Mike saw what he had seen play out many times as a police officer, as Laurel quickly did the math in his head and realized he had no case. So he fell back on ignorance, as people usually did.

"I've burned my leaves before and have never had any issues with the police," he said.

"I doubt anyone ever called it in before," said Mike. "But you can't burn your leaves here. I believe the proper procedure is to bag them and have the compost truck pick them up."

"What's your name, Officer?" asked Laurel. Still polite, but Mike could hear the threat behind his words.

"Officer Mike Dawson," he said, extending a hand. He'd kill him with kindness. That's what it would take with men like him. Laurel wouldn't refuse a handshake, and he didn't, taking Mike's hand and shaking it firmly.

"Dawson," Laurel repeated. "Are you new in town?"

"Yes, sir," said Mike. The fire still burned next to him. He felt the sweat build beneath his uniform.

"I was going to say, I thought I knew all the Laurel City police force," he said. "You must be the new recruit. Chief Miller told me about you."

"Did he?"

"Yes," said Laurel. "I told him you sounded like a great candidate."

Mike felt Janine behind him, but he didn't break his eye

line with Laurel. Laurel was testing him.

"Since you're new in town, I don't know if you know me—"

"You're Reverend David Laurel. Descendant of the founder of the town, and reverend of the Laurel City Holy Church," said Mike. "But you still can't burn leaves without a permit." Laurel stared at him, and Mike stared back.

"Is that a fact?" asked Laurel, a smile on his face.

"That's a fact," said Mike. "I don't make the rules. I just enforce them." A long silence hung between them, the fire roaring next to them. Mike held the stare, not breaking eye contact with Laurel. If he did, he'd be in Laurel's pocket. And that wouldn't do. Not on his first meeting. Laurel stared back, and smiled, and then suddenly broke eye contact, walking to where a hose was coiled up against the house.

"Then I better put it out," he said, loudly. "I don't want any trouble with the law." He quickly pulled the hose out and started spraying down the great burning pyre. The fire hissed and even more smoke poured out of it. Laurel continued to smile as he dumped water into the leaves.

"Glad to hear it," said Mike. "Thank you for cooperating."

"Oh, of course," said Laurel, the big smile still on his face, the same unpleasant one Janine had worn earlier. Mike turned to leave. Laurel's voice stopped him.

"Will I see you at service on Sunday, Officer?" asked Laurel. Mike froze and turned.

"That sounds great, Reverend," said Mike. "I've been searching for a new church."

"Looking forward to seeing you there," said Laurel, and turned his attention back to the fire.

Mike and Janine turned and walked back toward the

front of the house.

"Please lock the gate on your way out," said Laurel, from behind them.

They got back in the squad car.

"Jesus," said Janine. "That was fucking intense."

Mike sat down, his heart thudding in his chest. "I think I'm going to throw up."

6

It surprised Daniel when Dad asked him to go to church with them on Sunday.

He had been waiting for Daniel when he got home from his first day of school, several hours after they expected him. It had led to an argument, with them yelling back and forth, with Daniel retreating to his room. Marion still wasn't talking to him after he hadn't driven her home.

Dad had bowed on that. He knew how important football was to Daniel and had given ground on it. To try to keep the peace between them.

The guilt of leaving Marion high and dry had persisted for a while, but he deserved his own friends, and his own hobbies. He wasn't a chauffeur. She could work a job and buy her own car, like he had.

Still, he was excited to attend the church service. Isaac had invited him after a few more weightlifting sessions together. Daniel had enjoyed his old youth group, before things had fallen apart in Plinkett. This was a chance at a fresh start. Just like the football team.

Dad drove them early on Sunday morning. They were all dressed nicely, even Marion, in her finest black dress. She wasn't happy to go, but Dad had convinced her. She'd always do what he wanted, no matter what it was. She still ignored Daniel.

The car ride was quiet. They were running a little late to church service, and Daniel knew Dad hated to be late. They made it in the nick of time, the outer doors still open and welcoming on the cool fall morning. Stragglers leaked in, rushing to their seats, two older gentlemen greeting everyone coming inside.

The church was large. It was hard to avoid in Laurel City. Its steeple could be seen from anywhere in the area, and its bell was heard for miles at every quarter hour. Its construction was simple. Daniel believed it was the oldest building in town, but it didn't look shabby or old. It looked impressive. It had gone through many renovations throughout the years. Some changes to the church itself, plus the offices and associated buildings, looked relatively new and probably cost a fortune.

It was easy to see how they could afford it. As they entered, Daniel saw the crowd, with every pew packed full of people. He felt the eyes on him, on him and his family. He was imagining it, for sure. Imagining the hushed whispers that went around as they stepped into the sanctuary. His father's head tilted back and forth, looking for somewhere to sit. A deacon waved at them from the front of the pews.

"Newcomers!" he bellowed. "Please, we have a spot up front just for you." They walked past a couple dozen rows of pews, all filled, all talking amongst each other. Daniel's eyes scanned them, and he saw Isaac. Their eyes caught and Isaac nodded at him. Daniel nodded back.

They finally got to the front, a pew reserved for the new members of the congregation. They sat down, and it felt like sitting in the front row of a movie theater, the floor turning into stairs headed upwards onto the central platform, a gigantic pulpit right in the middle. Risers stood behind it, Daniel assumed for a choir, and the baptismal sat beyond that.

They sat down, and it felt good to have a seat, to have a place. The butterflies still hovered in his stomach. He looked over at Dad and Marion, and they both seemed anxious.

He studied the inside of the church. It was beautiful. Stained glass windows bordered each side, and the red carpet beneath their feet was soft and clean. Soon, the scattered noise of the congregation speaking to each other hushed, and he realized it was time for the service to start.

First was the choir and choir director. Everyone stood and sang the hymns. He didn't know any of them, but he did his best. The ensemble was big, with men and women wearing shining white robes, singing loudly. Their voices filled the space. They were great.

The choir left, and then it was time for fellowship. Everybody introduced themselves to everyone nearby. Wasn't much different from their service in Plinkett. Daniel shook hands with the people near him. A nicely dressed older couple sat behind him, and both their handshakes were soft. He could smell the perfume and cologne coming off of them.

Then came announcements. A church social would follow Saturday. A Fall Festival would take place October 31st. The Laurel Youth Experience had an upcoming field trip, and there was still time for any young men to register.

Then the crowd hushed again as Reverend Laurel strode out to the pulpit, dressed in his vestments. Daniel knew this was Isaac's grandfather, and Isaac's size made sense. Reverend Laurel loomed over his congregation.

"Hello, all," he said, his voice booming without a microphone, echoing through the sanctuary. "I'm glad to see you all today." He seemed to look pointedly in their direction.

He paused for a moment. "It's October. Fall is here. Leaves are falling and collecting into inconvenient piles on our lawns. But you all know what else October means. It means again we must fight against the threat of the occult. Of witchcraft, of Satanism. Of Halloween." His voice boomed on the last word.

"I know all of you regulars have heard me say this before. Every year I talk about this. But I want you, most of all, to listen. To all members of my congregation, I will reinforce the dangers of Halloween. Of allowing our community to fall into the black hole that is the worship of everything that is evil and wrong."

"I think it's especially important this year because I've heard news from some of you. Word has reached me, because in Laurel City, it tends to reach me. Word has reached me of people flaunting their worship of this evil. Of decorating their homes with flagrant worship of the undead and supernatural."

Was he talking about Dad?

Daniel looked to his father's face, and his jaw was tense. Daniel knew the look well. He had it the other night, when he was chewing out Daniel for leaving his sister without a ride. It was anger, it was frustration. But they sat there. The Reverend continued.

"I will not mince words. Halloween is Evil. And that is evil with a capitol E. I've heard it so many times over the years. I've heard it at seminary conferences. I've heard it from the congregation. People who I considered good Christians. Good people. And I've certainly heard it from the news, and television, and popular culture. I've been asked the same question over and over. That question is: what's the harm?"

He paused again, for effect, looking out over the audience. His dad's jaw was still clenched. Marion sat next to them, her eyes staring at the Reverend. They were cut tight.

"They say that it's innocent. They say that kids dressing up, trick or treating, of adults partying all night wearing costumes themselves, is just plain ole fun, and nothing else. They say—they say that its occult connections have been severed over the years. Now it's just candy and costumes. That's all it is."

He paused again. "But that's not true. Don't get me wrong. It starts out that way. It starts out as innocent fun with little kids. They don't know what they're doing. They dress up, and they get candy, and they spend time with their friends. So of course they have fun. But that's how it starts."

"It starts with costumes and candy, and then it turns into partying as they get older. And it turns into drug use. And what begins as a casual introduction into the darkness that lurks in the world becomes more than a once a year acquaintance. That darkness becomes a friendly face, one that stays with someone for the entire year."

"And then you get used to the presence of the occult. Of the supernatural. You get used to these stories, which directly contradict God's word. What starts out as simple fun isn't harmless anymore. Now you have children disobeying their parents, of rejecting tradition and all sense of morals, just because you thought trick or treating was harmless fun."

Daniel felt his father vibrating on the pew next to him. He glanced around and saw nodding heads, eyes looking up at the Reverend. The older couple sitting behind murmured their assent with everything the Reverend said. They agreed with him.

Halloween had been simple fun when he was a kid, like the Reverend had said. He had dressed up. Back when Mom was alive, they had all gone trick or treating together. That was before she passed and Dad started decorating, pouring himself into transforming their front yard, their entire house into a bastion of the spooky and weird. Every year he would begin a little earlier than the year before. As soon as the Halloween stores opened he was decorating the house. Before long, that's what their family was. They were the Halloween family.

And Mom was gone, and Daniel was older, and he didn't really care about dressing up anymore. It was just some candy. What was the big deal? He didn't know anything about it being evil. It didn't seem evil to him.

But it wasn't worth everything.

"I won't tell you Halloween leads to worship of the occult, even though it certainly has led certain people down dark, dark roads. But I will tell you, without a doubt in my mind, that it leads to you questioning God. It leads you to question God's role in your life. It is at the head of the road that leads to rejection of faith. It leads to the rejection of Christianity. It leads to the rejection of Christ."

The Reverend looked out over his congregation, and his eyes again met with Dad. A simple stare, that he held for a few seconds, before he glanced away again.

"Halloween is evil and is in direct contradiction of our faith. And I challenge anyone here to confront anybody trumpeting this celebration of evil. To tell them to their face what kind of evil they're spreading in our town and in our community."

Daniel could hear Dad now, his breath coming hard out of his nose. His face was red. Daniel had a momentary vision of his father charging up onto the platform, covered in blood, and tackling the Reverend. But he didn't.

"Our community is whole—"

His dad stood up then, his hand clasped around Marion. She quickly stood with him. The Reverend stopped then and smiled, a small smile, but a smile nonetheless. Dad only stared back for a moment, and then turned to walk out, turning at the aisle, Marion right behind him. He paused and realized that Daniel still sat. Daniel hadn't risen with them. He hadn't thought to. His father walked back, put a hand under his arm, and pulled him to his feet. Daniel didn't resist. He didn't know what would have happened if he had. They marched out in silence, the congregation staring as they left. His father didn't say a word on the entire drive home. After they got home, he found the rest of the Halloween decorations and started adding to what he already had.

Daniel didn't resist his father's pull. But as the day wore on, and Isaac texted him about what that was all about. Daniel didn't know. And he was right. He hadn't known what would have happened if he had resisted.

But he suspected.

He suspected his father would have left him.

7

Mike poked his head into Chief Miller's office.

"You wanted to see me, Chief?" he asked.

The Chief glanced up from some paperwork, a half-eaten breakfast sandwich still resting in its wrapper nearby. The Chief was in his mid-50's, with a soft smear of white hair on his head. He was clean shaven, and slightly overweight.

"Yeah, Mike, come in," he said. He spoke softly, but looked you in the eye when he talked. "Close the door behind you."

Mike did, sitting down in the worn pleather chair placed in front of the Chief's desk. The small office was cluttered, but Mike expected nothing else. The seat squeaked beneath him.

"What do you want to talk about?" asked Mike. It was

early Monday, and Mike had been getting ready to go out on patrol. His anger from the day before had largely dispersed. He shouldn't have marched out of the church service, no matter how angry he was, but he hadn't been able to help himself. Laurel had targeted him as soon as he had made him put out his fire. He had gotten him to attend his church and then humiliated him in front of the entire congregation. In front of his kids. He had walked out, and everyone had stared at him. And now that's who he would be. So be it.

But after a few hours of working in his yard, he had cooled down. Marion had helped. She always said the right thing.

"I saw you and Janine answered a call last Friday?" asked the Chief. He squinted at a piece of paper in his hand. "Out in Candlewood?"

"Yes, sir," said Mike. He held his breath.

"And you entered David Laurel's property and found him burning leaves?" asked the Chief.

"Yes, sir."

"And he didn't have a permit, and you told him to stop?"

"Yes, sir."

The Chief finally looked up from the paper, glancing at Mike, and then glanced back down at the paper, studying it. Silence hung in the air for a few moments. Mike didn't have the patience for this.

"Chief?" asked Mike. Miller glanced at him.

"Do you have any other questions? It was a routine call," said Mike. "Took us about five minutes."

Miller put the paper down on his desk and clasped his hands together. He started to talk, shut his mouth, and then started again.

"The Reverend talked to me after church service on Sunday," said Miller. *Christ. Of course Miller went to church there.* "Told me you and Janine barged onto his property without a knock on the door or a warrant. He said he hadn't meant anything by burning the leaves. He's done it for years with no trouble. And that was before your behavior at the service—"

"Let me stop you there, Chief," said Mike. "First, we knocked on his door, and rang his doorbell, and gave him a solid five minutes to answer. There *was* no sign of anyone home, aside from the gigantic plume of smoke rising from his backyard. Janine and I both confirmed we had probable cause, and walked to his backyard, where we informed him that burning leaves without a permit was illegal. It is illegal, correct?"

"Well, yes," said the Chief.

"Laurel tried to intimidate me with his position, and I reaffirmed that burning leaves was illegal. And then he put out the fire, which was large, and quite frankly, could have easily started more fires if a breeze hit it the wrong way."

"I understand that," said the Chief, his voice still soft. "But you didn't have to talk to him on Sunday."

No, I only had to be humiliated.

"I'm going to be honest with you, Chief," said Mike. "I couldn't be honest with my last superior, but I will be honest with you, because you're giving me a chance for a fresh start here. When I'm on the clock, I enforce the law when someone's breaking it, and especially when that someone is putting other lives in danger. Are you telling me I should have been lenient on Mr. Laurel because of who he is? Because his forefathers founded the town, because he's the reverend of your church? That I should have let him just continue that miniature forest fire he had started in his backyard?"

The Chief stared at him, a little taken aback. "Well, no, Mike," he said. "I didn't mean to imply that at all."

"Good," said Mike. "Because Reverend Laurel invited me to his church service after he put out the fire. Where he embarrassed me in front of the entire church."

"Now, I don't know about that," said the Chief. "He believes strongly about Halloween. This isn't the first time he's preached about it. It's a bit strong to say that he was targeting *you*. And he didn't make you march out in the middle of the service."

"Why did you want to talk to me, Chief?" asked Mike. "Was it to tell me to behave at church?"

"No," said Miller. "I—I don't want to seem antagonistic. After what the Reverend told me, after what I've heard from people around town—I just wanted to check in on you."

"Are you going to discipline me because I have Halloween decorations up?" asked Mike.

"No," said Miller. "But Laurel City is a small pond. And any time a new person shows up, there's a little ripple. You've only been here a few weeks, and there's already a wave coming out from you. I'm not saying you shouldn't celebrate Halloween. I don't agree with everything the Reverend says, but choosing this as your battlefield seems a bit short-sighted."

"You're telling me to fit in?" asked Mike. "Not to make waves? By not decorating my yard?"

"I'm telling you to pick your battles," said Miller. "Nothing more than that. As someone who once faced a similar situation."

Mike looked at the Chief, and there was no ill will in his eyes. Miller cared.

"I'll consider it," said Mike.

"Thank you," said Miller. "Good luck today."

*

"And then—then!—he stared right at me and says that Halloween is evil," said Mike. He thought he had gotten it out of his system, but his talk with the Chief had brought it right back to the surface.

"And you marched out in the middle of the service?" asked Janine.

"Yes," said Mike. "I wasn't going to sit there and take it."

"Half the town goes there, including the Chief," said Janine. "Probably why he talked to you about it."

"It's absolutely crazy," said Mike. "All of this over some damned leaves."

"Why do you think I was anxious before we went to talk to him?" asked Janine. "Reverend Laurel *is* Laurel City. More than the mayor, more than Chief Miller, more than anyone."

"And that doesn't bother you?" asked Mike.

"Of course it does," said Janine. "But like the Chief said, I pick my battles—"

"I can't just *not* celebrate Halloween," said Mike. "It's a part of me. A part of my life. Just because some zealots think it's evil—"

"You think you're the only one who's had to adjust to life in Laurel City?" asked Janine. "I'm Catholic, Mike. Well, lapsed, but still. Do you think there's a Catholic Church in

Laurel City?"

"I imagine not," said Mike.

"You'd imagine correctly," said Janine. "When I first arrived, the Chief asked me if I wanted to attend a service at LCHC. Just like he talked to you. Kindly and politely, with my best interests at heart. Chief isn't from Laurel City, but he found the best way to stay Chief and to belong in town was to go to church there."

"What did you say?"

"I politely declined," she said. "And he didn't push the subject. But then again, I didn't hang a disemboweled corpse from my front tree."

"It's October! It's Halloween season. This is the only time of year when it's acceptable."

"I don't disagree, but it's not worth fighting the entire town over," said Janine.

"Why not?"

"Why not? Because Laurel City is a nice place. The schools are good, the crime rate is low. My daughter likes it here. My job is secure. It's comfortable."

"But Halloween can't be the only thing that the town quietly enforces," said Mike.

"No, of course not," said Janine. "There's a bunch of little things that the Church frowns upon, and it quietly, or not so quietly, becomes town edict, but nothing I've wanted to fight over. Nothing worth upsetting the apple cart over."

"How old is your daughter?" asked Mike.

"She's seven," said Janine.

"What's her name?"

"Fiona."

"If the Church threatened her, you'd upset that cart,

though, wouldn't you?"

"Yes," said Janine, immediately. "But celebrating Halloween isn't hurting anyone."

"Not directly," said Mike. "But not everything is about what it's about."

"What?" asked Janine.

"Halloween isn't really about putting up tombstones in your front yard. Or candy, or scary movies. It's about celebrating the strange and different. It's the one time a year where you can dress up and march down the street as a monster, or a witch, or as your favorite comic book character and people won't think you're weird. It's okay to be different on Halloween. And when somebody calls that evil...I'm not going to trust them with my children. Calling it the occult or whatever is just window dressing. It's about suppressing individuality."

"You've thought a lot about this," said Janine.

"You think I'm weird," said Mike.

"I think it's okay not to celebrate Halloween. I used to have fun, just like everyone else, but then we moved here, and we just go to their Fall Festival. There's still candy and games, and people dress up."

"But it's safe," said Mike. "And I'm sure as long as you dress up like a Bible character or an athlete it's okay. But what if I showed up in drag? What if my daughter dressed like a witch?"

Janine paused. "They'd politely and kindly ask you to go home."

"That's what I mean," said Mike. "It's more than just Halloween."

Janine shrugged. "It was never worth fighting for me.

The longer you live in Laurel City, the more you get used to it. Every place has its trade-offs, and Laurel City is no exception."

"I don't want to get used to sacrificing what I believe in," said Mike.

"You're being melodramatic," said Janine. "It's just a holiday. We don't even get the day off. There's no Halloween in Laurel City, and that's okay."

Mike didn't answer, only scrinched up his face. He had an idea. They passed the community center on the edge of downtown.

"Can anyone rent out that community center?"

"Yeah, I think so," said Janine. "I went to a wedding there."

Mike smiled. He had a plan.

"What's that smile for?"

"This year, Laurel City *will* have a Halloween."

8

Laurel City Mall was packed on Friday night. Marion was surprised.

She had expected—well, she had expected a dump.

She and Cara sat in the food court, waiting for their theater to open. Cara had invited her out to a movie, offering to treat her for helping fend off the bullies. They had become fast friends in Marion's first week. She had offered to drive Marion home after Daniel joined the football team and Marion happily accepted.

The mall wasn't big, T-shaped with a handful of department stores. They had done a lap around it, stopping into the accessories store and Hot Topic, but buying nothing. They had a half hour to kill before they could see their movie, an adaptation of a YA thriller that Cara had *needed* to watch. Marion didn't really care about the movie. She just wanted to spend time with Cara.

"Is it always this crowded?" asked Marion. A big cinnamon bun sat between them, and they each picked at it, pulling off warm chunks of pastry.

"The mall?" asked Cara. "Not all the time. There's not many other places for people to go. And the only theater is here. There's a bar downtown, but that's about it. If anyone wants a real night out, they leave town."

"We had a mall in Plinkett, but it was sad," said Marion. "Half of the stores had gone out of business."

"I don't know," said Cara. "It's always been here."

"Thanks for inviting me out," said Marion.

"Thanks for going out with me," said Cara, before ripping off another piece of bun and eating it. Marion reached out for a bite and froze.

Wait a minute. Going out? Is this a date?

"Are you okay?" asked Cara. Marion had frozen, her fingers dug into the side of the pastry.

Marion forced a smile and then ripped off a piece, accidentally flinging it onto the ground.

"Fuck," said Marion. The butterflies in her stomach had doubled and then tripled.

"Man overboard!" said Cara. "I think it's alright. This thing is big enough to feed an army."

Marion smiled while her stomach churned. Cara's cell phone vibrated on the table. She glanced at it and then silenced it, letting it ring through.

"Junk call?"

"No, it's my dad," said Cara. "He not only has to put me through the wringer every time I leave the house, he also needs to call and check in on me, to make sure I'm not busy sinning once I'm out of his sight. The only reason he let me go out on a school night because it was with you. He thinks making new friends is good for me. If only he knew I was out with the big sinner in town."

"Is that what I am?" asked Marion.

"The first thing you did was threaten to curse our star football player," said Cara. "So you tell me."

Marion smiled. "I've never actually cursed anyone before." She nodded at the phone. "Won't your dad be angry if you don't answer?"

"Probably," said Cara. "But I'm not a baby anymore. I can't wait to graduate and get the hell out of here."

"Do you know what you want to do after graduation?" asked Marion. Counselors had already started scheduling appointments for college plans.

"Go to school," said Cara. "Probably study English."

"Do you want to teach?" asked Marion.

"I don't know," said Cara. "We're sixteen. Why should we know what we want already?"

"Well, I know what I want to do," said Marion.

"Really?"

"Yeah."

"Well?"

Marion stayed quiet. She suddenly felt embarrassed by her admission.

"You can tell me," said Cara. "I won't judge."

"I want to be a practical effects artist for movies," said Marion. "Or at theme parks."

"That's bad ass!" said Cara. "That'd be an awesome job. Where do you study for that?"

"There are a few special schools that teach it," said Marion. "Or you apprentice under someone for long enough to do it yourself."

"Man, that's cool," said Cara. "I think the theater should be open now. Want to go grab seats?"

They tossed what remained of the cinnamon bun and walked into the theater. The pre-show ad roll ran as they grabbed spots near the back. Some people trickled in, but it wasn't crowded. They shared a popcorn. Cara flipped up the armrest between them and planted the bucket in between them.

Marion opened up her mental tally and marked one for "definitely a date". They outweighed the "not a date" section, but she still didn't know. They chatted through the pre-show, ignoring almost all of it. As the lights dimmed, Marion took a small amount of joy every time their fingers grazed each other as they grabbed popcorn.

The movie started, the projector just above their heads, their seats against the back wall of the theater. Marion tried to pay attention. Cara's vision was glued to the screen. She had raved about the book it was based on, about a killer in a high school, picking off members of a friend group. Marion's gaze kept returning to Cara, her warm eyes staring at the action. The film's tension ratcheted up and up, and as the final girl was being chased by the masked killer, Cara's hand found hers in the dark and squeezed. Marion squeezed back reflexively.

This is a date!

It was decided. Friends didn't hold hands, not like this. Right? She didn't know. It had to be a date. It felt like one to her. She had only been on one before, but it had been a disaster.

That's because it had only been a date for him.

Conor Perkins was his name. He was a nice boy. Smart. They were friends. He had nervously asked her out, and she had agreed, mostly out of sheer terror of saying no and hurting his feelings. She liked Conor as a friend, but she had been fourteen, and didn't know any better. Didn't know anything. She had never been attracted to boys, and only meekly nodded whenever her few girl friends talked about the guys they had crushes on.

So she went out with Conor. They played mini golf. Conor's dad had dropped them off. The mini golf was fun, and they ate some ice cream that Conor paid for with his dad's money. They were sitting alone after mini golf, and Conor kissed her on the lips. She tried to kiss back. She really did. But it felt like kissing a house plant. There was nothing there, and as Conor's dad drove her home, she realized there would never be anything there. Not for Conor, and not for boys.

She liked girls. She had a crush on Alicia Kaufman, a girl with curly hair in the grade ahead of her. Alicia had a boyfriend, and they never talked, but that didn't matter. Marion knew there would be no boyfriends in her future. On the ride home, terror gripped her.

She was different. She had suspected it for a long time, but that terrible night with Conor Perkins cemented it in her mind, and she didn't say a word the entire way, and probably made Conor think he had done something wrong. She retreated into her room when she got home.

That's where Dad had found her, sitting in her bed, staring at a wall.

"How was your date?" he asked, peeking into the room.

"Fine," she said. What else could she say?

"It doesn't sound like it was fine," he said. "Is there something you want to talk about?"

"No," she said.

"Conor didn't, like, try anything with you, did he?" he asked.

"No, Dad," she said. Her face was tucked into her knees, her eyes behind her hair, but she watched the look on his face, one of confusion. But he didn't leave. He sat next to her, and he waited. He didn't say anything. He knew poking or prodding would only make her afraid. So he sat next to her. He sat *with* her.

After a few minutes, she leaned into him. He put his arm around her.

The terrible sinking feeling in her guts accelerated, spinning around and around, and she couldn't see a world with it inside of her. She needed it out, but she couldn't say the words, and she cried, softly at first and then louder and louder. He held her. She cried for a long time. Dad still said nothing, just letting her cry. He was patient with her. He always had been.

Marion had finally stopped crying, and they sat quietly, and the words just came out of her, because she couldn't hold them any longer, and Dad was the only person she could tell.

"I don't like boys. I like girls," she said. Her voice was quiet.

"Is that why you're upset?" he asked.

"Yes," she said. "I'm afraid."

"Afraid of me?"

"I don't know. Maybe a little. Scared of what will happen."

He hugged her tighter. "You don't have to be scared of me. You're allowed to like girls. It's normal. You're normal."

She started crying again, and this time buried her face in his shoulder.

Her heart leaped into her throat as Cara squeezed her hand. Marion swallowed it back down. They held hands even as the credits rolled.

"Did you like it?" asked Marion, as they walked to Cara's car, down a small corridor, hidden off the side of the mall. Their voiced echoed off the discolored bricks. Cara's hand found hers and grabbed it again.

"It was good," she said. "I don't know if it's as great as the book, but I want to see it again. Did you like it?"

"Yeah," said Marion. She couldn't help but smile.

The air was crisp, and Marion had forgotten to wear a jacket. She wore only jeans and a t-shirt, and she shivered. Cara wore a denim jacket over her plaid shirt. She pulled Marion closer to her as they neared her car. Marion could smell her shampoo, and her stomach danced inside her.

This is a date this is a date this is a date

They hid inside of Cara's car, and Cara turned the engine over and flipped the heat to high.

"I don't want to go home yet," said Cara.

"Won't your dad be pissed?" asked Marion.

"Probably," she said. "I'll worry about that later. Want to see my favorite place in Laurel City?"

"Sure," said Marion.

Cara drove, leaving the mall behind, turning off onto county roads, and then down an unmarked dirt road, miles away.

"Are we still in Laurel City?" asked Marion.

"Technically," said Cara. "But no one comes out here."
The car weaved down a skinny gravel trail, trees right up
against the path. Marion jumped when her side mirror
grazed a tree with a loud thump.

"Sorry," said Cara. "It's a tight fit. We're almost there."
The headlights lit the way, and trees surrounded them. Then
they emerged into a little roundabout, open to the front,
where the ground disappeared. Cara cut the engine.

"We're here," she said.

They left the warmth of the car, and Cara turned on the
flashlight in her phone.

"Be careful where you step," said Cara. "It's a long drop."
Marion could see that.

"Where are we?" asked Marion.

"Laurel City Ravine," said Cara. "There's an official park
off the highway, but the view here is better."

Marion's eyes adjusted to the moonlight, and the size
of the ravine came into form. It was beautiful. The granite
walls glowed white under the moon, spare trees and vines
hanging down. Marion could hear a faint trickle of water
from below.

"It's gorgeous," said Marion. She shivered again. The
temperature had dropped quickly.

"Here," said Cara, taking off her denim jacket and giving
it to Marion, throwing it over her shoulders. She could still
feel Cara's body heat in it.

"How often do you come out here?" asked Marion.

"Whenever I want to get away from my dad," said Cara.
"Helps me clear my head."

"Can I ask a dumb question?" asked Marion.

"Sure."

Marion took a deep breath and exhaled. "Is this a date?"

Cara looked at her for a long second and then laughed. "Do you want it to be?"

"Yes," said Marion.

Cara slid her hands around Marion's waist, over her t-shirt and underneath Cara's own jacket. She pulled her close, face to face, and they kissed. Their lips softly pressed together at first, and then they kissed again. Marion's heart thudded inside her chest. This was *not* Conor Perkins.

Cara pulled back and looked into Marion's eyes.

"Then it's a date."

9

Daniel already regretted agreeing to run errands with Dad.

"How's football practice been going?"

"It's been fine," said Daniel. Better than fine, actually. As soon as he hit the field, Daniel was the team's best offensive lineman. After two practices Coach had made him starting right tackle, protecting their quarterback's blind side, and the lead blocker on most of the running plays.

"When's your first game?"

"Next Friday. We had a bye this week," said Daniel. He was excited to be in a game that mattered again.

"I'll make sure I have the night off so I can go," he said. Daniel said nothing. In Plinkett, he had desperately wanted Dad to attend his games. To see how good he was. But now, after his conversations with Isaac, Daniel didn't know. Maybe it was better that he didn't go.

They drove through town in Dad's aging Explorer. He had said errands. Daniel had assumed that meant grocery shopping, but he had assumed wrong. They stopped at the craft store first.

Of course. Daniel should have known. More Halloween stuff. The store didn't have any of the typical Halloween decorations, but it had all the basics, which his dad would use to craft.

"Don't we have enough stuff at the house?" asked Daniel, trailing behind. Daniel's phone buzzed in his pocket. A text from Isaac.

You still coming tomorrow?

It had been after football practice, just the two of them in the weight room. Isaac had asked him to stay and work out afterward.

"What's the story with your dad?" asked Isaac, bench pressing his light rep.

"What do you mean?" asked Daniel.

"I mean him leaving service right in the middle of a sermon," said Isaac. "It's kinda crazy behavior."

Daniel had hoped Isaac wouldn't ask him about it. He was tired of having to defend his father. It had been the same story in Plinkett.

"I don't know," said Daniel. "Sometimes he does things I can't explain."

Isaac finished his reps and sat up. "I'm not blaming you. But it's disrespectful. Grandfather is a great man. How much weight do you want?"

"200," said Daniel.

"Only 200?" asked Isaac. "You can do more than that. Do

225. Push yourself."

Daniel nodded. 225 was a lot, especially after a couple hours of football practice. They threw the extra plates onto the bar and Daniel slid underneath it. He grabbed the bar, testing his grip, and then lifted it above him. He slowly brought it down to his chest. He had ten reps. It would be tough. He pushed up one.

"Why did your dad do it?" asked Isaac, looking down from above.

"My dad has a thing about Halloween. It's his favorite holiday. He's always loved it, even when we were little. But after Mom died…" Daniel pushed the bar up again, breathing out. He brought it down, pushed it up.

"Sorry to hear that," said Isaac. "I didn't know your mom had passed."

"It's okay. It was a long time ago. But ever since she died, he's kind of poured himself into it. They always decorated together. My sister really likes it too. I've never been that into it."

He pushed the weight up. Five. His breath came hard now, and his chest ached.

"You can do it," said Isaac. "Keep pushing."

"I don't know," said Daniel.

"No excuses," said Isaac. He put his hands under the bar, as Daniel struggled with his sixth rep. "Grandfather is right, you know. About Halloween. It can seem like nothing at first, but it leads people down dark paths. Your dad might be better off letting it go."

Daniel brought the weight down on his chest, and pushed, his heart pounding. His arms shook, but he got it up.

"Three more," said Isaac. "You can do it."

Daniel brought it back down and forced the weight up. It stalled halfway, and Isaac gently helped him finish the rep. "I'm right here. Two more."

The weight fell again. Daniel squeezed the bar, throwing all his strength into it. He pressed it up, and then held it, trembling. He couldn't lift it. Isaac slid his hands underneath again and pulled just enough for Daniel to finish the lift.

"Just one more," said Isaac. Isaac kept his hands under the bar as Daniel slowly lowered it to his chest. The bar made contact and he pushed hard, pushing all the air out of his body. The weight moved up, slowly, and Isaac helped Daniel finish his set. He racked it and the bench shook.

Daniel laid there, panting.

"Good job," said Isaac.

"Thanks for the help," said Daniel.

"We're a team," said Isaac. "We have to watch out for each other. You should come to a Youth Experience meeting. It's run by my dad. It's different from the main service. It's geared for us."

"I don't know if my dad would be happy with me going back," said Daniel, still catching his breath. He sat up. Isaac sat on the bench across from him.

"Sometimes the right thing to do is not the easy thing to do," said Isaac. "We do work in the community. All the guys are great. You should come this Sunday."

Daniel paused, still breathing heavily.

"I'll do it. I'll go," he said.

Isaac had smiled. "That's great! You won't regret it."

Yeah, still going

"It isn't for the house," said his father, throwing giant pieces of foam into the cart, along with every kind of red dye and paint they had. Daniel barely heard him.

He hadn't told Dad yet that he was planning to go back. Isaac replied.

Great!

His dad kept grabbing more and more things until the cart was piled high with all kinds of crafting supplies. If it wasn't for the house, what was it for?

The hardware store was next. It was a similar story, with his father piling up the cart with lumber, with nails and screws, and tons of paint and glue.

"Is this enough?" asked Daniel. Dad always went crazy around Halloween, but they had never gone to the hardware store for stuff.

"I don't know for now," he said, missing his sarcasm. "If I have to come back, oh well. I'm sure I'm forgetting something."

I should tell him. He could hide it from him, sure, but he would find out, eventually. He had a way of finding everything out. It was the cop in him.

Daniel didn't say anything, only followed behind him as he balanced more and more on the cart. They checked out, and his dad stuffed the SUV full of materials, lumber sticking out the back. He taped a red flag onto it.

"Is this going to take all day?" asked Daniel.

"Just one more stop," he said.

"What are we doing?" asked Daniel.

"You'll see," he said. "It's a surprise. In more ways than one."

Their last stop was at the community center, a square,

bland building.

"We're here," said his dad, and got out. He was smiling, almost giddy. What was going on? He had been so dour for the last week.

Daniel followed mutely. They walked inside and poked around until they found an office. A man with thinning hair and glasses sat behind a desk, working on a computer. His dad knocked on the door.

"Hello?" he asked.

"Officer Dawson?" asked the man behind the desk.

"I'm off duty. You can just call me Mike," he said.

The man got up, extending a hand. "Eric. Nice to meet you in person. Let me give you a tour."

"This is my son, Daniel," he said, gesturing toward him.

"Nice to meet you," said Eric, shaking Daniel's hand. He smiled. He always felt like a little kid with his dad, even now that he towered over him.

They followed Eric as he gave a tour of the building. It wasn't a gigantic place, but big enough for a town the size of Laurel City. The main space had a small stage and room for a few hundred people.

"This is our central hall," said Eric. "We most often see it used for wedding receptions and the like."

Eric led them down a hallway, to two connected meeting rooms, each only a quarter the size of the main hall.

"And these are our meeting rooms," said Eric. "We passed the bathrooms, and the kitchen is on the other side of the hall, in case you want to cook anything."

"This is perfect," said his dad, looking around each space as they moved through it. "Is there a cleaning fee?"

"It's included in the deposit," said Eric. "You're not planning on making a mess, are you?"

"Not if everything goes to plan," said his dad. "But no plan survives contact with the enemy, am I right?" Eric laughed. "Can't hurt to ask, you know."

"I understand," said Eric. "We are free on the thirty-first. Are you interested?"

The thirty-first? Halloween?

What was he doing now? Couldn't he leave well enough alone?

"Absolutely. Where do I sign?" asked his dad.

"Awesome," said Eric. "Give me a day or two to draw up the contract, and I'll email it to you. Sign it and drop it off with the deposit and we'll be good."

"Great," he said. "Now I can start really planning. Do you have a blueprint of the building? I'd love measurements of all the rooms."

"I think I have one somewhere," said Eric. "I can send it along with the paperwork."

"Awesome," said Daniel's father.

They went back to Eric's office. Daniel wanted to scream.

"Truth be told," said Eric, "I'm excited for an alternative to Fall Festival. I'm tired of having to dress up in some tame costume year after year. And you'll have actual haunt rooms?"

"That's the plan."

"I can't wait," said Eric. He shook hands with them, and they left. Daniel's mind boggled. He was organizing a Halloween party?

They walked back to the SUV. It all made sense. The crafts, the lumber. He would build a haunted house in the community center. Daniel didn't know what to say. His dad started on his way home.

They were halfway back, and Daniel finally found his words. "What are you planning?"

"A Halloween party," said his dad. "For the community. An alternative to the Fall Festival."

"Why?" asked Daniel.

"What do you mean why?" asked his dad. "Because I want to celebrate Halloween, and if no one else is going to throw a party, I will."

"But they don't celebrate it here," said Daniel. "Didn't you hear the Reverend—"

"Laurel can kiss my ass, Daniel," he said. "He doesn't own the town, and he doesn't get to decide what holidays I celebrate. And he doesn't get to make me feel guilty for celebrating Halloween."

His dad almost never cursed around them. Daniel felt his face grow hot and tears form in the corners of his eyes. It was happening again. Plinkett was happening again, and his father didn't care. He only cared about his damned Halloween.

"You're doing it again," said Daniel, squeezing his eyes until anger replaced the tears.

"What?"

"You're doing it again," said Daniel. "How can you not see it? Why can't you just let things be?"

"Doing what again? Slow down, Daniel. What's wrong?"

"You really don't realize it, do you? You ruin our lives in Plinkett, and then you drag us away from our friends, and now you're doing it again! Why does it matter if the town doesn't celebrate Halloween? Who cares? Go find something else to do! But you can't! You have to wreck our lives again. You have to turn the town against you." Daniel couldn't breathe. All his pent-up frustration had been released, a spigot once closed, now on full blast.

"Ruining your life?" he asked. "Not everything is about you, son. Sometimes you have to make a sacrifice, even if you don't want to. I did the right thing in Plinkett, even if it made life hard on us—"

They had arrived at the house.

"Could you think about us for once for a change? Think about me? I'd like to have some friends here, but everyone's already labeled me the son of the Halloween nut job!"

"That's not fair, Daniel—" but Daniel was already out of the car, walking to the house.

All Daniel heard was that Halloween was more important than him.

10

Neither of his kids wanted Mike to go to parent/teacher night at Laurel City High. Daniel was still pissed at him for the Halloween party, and Marion thought it was a waste of time for him and the faculty. However, it was the responsible thing to do, even if he wasn't worried about either Daniel or Marion's grades. It was also a way for him to meet some like-minded adults. Perhaps some liberal minds hid among the ranks of the teachers, who he could invite to the Halloween event.

They handed him a map at the front door, pre-marked with both of the kid's teachers circled in red pen. It proved handy, because Mike got turned around before he knew it. He had three hours to meet ten of them, so he'd have to get moving. He stumbled upon the first teacher by accident. Mr.

Watkins, Daniel's history teacher.

"Hello, Mr. Dawson," he said, a gigantic mustache covering his face. Mike smiled and shook his hand, but there was no hint of a returned smile. Had he been sitting in the congregation as Mike marched out with both his kids? Mike's eyes scanned the man's desk for any sign, but there was nothing but books and piles of paper.

"Daniel seems like a good student so far," said Watkins. "He pays attention in class, even if he doesn't seem particularly engaged in discussion. Is there something wrong, Mr. Dawson?"

"Sorry," said Mike. "I've never been here before. Just taking it all in."

"Yes," said Watkins. "You're the talk of the town. The newcomer." His voice barely changed, but Mike sensed some dark implications. Watkins only stared at him. Mike couldn't consider him a potential ally.

"Any other questions for me?" asked Watkins.

"No, I don't think so. Nice to meet you!" said Mike, and he retreated away from Watkins' dour stare.

Mrs. Kirkman was next, who was Marion's English teacher. She was no better. In fact, she was worse. She didn't bother to hide her distaste for him and his behavior at LCHC.

"Marion has been well behaved. She's a very attentive student," she said. Her miniature beehive seemed to defy gravity as she talked to him, every bob of her head threatening it to crash to the ground. "She falls very far from the tree, it seems. Why on Earth would you leave the service right in the middle of the sermon? It was so disrespectful to the Reverend, and I've heard about the decorations in your yard—"

She continued on, the beehive bobbing as she went, but Mike stopped listening. He only smiled and absorbed it. Eventually she had to stop to breathe, and that's when he made his escape, slipping out between her words.

Most of the faculty shared sentiments with those two. The majority had been in Laurel City for years, and the longer they had been there, the more entrenched they were in the ways of Laurel City Holy Church. He found a few smiling faces along the way, who weren't necessarily potential allies, but weren't enemies. The band teacher, Mr. Jenkins, who also taught psychology, seemed jovial, and happy to talk about The Clash after they exchanged pleasantries about Daniels' schoolwork.

"Wait a minute," he said. "Are you the Halloween man?"

"The Halloween man," said Mike. "I guess so."

Jenkins' voice suddenly dropped a few decibels. He almost whispered, looking around to make sure no one was listening in. They were the only ones in the room.

"That's awesome!" he said. "God, this town sometimes drives me crazy. Your decorations are great. Man, I wish I could decorate."

"Why can't you?" asked Mike.

"You know," said Jenkins. "This place." He gestured broadly, as if the answer was self-evident.

"If you want to do it, you should," said Mike. "What if I told you I was planning a Halloween party?" He whispered too. He couldn't help it. Every word felt conspiratorial.

"Really? Where?" asked Jenkins.

"The community center. Halloween night."

"Holy shit. You have iron balls," he said. "Can I come?"

The discovery of an ally amongst the stalwart Church

supporters was largely enough for Mike. He was tired after working all day and seeing all the different teachers, and the time left in the evening was winding down. Only one remained, and he considered just skipping her. It was Marion's chemistry teacher. Marion was almost never a worry in school. But he had seen everyone else, might as well see her. He went in expecting another enemy. Instead, he found Jenny Gibson.

She sat at her desk, her pen dancing over paper. She looked up and smiled as he walked in, standing up to greet him. She wore a simple sun dress that hugged her hips. Her brown skin glowed, and her green eyes startled him.

"Mike Dawson," he said, finding his words, extending his hand. She shook it.

"Jenny Gibson," she said. "Marion's father?"

"Yes," he said.

"Marion is a good kid," she said. "She talks a lot, but she's a good kid."

"Marion? Talking a lot? I don't believe it," he asked.

"I'm inclined to say that it's because she shares a desk with Cara. But it's not a big deal. They're never a problem."

"That's great to know—"

"Which is different from what I hear about you," she said.

"God, not you too," he said. "I walked out of a service. I didn't kill anyone."

"Don't worry," she said. "I'm not going to lambaste you about your sins against man. But someplace the size of Laurel City, word gets around quickly. You're the man with Halloween decorations in a town without a Halloween. They look good, by the way."

"So you've seen them," he said.

"My evening jog goes right by your house," she said. "I really like the disemboweled head hanging from the tree."

"Marion has as much to do with it as I do. Most of the rest of your faculty, hell, this entire town, seems to disagree. Everywhere I go, they stare at me like I'm a leper."

"You don't look like a leper to me," she said. She sat back on her desk and crossed her legs.

Is she flirting with me?

"It feels like it," he said. "It hangs over me, whatever I do."

"Have you not lived in a place like Laurel City before?"

"The last city wasn't huge, but it wasn't like this. Everyone notices everything. Are you from Laurel City?"

"Why do you ask?"

"Something tells me you're not from around here."

"Is it because I'm the only black girl in a fifty-mile radius?"

"That might have been a clue," he said. "Not the only hint, but it certainly was one."

She smiled and nodded. "Laurel City definitely has a predilection toward a particular color. I knew that going in, though."

"Why did you move here, then?" asked Mike. He leaned back against a desk. The quiet of the school suddenly reminded him of the hour. He looked at his watch. The parent/teacher meeting was over, technically.

"Don't worry about the time," she said. "I have keys. I'm usually here late. I moved here because of my folks. They retired to a community a few towns over, and I wanted to be close to them. And this is the work I found. Not a lot of jobs for a chemical engineer in Laurel City. Plenty of science teachers openings."

Mike nodded. "It pays the bills."

"It does," she said. "And the cost of living in Laurel City is pretty low, I'll give it that."

"It's not entirely without its benefits," he said. "I keep finding new ones, which is nice." He looked her in the eye, and she met his gaze, and held it for a second.

"I'm throwing a Halloween party," he said. "Would you like to come?"

"We just met," she said, with a raised eyebrow. "And you're already asking me out?"

"It—it's going to be for the community, you know," he said. "I didn't mean to be too forward. I apol—"

"Relax," she said. "I'm just teasing. I will absolutely attend your Halloween party. This damn town is too boring. It's about time somebody spiced it up."

"Great," he said, smiling. "Maybe I'll see you around, maybe, before then. I should probably get going."

"Did I scare you?" she asked. "Mr. Halloween got spooked?"

"Ms. Gibson—"

"Jenny, please," she said.

"Jenny," he said. He paused and smiled. She was too fast. He couldn't keep up. "I should go home, before I embarrass myself further."

She rolled her eyes. "Would you mind if I stopped by your house sometime? To take a closer look at your decorations?"

God, I'm an idiot. She's asking herself out for *me.*

"Yes, of course," he said. "This Saturday? I'm going to be working on stuff for the party in the garage, probably with Marion."

"I'll stop by," she said. She climbed down from her desk, her long legs untangling. She gave him her hand again.

"It was nice meeting you, Mike" she said.

Mike took her hand, skin to skin. He couldn't help but smile.

"Nice to meet you, Jenny."

11

"The challenges facing young men today have never been greater. Everywhere they look, they see different people telling them how to be a man. Telling them to weaken themselves for the sake of some woman. For the sake of some subculture. For the sake of the world. But no one is telling them to be stronger. To take what makes us inherently masculine and to cultivate it."

There were only ten in the room, including Abraham Laurel. The nine boys sat in a semicircle around him, all facing him. Abraham faced them. He was big, just like his son and his own father. He was wider than Isaac. Some of it was fat, but there was muscle underneath. Isaac told Daniel that his dad had played college football, and Daniel believed it. Abraham stood as tall as him, and very few did.

Isaac sat next to Daniel, who had introduced him to the other guys. Daniel recognized some of them from school, but the other half were younger, with two being no older than thirteen. They had all eyed him warily. He knew the word about Dad had gotten around. They all had seen him walk out of the service a couple Sundays back.

But the anxiety had relaxed once he met Abraham. Abraham spoke softly, with a calm assurance that immediately set Daniel at ease. He spoke confidently.

Daniel believed in God. When he reached into himself, when he searched inside for a solid foundation and facts, God was there. Immutable, undoubtable. He felt Him there.

Daniel believed in God. But he didn't always believe in the several preachers he had heard over the years. They didn't speak the Word of God. They spoke *about* the Bible, or *about* doing the right thing, but they lacked something. Something was missing from them. So he didn't listen. Because why should he?

Daniel *listened* to Abraham. He had the something, just like Reverend Laurel had during his sermon. Daniel could swear he even heard Isaac have the same quality once in a while. It was in their blood.

Daniel felt like he belonged as soon as he met Abraham, and he had welcomed Daniel to the Laurel Youth Experience. For the first time in Laurel City, he felt at home.

"It's in the Bible. Over and over again," said Abraham. "Men are to be emboldened by God's Word. To be strong, like David, in his fight against Goliath. To be strong like Samson, with his mane of hair, in his fight against the Philistines. And yet, more and more sources pull at our masculinity. Try and rip it away. To make us 'modern men'. To be truly modern men, we have to look back, not forward. We need to follow the Lord's Word. It will lead us to be men of God."

He stood up. "Let's pray." Daniel closed his eyes and bowed his head. Abraham's words washed over them.

"Dear God. Let us be true men of God. Let us not be swayed by the many temptations of modern life. By the appeal of women on Instagram, or on the street. By the liberal culture that encroaches on us more every day. Let us live by Your Word, and by Your Edict. Amen."

"Amen," said Daniel, and everyone said it alongside him.

They all stood up. Daniel needed to go home. His dad would be suspicious. He had said he was hanging out with friends, but leaving so early in the morning, on a Sunday, would probably set off alarms. He had changed into dress clothes in the church bathroom, stuffing his casual wear in his backpack.

"Are you staying for touch football?" asked Isaac. "You have to stay. I can't lose with you on my team."

Daniel nodded without thinking. "Sure," he said. Another hour wouldn't hurt. Dad wouldn't care. He didn't notice anything about Daniel's life, anyway.

The rest of the fellas were waiting for him in the field adjacent to the church, mostly grass with some dirt paths laid out around it.

"Witch boy finally arrived," said one of the guys. Jason, Daniel thought his name was. He had been quiet when Isaac had introduced him. Daniel ignored him.

Isaac looked at him and narrowed his eyes. "This is my secret weapon, boys," said Isaac. "You don't have a chance with him on my team."

"He's the size of a house," said Sam, another boy. "It's not fair."

"You can have the extra man," said Isaac. "Billy. Flip." Billy, one of the younger guys, moved to the other team. It was now five versus four. Isaac, Daniel, and two other kids, Mark and John. They hadn't made much of an impression on Daniel, and neither were as big as Isaac, let alone Daniel. They huddled up, back against one side of the field.

"Theo will fall back and play safety. He always does," said Isaac. "Mark, line up on the right, across from Sam. He's slow as molasses. Run a post route, as hard as you can, and lead Theo to the left. I'm going to run a crossing route, from left to right. Jason will cover me."

"What do I do?" asked Daniel.

"Line up on the right, inside of Mark. Run a little button hook. Stay close enough to keep two men on you. John, look for me coming across the middle. Lead me a little, Jason will cover me tight. Daniel, when you see him, screen him. He'll slam into you, and I'll be gone."

"What are you talking about? Halloween plans?" asked Jason, prodding at Daniel again. They lined up. There was no rushing, so the five boys all sat in coverage. Jason lined up across from Isaac, as Isaac said he would. John looked them over and hiked it himself, falling back. They all moved.

Mark ran hard, and he quickly passed Sam. Theo saw him get open and moved to the left to cover him. John faked the pass, and they both bit. Daniel ran a short button hook and sat in space. Billy stood nearby, trying to read John and tip his pass. Steven covered Daniel, but Daniel was a solid foot taller than him. He could catch a pass at will.

Isaac had crossed the field, and John switched his vision

at the last moment, throwing the ball in front of Isaac. John wasn't a quarterback, but he got it close enough for Isaac to catch. Jason trailed him and tried to reach out with two hands. Isaac was a fingertip ahead of him. Isaac saw Daniel, who had boxed out his man, and slipped around him.

Daniel took a step in as soon as Isaac passed him and Jason ran into a brick wall, his eyes only on Isaac. He hit the ground with a thud, Daniel looming over him. Isaac's plan had worked. Without Jason on him, he was gone, sprinting toward the end zone, not a player within twenty yards of him. He kneeled and pointed to the sky, and then came trotting back, a smile on his face.

"What did I say?" asked Isaac. He tossed the ball to Jason, who had picked himself up off the ground.

"You only scored because of him," said Jason, talking to Isaac, gesturing toward Daniel. "You're willing to dirty your hands with some sinner." Venom poured off every word, but Isaac didn't answer. Daniel saw the look he gave Jason, though, a quick narrowing of the eyes, and then a release.

They lined up again. The offense huddled.

"Play zone," said Isaac, to the three of them. "I'll cover deep, you play up front." The offense lined up, two receivers on each side. Jason lined up on the far left, and the quarterback started the play, fake hiking it from the imaginary center. Daniel fell back, trying to keep an eye on his part of the field. The four receivers crossed each other. Daniel tried to read the quarterback. Jason ran in front of him, and the football was in the air, heading toward Jason. Daniel saw a blur of motion in the corner of his eye. It was Isaac, running at full speed.

Jason's hands touched the ball and then Isaac hit him,

spearing him. Jason wasn't a small guy, but Isaac dwarfed him, and Jason hadn't expected the tackle. The football flew out of his hands, and Isaac drove him into the ground with an audible empty thud.

Isaac got up quickly, stretching his neck. He stood over Jason, who blinked, trying to collect himself. Daniel would have bet on a concussion. He'd be surprised if Jason didn't have a cracked rib.

Isaac looked down at him, but spoke loudly enough for everyone on the field to hear.

"Daniel is not his father," said Isaac. "And he won't be treated like he is. Understood?" Jason had collected himself enough to nod wearily, grimacing in pain. Isaac extended a hand to Jason, and Jason took it. He didn't look at Isaac now, his head down. Daniel didn't know if out of shame, or because he was still dazed, but Jason didn't say another word the entire game. Isaac's team won handily.

Abraham was waiting for Daniel when he came back in to change and get his stuff.

"I'm glad you could join us today," said Abraham. The small meeting room was empty except for them.

"It was good," said Daniel. "I'm happy Isaac invited me."

"He's talked a lot about you," said Abraham. "He's happy he finally has a friend on the football team." That surprised Daniel. Isaac seemed like the popular type.

"Isaac's helped me a lot," said Daniel. "It's been hard, you know, moving to a new town, and everything."

"About that," said Abraham. "Is everything okay at home? After what your father did at the service, and what I've heard from people around town—"

"Everything's fine," said Daniel. "It's just my dad. He can

be really stubborn. Halloween is one of his favorite things. I've tried to talk to him about just giving up on it, but he won't listen."

"That's admirable," said Abraham. "But you're not responsible for him. He is *your* father, and not the other way around. He should be more diplomatic in a new town."

"I told him that," said Daniel. "But he's not listening anymore."

Abraham sighed. "That's unfortunate. But I'm glad you found Isaac, and us. I know you've only joined us this one time, but I wanted to invite you to our camping trip next weekend. We're going to McCrea's Falls early Saturday and coming back late Sunday. It'll be a lot of fun."

"I don't know if Dad would appreciate me going to that," said Daniel.

"You're eighteen, correct?"

"Yes," said Daniel.

"Then you don't need his permission," said Abraham. "Does he know you're here?"

The question hung in the air.

"No," said Daniel. "He doesn't."

"Would he have stopped you from coming today?" asked Abraham.

"Probably not," said Daniel. "But I didn't want to cause any more trouble between us."

"Sometimes, you must stand firm and proud in your beliefs," said Abraham. "I'm lucky. My father has always supported me, and I try and do the same for Isaac. I imagine it's rough when you don't have that support from family."

Daniel wanted to reject that. He would like to say that his dad had always supported him. Had always done the best for him. But the words wouldn't come.

Had he always supported him? *Had* he always done what was best for Daniel?

"I'll think about the trip," said Daniel, finally. "I should get home."

"That's fair," said Abraham. "But remember, Daniel. Regardless of what happens between you and your father, you'll always have a family here. Laurel City can give you a new family. One that will support you."

12

"A zombie?"

"Boring."

"A scarecrow."

"Scarecrows don't scare anyone."

"That's not true. Harold from Scary Stories to Tell in the Dark is creepy."

"Can *we* make Harold?"

"No, probably not."

"Then it's a no."

"Pumpkinhead?"

"Dad, we need to build this in less than a month, and plan the whole rest of the party. Pumpkinhead would take us months to make. Think simple, but effective."

"Scary clown—"

"Please, so overdone—"

"Let me make my case. It's classic. It allows for a lot of fun creativity on our part. And everyone is afraid of clowns. We want something people will take selfies with. I think it's perfect."

"Hmm," said Marion. He had a point. They could do a lot with a clown. *She* could do a lot with a clown. John Wayne Gacy, Pennywise, The Joker. She could do something different. Maybe more classical, with a secret edge?

"See?" said her dad. "There's a lot of ideas there. It's iconic and recognizable. Doesn't make it bad."

"I'll brainstorm some stuff," she said.

Marion and her dad stood in their garage, two sawhorses with a piece of plywood on top serving as one workstation, a workbench as the other. Dad had fastened a big whiteboard to the back wall of the garage, and on it they planned Halloween. The plans for the house and the front yard had been sketched on it, but they'd erased them. They had to think big this year.

This had been their routine for years now, with Marion and her dad meeting in the garage as soon as the first pop-up Halloween store arrived. They'd sketch out their ideas for decorating the house, and for the party they'd throw every year.

Both Mom and Dad loved Halloween, and Marion had loved it too, right from the beginning. Christmas and Thanksgiving were always important, and she liked them too, but Halloween was special. Everything that was strange was acceptable during Halloween. They had encouraged her into helping with the decorations. At first, it was just fun to play with goop, but it sparked her artistic side, and every year she got to decide what to make of their centerpiece.

And then Mom passed away. And Dad didn't want to do anything. He had been a zombie. She didn't realize it then, but he held it together because of her and Daniel. He carried all that grief, and sent them off to school, and picked up Daniel from football practice. But he still wasn't the same.

She dragged him into the garage. It was the first Halloween since the accident.

"What is it, Marion?" he asked. It was early on Saturday, the first week of October. She had held him by the hand and pulled him outside. She had gotten up before him and set up their workstations.

"What's going on—" and then he saw the garage and realized the calendar. He didn't say anything.

"We're starting a little late, but we still have time to decorate," she said. "I've already got some ideas. I was thinking we could do a spooky campground, like Camp Crystal Lake? We could do a big Jason, right in the middle, holding a machete up—"

Dad wasn't looking at her then. He was bent over, both his hands leaning on the edge of a workbench. He looked hurt, like someone had punched him in the gut, or that he was about to be sick.

"Are you alright, Dad?" she asked, and then she saw that he was shaking.

Ever since the accident, Marion had never seen him cry. Even at the service, when he gave her eulogy, he had remained firm and strong, as he talked about the greatest woman he had ever known.

"I—can't—" he mustered before he started sobbing, his hands over his face. Marion didn't know what to say, so she just hugged him. She had been ten. What could she say?

He stopped, after a while. He hugged her back and re-treated inside. She didn't know what to do, so she stayed out in the garage and worked. Marion hadn't known if he would come back out. But after a couple hours, he did. He came out, and they put together their Halloween.

Their first Halloween in Laurel City would be bigger. They had more than a house to decorate. They had an entire community center.

"If we're going to have a scary clown as the centerpiece, we should do a carnival theme," said Marion. "We can have spooky carnival games, and then the two set-piece rooms can be a freak show or a sideshow or something."

Dad wrote everything down on the whiteboard as Marion dictated. They had done this for years now, but the board was filling up, as they colored in the schematic of the community center with all the different ideas and decorations they would need.

After a couple hours, the board was filled, and they still had space to fill in the center's schematic. Dad went inside to get a drink, and she stared at it. It was impossible. Building all of this and getting the word out to the town. It was impossible.

Dad came back out with two sodas in his hands.

"Here you go, killer," he said.

"We can't do this," said Marion.

"It doesn't have any calories, it's totally fine," he said.

"Not the soda. The party. It's too much work. We couldn't do this in three months, let alone one. Unless you plan on making it your full-time job, and I'm going to drop out of school."

"I mean—" he started, and then dropped off, staring at everything on the board. They had never done anything nearly as audacious as this. "It is a lot."

"Even if we spend every waking hour on it, we don't have enough time."

"We can't not do it," he said, finally. "Failure is not an option. We'll just have to prioritize the most important stuff, and hope we can get to the rest."

"And we need to get people to come too," said Marion. "I would say we could post fliers, but I don't know how long they'd stay up."

"We need a street team," he said. "Fliers, community boards, social media. We have to spread the word of this far and wide. I *know* there's demand for this. Laurel City is under served. Not everyone goes to LCHC. A few hundred people will fill the place."

"Leave that up to me," said Marion. She had an idea.

"You sure?" he asked. "It's a lot of work."

"I'll get help," said Marion. "We'll need more people, but we *can* do it. As for getting folks to come, we could have a costume contest. With prizes. It might draw people in."

"That's an excellent idea," said her dad. "And it doesn't require any extra work from us, aside from sourcing prizes."

"What should they be?"

"Gift cards?" he asked. "People like gift cards."

"Yeah, but they're boring," said Marion. "We can do better."

"Boring but useful."

"People don't want *useful* prizes," said Marion. "People want *exciting* prizes."

"I'd love to get a gift card," he said. "We could go to Olive

Garden—"

"The food is terrible at Olive Garden," said Marion.

"But the breadsticks! As many as you want!" he said.

"Quantity does not equal quality, Mike," said a third voice from behind them. Marion turned to see Ms. Gibson standing just outside their garage, wearing workout clothes and running shoes. Her curly hair was tied in a tight knot.

"Hi, Ms. Gibson," said Marion. "Someone with sense has finally arrived."

"I, for one, don't like a metric ton of salt on my bread," said Ms. Gibson. "May I come in?"

Dad was still trying to find his words.

God, Dad, you're embarrassing. "Sure, Ms. Gibson. We were planning our Halloween party," said Marion.

"They're not *that* salty," said her dad, finding his tongue again.

"They taste like the Dead Sea, Dad," said Marion.

"That looks like a lot of work," said Ms. Gibson, gesturing toward the whiteboard. "How do you plan to make the clown?"

"I don't know yet," said Marion. "Depends on the design. And how much of him is hanging out of him."

Ms. Gibson smiled. "Do you have a go-to recipe for guts?"

"Depends on the consistency we want. Sometimes you want slimy guts, sometimes you want firm guts that will hold their shape."

"Is there something I should know about you?" asked her dad, looking at Ms. Gibson.

"Probably," she said, smiling. "I'm stopping by to say hi."

"Hi," he said. "Oh, right. Excuse us for a second, sweetheart." Dad walked Ms. Gibson back out to the sidewalk where they talked. Marion returned to her work, taking a sketch pad out and starting to brainstorm ideas for the clown centerpiece. It should be big, at least eight feet tall. How high was the ceiling in there? They'd have to go back for exact measurements. How much of this would need to be assembled on site?

She couldn't help but glance back at Dad and Ms. Gibson talking on the sidewalk. Her dad was barely recognizable. He was smiling. Not that he didn't smile normally, but he didn't smile like this. It was uninhibited. She knew her dad. He was guarded about how he shared his emotions with most people. Ms. Gibson had already cracked through it.

He glanced at her, and she turned back to her work. After ten minutes or so, Ms. Gibson jogged off and Dad returned to the garage.

"How's the clown looking?" he asked.

"I'm thinking about a vintage Ronald McDonald look. Like those creepy pictures of old Halloween costumes? An old looking clown. With maybe only a little bit of gore. Like maybe the red touches on his costume are actually covered in blood, but only on a second glance."

"That sounds great," he said, looking back at the white board. "So."

"So?" asked Marion.

"I'm going out on a date with Jenny," he said. "Ms. Gibson."

"I know who you're talking about, Dad," said Marion. "It's not a mystery. You should have seen your face when she walked up."

"That obvious, huh?" he asked.

"Yeah, it was pretty embarrassing, actually," she said.

"Thanks," he said. "Wouldn't want me to get a big head or anything. I can always rely on my loving daughter to bring me back to Earth."

"It's what I'm here for," she said.

The garage was quiet again, as they each started drawing up plans.

"Is that okay?" asked her dad, out of the blue.

"Is what okay?" asked Marion.

"Me dating your teacher," he said. "Me dating in general."

"Of course," said Marion. "She's nice." He nodded, a small look of relief on his face that he failed to hide. They worked together most of the rest of the day, occasionally breaking the silence with a joke or a question about parts needed. They worked together on making Halloween happen in Laurel City.

13

"Hut, hut, HIKE!"

The center snapped, hiking the ball to the QB, who pivoted in the grass and handed the ball off to Isaac, who charged to the right of the center, in between the right guard and tackle.

Daniel pushed forward at the call, driving the defensive end back. The end was smaller than Daniel, but he was quick, and he swiped away Daniel's hands, and swam around him, wrapping his arms around Isaac's knees as he tried to run past. The end locked Isaac's legs together, and he went down. The whistle blew, and it was fourth down. Daniel, Isaac, and the rest of the team hurried off the field as special teams ran on.

Daniel caught his breath as he walked to the water cooler, taking a swig from a cup, swishing it in his mouth, and then swallowing. He downed the rest of the cup and then threw it away, sweat pouring off of him. The steam rose off him in the cool night air. He looked to the crowd, which was watching the Laurel City defense. His eyes scanned it, looking for his father. He had said he'd try to make it, but it would be difficult because of his schedule. There was always something more important—

"Daniel, what was that?" asked Isaac, walking up from behind him, grabbing a cup.

"The end—"

"I don't want to hear it," said Isaac. "You're destroying guys in practice, but suddenly you can't clear a path? We're getting wrecked out there, and they're all coming straight through you."

"I'm trying—"

"You want to be on the team or no?" asked Isaac. "I vouched for you."

Daniel looked to the stands again.

"Your dad's not out there," said Isaac.

Daniel wheeled on him, a sudden anger arising in him.

"That's what I want to see," said Isaac, not backing down. "Where's that anger out there?" Isaac pointed to the field. "There's no one on that field stronger than you. Get your head screwed on and prove you belong here."

Isaac walked away, back to the edge of the sidelines, standing next to Coach Holland.

Daniel felt his chest tighten, felt the rage still in him. He looked to the stands one last time, and he realized Isaac was right. His dad wasn't there, and he wouldn't be there. He'd chosen something else, again.

The Laurel City defense stymied the opposition, and their offense had possession again. Daniel ran onto the field, huddling up. Their QB called a play, another running play. It was coming right behind Daniel, and Isaac caught his eyes again as they broke the huddle, nodding at him.

They lined up the play, and Daniel put his hand down on the grass. He thought about his dad not being there, of leaving town, and he coiled up that emotion in him.

"Hut—hike!" yelled the QB, and the center snapped the football. Everything moved quickly. Daniel exploded off the line of scrimmage, grabbing the defensive end inside the shoulder pads, running faster than before. The end tried to swipe them away, but Daniel held on, getting underneath him and driving him off the ball, almost lifting him off the ground. They moved backward into the charging linebacker and Daniel threw the end into him, before moving onto a safety who had collapsed in. He made contact and then everyone started cheering, screaming loudly. Daniel turned and saw they had sprung Isaac, sprinting up the sideline, no defenders within range. The crowd roared, louder and louder, and then erupted as Isaac scored. Daniel ran down the field, joining in celebration with his teammates. Isaac found him in the fray.

"That's how you prove yourself," said Isaac.

*

"Surprised you're not near the fire," said Isaac, a voice coming up from behind Daniel.

"Didn't feel like it," said Daniel. Isaac sat next to him in the field, the grass rising above their heads. The victory party would go all night, out on the QB's family's land.

"Jessica likes you, if you're looking for a date for homecoming," said Isaac. "She's sitting by the fire."

"Yeah, I know," said Daniel.

"Not your type?" asked Isaac.

"I'm only going to be here a year," said Daniel. "I don't want to get too connected."

"I mean, it's only a dance," said Isaac. "Doesn't have to be more than that."

"I've got enough to worry about," said Daniel.

"Suit yourself," said Isaac. A silence settled between them. Daniel could hear yelling from behind him, closer to the fire. He took a swig of his beer. Isaac drank water.

"You were good out there tonight," said Isaac. "I apologize for being rude with you, but someone needed to snap you out of it."

"It's okay," said Daniel. "You were right. I was making stupid mistakes. Could have cost us the game. I was in my own head too much."

"Happens to the best of us," said Isaac.

"Doesn't seem to happen to you."

"Just because I don't show it doesn't mean it doesn't happen," said Isaac. "My father always said self doubt is normal, but that you should never let that doubt overwhelm your self-confidence. That you should always project complete belief."

"You're good at it," said Daniel.

"It's hard sometimes," said Isaac. "But I'm going to be here for the rest of my life. And people have long memories."

Daniel looked to Isaac, both of them shrouded in shadow, the only light coming from the distant fire and the stars.

Was it doubt he saw now?

"Do you ever regret being a Laurel?" asked Daniel.

Isaac didn't answer at first, taking a sip of water. "It's hard. Everyone watches you, all the time. They know who you are, and what you're doing, and who you're doing it with. And my father and grandfather aren't hard to find. There was a time. I was eight. I had gotten a bike for Christmas, and I had the run of the town. I became friends with a kid named Jon. He had a bike too, an older one, and we spent every day riding around. One day, I followed Jon to an abandoned house, out on the edge of town. We went inside. The place was old, falling apart. Jon started throwing rocks, breaking windows. I joined him. I didn't really think about it. But the next day, my father called me aside."

"Someone told him," said Daniel.

Isaac nodded. "Someone saw us and put two and two together. And I'll never forget not what he said, but how he said it. Because he spoke in cold truth. There wasn't frustration or disappointment or anger. But he forbid me from seeing Jon anymore. Told me he was a bad influence. Jon lived in Laurel Manors, and it isn't becoming for someone like me to be there."

"What's Laurel Manors?" asked Daniel.

"It was a trailer park, back then," said Isaac. "It's gone now. The Church bought the land. And I didn't understand it then. But he was right. As a Laurel, I have a responsibility. I always have to portray the appropriate image. It isn't about what I want. It's about what people see."

Daniel looked to him, and Isaac took another sip of water before looking back.

"So no," said Isaac. "I've never regretted my name. Only

what it requires of me."

Another silence. Daniel took another swig.

"Thanks," said Daniel.

"Thanks for what?" asked Isaac.

"For being my friend," said Daniel.

"Thanks for being mine," said Isaac. "Another thing that comes with the name."

"What do you mean?" asked Daniel.

"Friends," said Isaac. "Sometimes we don't get them."

14

Mike was taking a break from working on Halloween when David Laurel showed up at his door.

The doorbell rang, and he stood there, his foreboding figure waiting on his front porch.

"Can I help you, Reverend?" asked Mike. "If you're looking for the essential oils night hosted by Mrs. Baker, that's three doors down. Only sinners here, worshiping our pagan gods. Unless you're interested in a blood sacrifice?"

"You're very funny, Mr. Dawson," said Laurel. "I just want to talk. I think we've gotten off on the wrong foot." Mike sensed the veil of kindness that always wrapped Laurel, the same one he had recognized when he made Laurel put out his fire. Maybe Laurel had changed his tune. Mike doubted it, but maybe he could have some fun with him, on his own turf.

"Alright," said Mike. "Come in." He opened the door and gestured inside.

Mike led him to their living room.

"Would you like something to drink? Bud Light? Rum and coke?" he asked.

"No thank you," said Laurel. "I see you don't have decorations inside."

"Not really," said Mike. "We keep it all out for the world to see. Open and honest."

"I can appreciate that," said Laurel.

"Well?" asked Mike. "You wanted to talk? Talk."

Laurel pursed his lips. "I've heard about your plans for Halloween." He said nothing else, as if that alone was enough to make Mike understand his reasoning.

"Yeah," said Mike. "Should be a good party. We have big ideas for it."

"Who's we?" asked Laurel.

"My daughter and I," said Mike. "We always do it together. She's very talented."

"What about your son?" asked Laurel.

"What about him?" asked Mike. "He doesn't really like Halloween that much, if that's what you're asking. It also has nothing to do with why you're here. Or why you invited me to your church and then singled me out and insulted me in front of the entire congregation."

"That was—"

"And don't say that it was unintentional," said Mike. "Because I'm not an idiot, and the tricks you use on your flock won't work on me. I made you put out your fire, and I decorated my yard, so you killed two birds with one stone, and hoped I would crawl home with my tail between my legs. But it didn't work, and now I'm throwing a big shindig that's got you upset. Right?"

Laurel sighed and stared at him. "You are direct, aren't you?"

Mike smiled. "I don't have time for bullshit."

"Very well. I'd like to reconsider your party."

"Reconsider what? We're pretty happy with the ideas so far. Marion is absolutely killing the clown centerpiece. It's out in the garage, if you want to take a look—"

"Please, Mr. Dawson. I'd like you to cancel the party."

"Why would I do that?" asked Mike. "I've already paid the deposit on the community center, and I don't know how much you think a cop's salary is, but the deposit is not a negligible amount of money."

"If it's a problem of capital, the Church will gladly pay back—"

"It's not about the money," said Mike. "Why would I cancel the party?"

"Because it's the right thing to do, Mr. Dawson," said Laurel. "It's the right thing to do for the community and for you."

"Is that right?" asked Mike. "I'm not so sure about that, on either count."

"Halloween is a threat to our way of life, Mr. Dawson," said Laurel. "The children—"

"Won't *someone* please think of the children?" asked Mike. "I heard your sermon already, Reverend. Your empty fear-mongering won't work on me. I'm an upstanding member of society. I obey the law and look out for my fellow man. In fact, it's my job. And I've celebrated Halloween my whole life. I don't worship demons, and I don't practice blood magic. Once a year, I decorate my house with spooky stuff and dress up in a costume. That doesn't make me Satan."

"I never said it did," said Laurel.

"Ehh, you kinda sorta implied it in that sermon the other day," said Mike.

"Mr. Dawson, let me be straight with you."

"I'm all ears."

"In my sermon, I speak of the dangers of Halloween because I am speaking to the people of Laurel City as a whole. I cannot be specific to the intelligence of any particular member—"

"So all those dummies in your church can't be trusted to celebrate Halloween because they'll confuse the costume devils for real ones?"

"I'm tiring of your humor," said Laurel.

"The door's over there," said Mike, pointing. "You can leave if you want."

"I'm simply saying that if you cancel your party, the Church will refund your deposit, and allow you to host a party here, in your home, for anyone who'd like to attend."

"Why do you keep saying 'the Church'?" asked Mike.

"What?"

"You keep saying 'the Church' will do this, or 'the Church' will do that. Who runs the Church?"

Laurel only stared at him.

"Right. You run it," said Mike. "I'm sure there are other people involved, but at the end of the day, you make the decisions. So what you're really saying is that *you* will allow me to have a party in my own home, which is my property, that is, if I cancel the party at the community center, which is *also* private property."

"Or you can simply attend the Church-run Fall Festival, also running on October 31st. We will have games, a bake sale, and a reenactment of Christ's miracles, put on by the children. Costumes are encouraged, as well."

Mike laughed. "What kind of costumes?"

"Any Biblical or historical figures. Athletes or soldiers. Characters from film, provided they're not obscene—"

"But nothing scary?" asked Mike. "Or grotesque? Or aberrant? Or weird?"

"It's a family event, Mr. Dawson. Why would you want to dress up like something like that?"

"Because it's fun, Reverend. Because sometimes, people want to indulge in the strange parts of themselves that they have to hide away. Because it's important to carve out a space for that. Healthy, even."

"I don't know what you're talking about," said Laurel. Mike studied Laurel's face. He wasn't listening to any of this. Mike could frustrate him, but he wouldn't change his mind. It was too late.

"I bet you don't," said Mike.

"Fine. If you won't listen to reason," said Laurel. "The Church has a lot of power in town—*I* have a lot of power in town. What would it take you to cancel your party?"

"Now you're trying to bribe me?" asked Mike.

Laurel again said nothing.

"I'm sure if I tried to mention this to your parishioners, you'd deny it, and they wouldn't believe me."

"I can ensure you get a promotion and a pay increase," said Laurel. "Chief Miller is a devout member of the Church.

I can ensure your children get good grades at school. I can even make your taxes go away."

"All of that, just so I cancel a party?" asked Mike.

"Yes," said Laurel. "I care about the welfare of Laurel City. I will do anything to keep it safe for its residents, and for its future."

"And if I don't cancel?" asked Mike.

"The same power can punish. Your life in Laurel City can be difficult. You can be ostracized from community events. Your career as a police officer will be stymied. Your children will face hardship at school."

"You'd go after my kids?" asked Mike. "All this from a man of God."

"I care about Laurel City," said Laurel. He believed what he said, Mike could see that. And Mike knew getting angry would only make Laurel happy.

"That's a shame," said Mike. He pulled out his phone from his pocket. "Because your parishioners might not believe it coming from me, but they might believe it if they hear it from you."

"You—"

"You bastard?" he asked. "Reverend Laurel, you wouldn't use such vile language against a fellow man, would you?"

"How dare you record me without my permission!" said Laurel. His face reddened.

"It's my house," said Mike. "I can do what I want here. Private property supersedes your right to privacy."

Laurel stood up now, flustered and angry.

"I will have those decorations declared obscene!" said Laurel. "I will—"

"Again, private property," said Mike. "Much like the

community center, the law is on my side. I'm a cop, Reverend. I know my rights better than anyone. I'm real impressed that you came to my house, and thought up this whole speech, trying to sway me. But I'm not canceling my party. You're invited, if you'd like to attend. We're having a costume contest. The winner gets a one hundred dollar gift card of their choosing. See, Marion thought a gift card was kind of boring, but when I said it could be *any* gift card, and it was a hundred big ones, she changed—"

"This is Laurel City!" said Laurel, blustering now. "I am David Laurel, son of John Laurel, descendant of Elijah Laurel. We founded this town, and I will not allow pagan deviltry in it."

Mike stared at him and smiled. "I don't care, Reverend. You don't own the city, and you don't control me. Go back to your little fiefdom, and never come back to my home, or I'll have you arrested."

15

It was late, and the Laurel City Holy Church was empty except for Reverend David Laurel. He sat at his desk, deep in the church, reading through their most secret possession.

"I can't believe the disrespect," he said aloud, not realizing he muttered to himself. He looked at the clock. It was almost midnight.

Where the hell was Abraham?

This was all Miller's fault. After all the trouble last year, he should have known better. But David had trusted him. He had trusted him to vet the new officer. But then again, how could he have known? No one asks questions about Halloween during job interviews. Maybe David himself should have sat down and talked to him before all of this.

No. It wouldn't have solved anything. Dawson was the

kind of trouble that was inevitable. No one could have predicted how stubborn a newcomer could be, about Halloween of all things. If it wasn't Halloween, it'd be something else. Someone would have a problem with displaying the nativity scene by the firehouse, or using city funds on church renovations, or they'd get another person like Sarah Hamilton. People who didn't understand the history and tradition of Laurel City and put their nose where it didn't belong.

Well, they took care of Sarah Hamilton. God had shown them the way. And He would do the same with Dawson.

Where the hell was Abraham?

He ran his hands over the pages of the Book. He could feel its power, raw and dangerous. His own father had shown him the way of the Book, had shown him how God had blessed their family with this authority. The Book was bound in red leather, a foot tall and wide, over six inches thick. The Book was ancient, but the pages stayed fresh and pliable.

But he could also feel the danger within. He knew in untrained hands the Book would be a threat. Only he could use it correctly. Over the years he had grown to know it, which pages to study, and which to avoid. God had shown him the path. God had blessed the Laurels. He had doubted at first. It was the way of things. He had been only nineteen then.

"I don't know, father," said David. *"This seems—wrong."*

"Do you doubt the Word of God?" asked his father John. They stood in the small room, lit only by candles. The walls were brick, and the floor was simple wooden boards, stained and smudged. They had been laid when the church was built and had never been cleaned. His father had told him this. His father had told him many things.

"No, father," said David. "But the Bible is the Word of God."

"You are still young, and there are still many things you are yet to comprehend. But the Bible is but one Book. It is the one that we present to the world, and to the congregation. But there are others that belong only to us. To God's chosen. We were ordained to create Laurel City, and to protect it. This Book is our tool. Do you understand?"

I will try had been his answer, and he had tried. His father had died twelve years ago, and he had gained full control of the Book. Many things had changed since he was nineteen. Even from twelve years ago, when his father had passed into God's hands. Laurel City had changed.

It was subtle and slow. New people came in from outside. The town grew, and then shrank, and then grew, and David knew it was God's influence to keep the small town alive, when so many were dying around them. They had no cottage industry to carry them, but still they thrived.

But as the town flourished, the congregation dwindled.

He looked out at the pews every Sunday, and every Sunday they were filled. But he had to remind himself that not even twelve years ago they were packed for two services every Sunday, an early and late service. They only had the late service now, after attendance at both had declined, and he had made the call to combine them. Now the church was full again, but did the congregation realize that there were so many less of them? If they did, they hadn't mentioned it to him. The town was losing faith, literally. Dawson and Halloween was just the most recent strike in the war.

They had to make a stand. He had thought Sarah Hamilton would have been enough, but it wasn't. They would have to go further.

"Father," said Abraham. He stood in the doorway to his office. David jumped. "Sorry. I was waiting for you to notice me—" He saw the Book on his desk, the pages open.

"I didn't realize," said Abraham. "I didn't realize it was—"

"Why else would I possibly invite you to the church at midnight?"

"You usually give me a heads up—"

"Never mind that. Did you bring Isaac?"

"Yes," said Abraham.

"And the dog?"

"Yes," said Abraham. "Why do we need the bulldog?"

"Why do you think?" asked David. "Because it's time for Isaac's initiation."

"He's not ready," said Abraham. "He hasn't even graduated high school yet."

"He's only two years younger than when I learned, and we require him now. The talk with Dawson didn't go well."

"It's only one Halloween party, father. Is this really necessary?"

"Only. That's how it started with Sarah Hamilton, too. Only one journalist looking into our family history."

"Now father, how was I supposed to—"

"Szt. He is directly defying us, and he is organizing. It will begin with him, and friends, and then it will expand, and next year it will be bigger, and people will pick sides, and so on. We must make sure we win this battle, and that we win it decisively. Isaac has befriended the Dawson boy?"

"Yes," said Abraham. "And I've invited him to our camping trip next weekend."

"Good," said David. "We'll need him for leverage."

"I still don't know—"

"I don't need you to know anything, Abraham. I only require your *belief*. Go get Isaac and the dog. Meet me in the room."

Abraham left after a short pause. David worried about him. He'd struggled his entire life with it. It had taken Abraham three tries to be initiated. He had gotten it though, but he hadn't started until he was twenty-three, and back from seminary school.

College had been the problem. I had started him too late. I won't make that mistake with Isaac.

He ran his fingers over the Book one more time, over the right page. Contact was important. He felt God in those pages, and touch ensured faith. He shut the Book and took it.

David walked deep into the church, down hallways, to an unmarked wooden door, no different from every other door. This one was always locked, and David found the key in his pocket without thinking and unlocked it. He shut it behind him. Abraham had the only other copy. He stood in a small brick room, with a heavy metal door in front of him, padlocked shut. A different key unlocked this one, completing the set. After tonight, Isaac would get copies of both.

Only if he could handle it.

He could handle it. He was strong and believed in their name. He *would* handle it.

The heavy padlocked door opened soundlessly. David looked after the doors, because no one else could. A small set of stairs led down into an old brick chamber with a dirty wooden floor. The floor was older than the church, set into the ground by his great-great-great-grandfather's hands. This was the true bedrock of Laurel City, and the church an extension of that foundation.

The room was dark, and David lit the many candles that were the only source of light. By the time he was done, hundreds of flames provided enough light to read by. Then he waited, the Book open on a small table. It only held the Book.

David heard the metal door open above him, and Abraham and Isaac walk down the stairs.

"You can't tell me why we're here?" asked Isaac. "I've got to get up early tomorrow to go running with Daniel. And why did I have to bring Bubba?"

"Patience, Isaac," said Abraham. "Your grandfather will explain everything."

They came down, and Abraham guided Isaac to the center of the room, before he stood behind David.

"What's going on, grandfather? Where are we?" asked Isaac. Bubba, a white pure-bred bulldog, sat at his feet. Isaac held a leash attached to his collar. Bubba licked himself, oblivious to everything.

"All your questions will be answered in time," said David. "Most will be explained if you listen."

"The Laurels founded Laurel City. They were led here by the Word of God. They founded the Laurel City Holy Church, and we continue that legacy to this very day."

"I know all that, grandfather," said Isaac. "Dad has been telling me it since I was born."

"That is only a portion of the story. This Book serves as the rest," said David. Isaac's eyes glanced at the Book, flitted away, and then back again, unable to look elsewhere for long. It was the power of the Book. It's magnetic strength affected everyone, Laurels stronger than most. It had grown accustomed to their blood.

"What is it?" asked Isaac.

"Do you believe in God's Power?" asked David.

"Of course, grandfather," said Isaac.

"Do you believe that God has a hand in all things?"

"Yes," said Isaac.

"Do you believe that God gives man control of his domain on Earth?"

"I—I think so," said Isaac. "I'm not sure what that means."

"It means that God provides us with resources, and with the wisdom to use them correctly. To ensure the survival of His Word on Earth," said David.

"Then yes," said Isaac.

"This Book is control, Isaac. God led your distant grandfather to this Book, and then brought him here, to start the Church and town, using the Book whenever necessary."

Isaac drifted toward the Book. He was not aware he did it. David saw it and did not stop him. He would need to touch it before the night was through. It would need to know him before they could finish.

"What does it do?"

"It does many things," said David. "It can call upon many powers, some of which are too dangerous for our world. I have held the Book for only twelve years, since your great-grandfather's passing, and I have only gleaned the merest knowledge from its pages. When I pass into God's hand, your father will take control of it. And then you."

Isaac reached out his hand. He didn't realize he did it, the leash held slack in his other. It called to him, like it had called to every Laurel over the years.

"Tonight, we will initiate you in its use. So touch the Book."

Isaac's fingers grazed the page. His face changed imperceptibly, but David knew it. He had seen the same on Abraham. He had felt it, himself.

Isaac stepped back, into the middle of the room, over the dirtiest part of the floor. David pulled out a knife. A large one, with a five-inch blade. He handed it to Isaac, who took it.

"What is this for?" asked Isaac. Bubba still licked himself next to him.

"All things in God require sacrifice."

16

"How's Halloween going?"

Janine and Mike drove through town on patrol.

"We're building," said Mike. "Me and Marion. But we need help, frankly. There's still time to get in on the ground floor, you know?"

"I'm not crafty," said Janine, her eyes on the road.

"You don't have to be crafty," he said. "Anyone can hammer two boards together."

"You'd be surprised," she said. "I'll ask my daughter. See if she's interested in helping out."

"It's my favorite part of Halloween," he said. "Spending time with Marion. Good father/daughter bonding."

"She likes it too, huh?" asked Janine.

"Yeah," he said. "She's so talented. She's way better at the effects stuff than me. I just enjoy it, but she's *good* at it."

"Is she good with younger kids?" asked Janine.

"Marion? I don't know. Probably," said Mike. "She's patient with me, and I'm dumber than a kid sometimes."

"Maybe I'll bring Fiona around on the weekend. See if she enjoys it."

"That'd be great," said Mike. "We need all the help we can get."

The radio buzzed, and Janine hit the button.

"Come in," she said.

"We've got reports of an animal attack at Johnson's Pets, over in the old Crowne Plaza."

"Did one of their dogs lose it, or something?" asked Janine.

"Don't know," said the radio.

"We'll check it out," said Janine, and sped over.

"As far as I know, Johnson's only sells puppies," said Janine. "Don't know why you'd call in an animal attack if a puppy bit someone."

They found out when they got there. Johnson's Pets was tucked in the corner of a strip mall, between a Family Dollar and a grocery store. The sign was bright green, with a cartoon puppy poking his head out of the O in store.

Both of the front windows were smashed. Johnson's kept puppies in the front display, to attract customers. Mike couldn't recognize what was left of them. He smelled it as soon as he got out of the car. They both slipped on latex gloves.

"Oh my God," said Janine, covering her mouth. Broken glass was everywhere and gore covered the displays. Strips of yellow fur were strewn about, like a stuffed animal had been ripped apart. He had never seen anything like it.

It was worse inside. Simon Johnson waited inside for them.

"Thank God you're here," said Johnson. Johnson looked to be in his mid-50s, and seemed like he'd been woken up out of bed. "I can't believe this. All my animals—just gone."

Mike looked around the modestly sized store. Blood and guts covered over half the place with corpses strewn everywhere. Some lay in their cages still, while the remains of others had been thrown across the area. One entire wall was glass cages, where most of the puppies were kept. All were broken, and none of the dogs remained alive. There were open cages where they kept what looked like rabbits, guinea pigs, and ferrets. All were destroyed, bloody hay all over the floor nearby.

Something buzzed Mike's head, and he instinctively ducked.

"Parakeet," said Janine.

"Whatever it was, it didn't get all the birds," said Simon. "A silver lining, I guess."

As they walked deeper in the store, random shelves were knocked over, with pet food bags ripped apart. The stink of gore was weaker as they stepped through the store, replaced by the scent of saltwater.

"All the saltwater tanks," said Simon. "All broken. All the fish dead. Reptiles, too. I'm out almost everything."

"Have you touched anything?" asked Mike.

"No," said Simon. "I wanted to wait for you. I only got here half an hour ago. Heather opened, and she called me in. She's sitting in the back office. She's pretty shaken up."

"I can't imagine," said Mike. "Any signs of burglary? Any

money missing?"

"We don't keep a lot on hand," said Simon. "Only enough to make change. But none of it is gone. Nothing stolen, either. A person couldn't have done this. The animals were ripped apart. All of them. It was like it went after anything alive."

"Where's Heather?" asked Janine. "Let's talk to her."

Heather sat in the back office, the door closed. She was young, just out of high school, with short blond hair. She stared down at her phone, her face red from crying. Simon poked his head in.

"Heather? The police are here. They'd like to talk to you, and then you can go home," he said. She nodded, and then Janine and Mike went inside, closing the door behind them. It kept the smell outside.

"Hi, Heather," said Janine. "I'm Officer Hernandez, and this is Officer Dawson. We just want to ask you a couple of questions."

She nodded, stuffing her phone in her pocket.

"Will you be okay?" asked Janine. "We don't have to do this now—"

"I'll be alright, Officer," she said. She looked up at them, and her eyes were red. "They were like friends, you know?"

"I'm sorry," said Janine. "Just tell us what you saw when you got here."

"It was 6:30. I get here at 6:30 to open the store by eight. The sun was just rising, and nobody else was around. I feed all the animals, clean their cages, give them medicine if they need it, usually. But I saw the glass broken when I pulled up and knew immediately something was wrong. And then I saw all the blood. It was everywhere." She pulled out a tissue from her pocket and wiped her eyes and blew her nose. Mike couldn't imagine how terrible it was, to help raise all these animals, to take care of them, and find them destroyed, all at once. And not just dead, but torn apart.

"Did you notice anything else?" asked Janine.

"Yes," said Heather. "I saw the thing that did it."

"What? You saw it? What was it?" asked Janine.

"I don't—I don't know," she said. "It was black."

"Was it a bear? Or a coyote?" asked Janine.

"No," said Heather. "It walked on two legs. It was on—on top of one puppy in the window, and its arms were inside the dog, just ripping, pulling it apart, throwing it everywhere, and I pulled up, and my headlights hit it, and it looked at me, and it was black—"

"Bipedal?" asked Janine. "There's no animal that does that. It had to be a person, then. Dressed in black."

"It wasn't human," said Heather. "It couldn't be, there's no way, no person could look like that, no matter what they did—"

"Slow down, Heather," said Janine. "Describe it."

"It was black. All black. Dark. It—it absorbed the headlights. Like, I could still see it, but the light that hit it just went in. But it walked on two legs. It was maybe four feet tall. Its arms—they ended in prongs. Two sharp claws. Like a barbecue fork." Mike studied Heather while Janine interviewed her.

"What happened next?" asked Janine.

"It ran," said Heather. "It disappeared in a flash. I blinked, and it was gone, out of the window display and past my car."

"What did you do then?"

"I sat in my car for a good fifteen minutes," said Heather.

"I didn't know if it was still around, or if there were more of them inside. But I sat there, and I waited, and then when nothing moved for a while, I called Simon. He showed up, and we went in together."

"Did you find anything else?" asked Janine.

"No," said Heather. "We looked around a little, but I just started crying, and I couldn't—I couldn't take it anymore. I sat down in here and waited for you."

"Thank you for your help," said Janine. "Call us if you remember anything else." They went back outside, and Simon dismissed Heather. She left out the back, so she wouldn't have to see the horror again. Janine talked to Simon, and Mike went to the wall of windowed cages. He wanted to inspect the bodies. See what kind of damage had been done to them.

The smell of copper came back strong, and his early morning coffee surged into his throat. He swallowed it down with a grimace. He would not throw up. Not here. He went window by window, all broken and shattered, looking at each corpse.

The puppies had been small, all young, all pure bred. The price tags were still up, with some dogs costing over a thousand dollars. Mike couldn't imagine spending that much on a dog, especially when you could easily adopt one for free.

Finding anything substantial from any of the bodies was challenging. The thing, whatever it was, had been thorough. Every single animal had been targeted and destroyed. Mike stepped back into the kennel area behind the display cages, and the smell of gore and feces was so strong that he doubled over. His coffee didn't come up again, though.

Pieces of meat were everywhere, some with fur attached.

He found a rear hindquarter, separated from the rest of the dog's body, and he crouched to examine it.

The bite and claw marks were evident at closer inspection. The tears were ragged, not clean. No human did this. This was the work of an animal. He heard a noise from a kennel tucked up against the far corner of the room, and his hand went to his gun instinctively. He crouch walked over to the enclosure, set on the ground, the cage door swung open. Was there more than one of them?

He looked inside, hand on his holster, but he saw nothing, only a tipped over bed and two empty bowls. Then the bed shifted. He reached out a cautious hand and lifted the edge. A set of eyes stared back at him. A golden retriever puppy peeked out. It had hidden underneath, and the killer had missed it.

Mike reached in and grabbed her. The puppy was anxious, but as soon as Mike brought her to his chest and held her, its tail wagged slowly, and then it licked his face. He carried it out into the main area.

"I found a survivor," said Mike.

"She likes you," said Janine. She turned back to Simon. "Did Heather tell you about the animal she saw?"

"Yeah," said Simon. "She told me."

"You don't believe her?" asked Janine.

"A bipedal animal? Completely black, with hands like barbecue forks?" asked Simon. "Heather's a great manager, and has a good head on her shoulders, but no, I don't believe her. I understand, I do. She saw all those dead animals, and she imagined something terrible. Something horrible enough in her mind, that could do a thing like this. But I think it was just a rabid wolf. Only thing that makes sense.

Or maybe a bear, but we don't get them much anymore. Farmers out in the country still see wolves though, from time to time."

"You think a wolf could break through glass?" asked Janine.

"They're strong as hell, officer," said Simon. "And if they were driven mad by rabies, I think it's possible."

"It wasn't done by a person," said Mike. "There are claw and bite wounds on the animals. What do you want to do with the dog?"

"Do you want her?" asked Simon.

"What? Really?" asked Mike.

"Insurance will cover everything," he said. "It'll be a mess. I'm gonna need a bio-hazard crew to dispose of the bodies, clean the entire place. Replace all my inventory. I don't have anyplace to put the dog. You can have her free of charge. She's been through enough."

"I'll take her," said Mike, the puppy licking him, as if on cue.

They returned to the car, with Janine starting the paperwork and radioing back the details. Mike put the puppy in the back seat. They could drop her off at his house.

"What are you putting down as the attacker?" asked Mike.

"Rabid wolf," said Janine. "You heard Simon. It makes as much sense as anything."

"But you don't believe it," said Mike.

"No," said Janine. "Heather believes what she said."

"There's nothing on Earth that looks like what she described," said Mike.

"You're right," said Janine. "There's not."

17

"This is your street team," said Cara. She opened the door to the classroom. She revealed a couple tables filled with five kids combined. Two boys played Magic: The Gathering on one smaller table, while the three others moved characters around on a dungeon-tile map.

School had ended twenty minutes ago, and the five of them sat in an empty science classroom.

"The bigger kid playing Magic is Justin, and the boy across from him is Gene. The three kids playing Descent are Laura, Mandy, and Ben. This is the Laurel City High School Gaming Club."

Justin was big, even sitting down, looming over the table with broad shoulders. He was black, with close shorn black hair. His huge hands delicately held his Magic cards. He wore a My Hero Academia t-shirt. Gene, across from him, was almost his exact opposite. He was small, Asian, and dressed in a polo shirt three sizes too big. His huge glasses covered his face. He held a lot of cards and was shifting them back and forth.

Laura had a giant cloud of bright red hair, corralled by several scrunchies. She wore overalls over an old t-shirt. Laura wore a dress with a simple flowery print, and she smiled as Ben described something in the game. Ben had sandy hair, overgrown, and he wore a band t-shirt. Marion couldn't make out the band name.

"Is this all the members?" asked Marion.

"No," said Cara. "There's also me. And now you."

"I've only played Settlers of Catan before," said Marion.

"It's no problem," said Cara. "Most games are better than that. We'll teach you how to play." Marion felt unease at meeting so many people at once, but Cara squeezed her hand and smiled and the anxiety disappeared.

"They're all interested in helping with the party?" asked Marion.

"Oh, um, I haven't asked them yet," said Cara. "But I'm sure they will. They're all good people. Come on."

Cara pulled her inside the room. No one noticed, all of them continuing their games.

"Hey guys," said Cara, speaking up. "Guys!" They all looked up, broken from the trance of gaming. "This is my girlfriend, Marion. She's joining the club."

There was a short chorus of "hi's" from the group, and then they went back to their games.

"They're not the most outgoing, but they warm up once they get to know you," said Cara quietly. Cara walked up to

Justin and Gene.

"Are you guys almost done?" asked Cara.

"We would if Gene would just concede," said Justin. "I have an infinite combo, dude. You can't win."

"You haven't shown me a win condition yet," said Gene. "Why would I concede?"

"Okay," said Justin. "I loop fifty times, until I gain 300 life, and then I play Dawn of Hope. I loop fifty more times, and make 100 soldiers, and then attack. Better?"

"Fine, I concede," said Gene.

"You weren't even holding a counter?" asked Justin, rolling his eyes.

"It's the principle of the matter," said Gene.

"We're done," he said. "What were you thinking?"

"Maybe a game of Resistance, with everyone?" asked Cara. "So Marion can get to know everybody."

"I prefer Avalon," said Gene, quietly.

"You're the only one, Gene," said Justin. "Fine with me. I don't know how close they are to wrapping up. Not like they haven't played Descent before."

Mandy responded from the table. "It's steady and reliable, Justin."

"And boring," said Justin. "Just play D&D."

"You don't need a DM for Descent," said Laura. "Unless you want to DM for us?"

"That's a lot of work," said Justin. "And I'm not buying all those books."

"We can pause the game," said Ben. "I'll take a picture with my phone and we'll finish the adventure tomorrow."

They put away everything and Ben grabbed Resistance from the closet. They all sat around the biggest lab table.

"So…how do you play?" asked Marion.

"I'll explain," said Cara. "Resistance is a social deduction game. We'll split up into two teams, the blue team, the good guys, and the red team, the bad guys. The trick is that the blue team doesn't know who's on their side, while the red team does. We'll pass out cards which tell you which team you're on. Do not reveal this information to anyone, and I mean anyone. It can spoil the game if someone finds out, so keep it secret at all costs."

"How do you win?" asked Marion.

"Don't trust Cara," said Gene. "That's how you win."

"I'm on the red team one time, and now you can never trust me again," said Cara.

"You lied to my face," said Gene.

"That's the game, Gene," said Cara.

"I thought I could trust you," he said, shaking his head. Marion couldn't tell if he was being serious or not.

"But we go on missions and try to figure out who's who. The blue team wants to succeed on missions, and the red team wants to fail. We'll do a practice round to make sure you understand."

They set up the game and dealt cards. Marion understood it quickly enough, and they played. She was on the blue team. At least she didn't have to lie about her intentions.

Two rounds went by, with the blue team succeeding on both.

"Easy street," said Cara, passing the leadership chip.

"Sounds like what a spy would say," said Mandy. "Marion, is yours the house with all the Halloween decorations?"

"Yeah, it is," said Marion.

"I knew it!" said Mandy. "They look awesome."

"Thanks," said Marion. "I made most of them. A few things are store bought."

"Really?" asked Laura. "That's cool."

"I heard people are freaking out about them," said Ben.

"The Church," said Marion. "The reverend came over and tried to talk my dad out of hosting a Halloween party at the community center."

"Wait a second," said Justin. "You're throwing a Halloween party? In Laurel City?"

"Well, me and my dad," said Marion.

"Wouldn't be surprised if God struck the whole town with a thunderbolt," said Gene.

"Who's invited?" asked Justin.

"Everyone," said Marion. "We love Halloween, and we wanted to throw an actual Halloween party, not some Fall Festival crap with a bunch of Jesus costumes."

"Hell yeah," said Laura.

"So we're invited?" asked Ben.

"Yeah, absolutely," said Marion. "Actually, I was wondering if you guys would help."

"Help with what?" asked Justin.

"Help with getting the word out about the party," said Marion. "We're still new in town. We don't know many people."

"How would we do that?" asked Mandy.

"Put up fliers. Talk about it online. Tell your friends," said Marion. "We've got our hands full trying to decorate the community center, so we need help."

"That sounds great," said Laura, smiling. "I'll help."

"Yeah, sure," said Ben. "If it bothers the Church, I'm in."

Gene nodded his assent.

"I'll help," said Mandy.

Marion looked to Justin, who sat with his arms crossed, thinking.

"Will there be costumes at this party?" he asked.

"Of course. It's Halloween," said Marion.

He nodded.

"As anything, right? Not just some boring disciple?" he asked. His wheels were turning.

"Yeah, anything you want," said Marion. "We're having a costume contest."

"Then I'm in," said Justin.

*

"You've been so nice to me," said Marion.

"What do you mean?" asked Cara.

"You drive me home every day," said Marion. "You introduced me to all your friends. You're helping with this crazy Halloween idea."

"It's not a big deal," said Cara. "I can be myself around you. I've never really had that before." Cara reached over and grabbed Marion's hand.

"You called me your girlfriend in there," said Marion.

"Yeah, it just kinda came out," said Cara. "If you're not comfortable—"

"No, it's good," said Marion. "It felt right." Cara smiled.

"Is it okay if we stop at my house for a minute?" asked Cara. "I just need to run in and get something, and then we can head over to your place."

"Sure, that's fine," said Marion. "Am I ever going to meet

your folks?"

"Maybe," said Cara. She didn't say anything else. Marion looked at her, and the previous smile had vanished. She reached over and grabbed Cara's hand and squeezed. Cara squeezed back.

Cara parked on the curb at her house.

"I'll be right back," she said, and then hurried over her front lawn, and disappeared inside. It didn't look all that different from Marion's, a ranch-style house on a big lot. No Halloween decorations. There was a sign, though. Marion squinted to read it in the early evening sun. "Hallowon't" it said, with a Jesus cross for the T at the end.

That explains why I haven't met her parents yet.

The minutes crawled by, and Cara hadn't come out. Marion saw shadows move in the windows. She rolled down her window, and she could hear the distant sound of shouting from inside. The pit of worry in her stomach doubled. She waited another minute, and there was still no sign of Cara. Marion thought back to her first day of school, where she had marched straight at Isaac and the group of boys. She summoned that girl again and got out of the car. Marion marched toward the front door. As she approached, she could hear the yelling.

"I know what you're doing out there, with those Satan worshipers!" yelled a male voice. Cara's dad. "You can't fool me. The more time you spend outside of the house, the worse you get. You're being corrupted!"

Cara replied, but Marion couldn't understand her, being much quieter. She heard her crying, though. Marion took a deep breath and knocked loudly on the door. The house shook with stomps as Cara's dad approached.

A man with white hair and salt and pepper stubble answered, red faced and furious. His head was block-shaped, and he wore a plaid shirt and suspenders attached to worn out jeans.

"Ah, here she is now," he bellowed. "I know who you are, young lady, and you will not be corrupting my daughter any longer!"

Marion didn't know what to say, struck by confusion. She couldn't imagine answering the door like that.

"Are you okay?" she asked, the first thought that escaped her lips. He didn't look okay.

"*You* ask me that?" he yelled. "I'm great. I'm filled with God's glorious light, which is more than I can say for you and your father. You should be ashamed of yourself."

Cara suddenly barged past her father and grabbed Marion by the hand, pulling her back to the car.

"Go home, Marion," said Cara. Her dad stared from the doorway.

"You're my ride," said Marion.

"I'm sorry," said Cara. "My dad, you don't understand."

"But—"

"Go. Please, go," said Cara, and hurried back inside. Her dad slammed the door behind him.

Marion stood next to Cara's car and looked at the house. She could still hear Cara's dad yell. She waited, but Cara didn't come back out.

Marion's home was just over two miles away. She walked home. She was done crying by the time she got there.

18

"Geronimo!" yelled Jason as he jumped off the huge rock that loomed over the swimming hole. He fell thirty feet through the air and plunged into the water, the impact echoing back up to Daniel and the few other boys who hadn't leaped yet.

They had hiked for hours to get to their campsite. They had left early in the morning that Saturday, before the sun was up. Daniel had told his dad he was camping. But not with the Church. His dad hadn't questioned him at all. A part of him felt relieved that he could keep his secret. The rest of him saw it as another thing his father couldn't be bothered to care about him.

They set the campsite up, multiple big tents erected to house the Laurel Youth Experience, the nine boys and Abraham Laurel.

Then they came to the stone, the rock of creation Abraham had dubbed it, an annual camping trip tradition, where each boy would jump off into the swimming hole far below. A leap of faith, Abraham said.

Daniel was the newest kid, and so he would go last, last before Abraham himself. Isaac had gone first, jumping off without hesitation. Isaac had been quiet on the drive and the hike. Daniel had tried to start a conversation with him a few times, but he hadn't responded with much. Daniel had learned of the Reverend's discussion with his dad. Isaac had to have known about it.

The last kid aside from Daniel jumped, the youngest boy among them. He held his nose and plummeted into the chilly water, shouting with joy as he emerged from beneath after a few moments.

Daniel stood a few feet away from the drop. He could do this. He could do this. He walked out to the end carefully, one foot moving inch by inch until he toed the edge of the rock. He looked down.

It's so far down. He could barely see the rest of the boys, their small heads breaking the surface of the murky green water. The back of his knees ached, and his heart leaped into his throat. His vision swam, and he took a quick step back. He would pass out, and fall, and that'd be it for him.

"You okay, Daniel?" asked Abraham.

"You okay, Daniel?"

Daniel stood on the first rung of the ladder, looking up. The top seemed so high, and the roof even higher. He lost his football up there. It laid in the rooftop's crook. He could see it. Daniel just couldn't *get* to it.

Not without climbing the ladder. And that felt impossible. He was eight, and it was impossible.

Dad asked him again. "Are you okay, Daniel?"

Daniel's head whipped around. He didn't even realize his dad was there.

"Because you've been standing on the same rung for a good five minutes," said his dad.

"My ball is on the roof," said Daniel. "I threw it too hard and it took a weird bounce. Mom told me I could use the ladder."

"As long as you're careful, it should be okay," he said.

"I don't think I can climb it," said Daniel.

"It's scary," said his dad. "If you want to try, I'm right here. I'll hold the ladder for you. Do you want to try?"

Daniel looked up and nodded. His father grabbed the steps, steadying it.

"I've got it," he said.

Daniel took a slow step to the next rung. He glanced down at Dad, who still held it. His dad nodded at him.

Daniel took another step up. The anxious worry in his gut hadn't gone away, the ground a thousand feet below him. Two more rungs, and then the top. He inhaled deeply, exhaled, and then stepped up, and then once more. He was at the top, and his heart pounded in his chest. He looked down, and the world fell out beneath him. He closed his eyes. He couldn't see it. He saw the roof, now an arm's reach away. All he had to do was swing a leg over, crawl toward it, and get his ball.

But he couldn't. He stared at the edge, but his foot wouldn't budge, not anymore.

"I can't do it," said Daniel.

"You sure?" asked his father.

"Yes," said Daniel, his voice barely above a whisper.

"It's okay," said his dad. "Swinging over is the hardest part. Climb down slowly."

Daniel carefully took a step down, his hands and feet never leaving the rungs at the same time. He could breathe again on the ground. He sighed.

Dad climbed the ladder. "Can you hold it for me?" he asked.

"Sure," said Daniel. He grabbed it and held it down with all his strength.

His dad climbed slowly, much like Daniel did. He made his way to the top, took a deep breath, and then swung a leg over to the shingled roof. He quickly stepped over and he was on it. He stood up, walked over to the ball, and picked it up, tossing it to the ground. It bounced near Daniel and came to a stop.

Dad went back to the ladder, inhaled deeply, and stepped over, swinging back to it. He climbed down.

"Thanks for holding it, buddy," said his dad.

"Sorry I couldn't do it, Dad," said Daniel.

"Don't be sorry," he said. "You got a lot farther than I would have at your age."

"It's scary," said Daniel.

"It is," said his dad. "But it's okay to be afraid of things. It's normal."

"Daniel?"

"I'm afraid of heights," said Daniel. "I can't even climb a ladder."

"I used to be the same way," said Abraham. "One day, my father had me climb a tree, the tallest tree in the city. And I was terrified. I couldn't imagine even standing on the lowest branch. But my father waited there. We weren't going home until I climbed the tree and conquered my fear. He told me that my faith in God would keep me safe. And I sweat, and I cried, and my stomach turned itself in knots, but I climbed that tree."

"It's so far down," said Daniel.

"It's a leap of faith, Daniel," said Abraham. "God will protect you, if you believe in Him. You do have faith, don't you?"

Daniel nodded. His heart thudded in his chest. He couldn't let them down. They had accepted him. He backed up, ran to the edge, and jumped as far as he could.

I'm gonna die I'm gonna die I'm gonna die

His eyes were open the whole way down and he fell so fast, and the small figures of the boys grew larger and larger and he hit the water with an incredible splash and he was underwater and then he swam up and he took a breath.

Everyone cheered.

*

They sat around the campfire later that night. A chill had settled in and the warmth felt good. They cooked their dinner over it, hot dogs with marshmallows afterward. They joked around as they ate.

"Let us pray," said Abraham. Everyone bowed their head and closed their eyes. Daniel could feel the fire and the smoke with his eyes closed.

"Dear Lord," said Abraham. "Thank you so much for our meal, our meal that we cooked ourselves over Your fire. Thank You so much for this fellowship, of young men coming together in celebrating Your Earth and Your Creation. None of this would be possible without You. Amen."

"Amen," said Daniel, alongside everyone else.

They all ate for a while, all talking with each other. Daniel had gotten to know the other boys beside Isaac, and they all teased each other. All the talk about his father had stopped after Isaac's defense of him at the football game. Daniel felt like he belonged. He *wasn't* an outsider.

"Young men," said Abraham loudly, and the guys all quieted down, looking toward him, over the dancing orange flames of the fire. "Every year, the Laurel Youth Experience comes to this exact spot to renew our love and faith in God. Every year, my heart swells to see the future of our great city embracing brotherhood. But none of that comes for free. It requires hard work. Dedication. Sacrifice."

Daniel saw Isaac twitch on that last word. Isaac had stayed quiet throughout the day. His sunken eyes looked more pronounced in the fire's glow. Daniel had asked him earlier if he'd slept last night, joking with him, but Isaac avoided the question.

"And this trip is to both focus on that hardship, but also to celebrate triumph over it. I want each of you to talk about something you've struggled with in the past year, and how you've overcome it. John, we can start with you, and go clockwise around the fire."

John started talking about his grades, and Daniel tried to listen, but all he could think about was what he would say when it was his turn. What *could* he say? What had he triumphed over? His life had been thrown into disarray over the past year, between the controversy in Plinkett and moving to Laurel City. That *was* his life.

John finished, and it moved onward, each boy talking about what they had struggled with this year. It got to Isaac, with Daniel up next.

Isaac stared at the fire, his face blank.

"Isaac?" asked Abraham. "It's your turn." Isaac looked at him and nodded. He stayed silent for a moment longer.

"My issue has been relatively recent. With who I am, and with what's expected of me as a future leader of Laurel City, and Laurel City Holy Church, I've had to be that leader my entire life. And that's good. It's made me strong and confident. But recently…I've had to sacrifice something important to me. I've done things I wasn't sure I was capable of. I've made tough decisions. And it's been hard."

Daniel looked over to Abraham as Isaac spoke, and Abraham's face looked concerned. No, concerned wasn't the right word. Afraid? Daniel couldn't tell. Isaac continued.

"But I've realized that it's for the best in the long run. That tough choices now prepare you for the hard choices that will come down the road. And there always will be more of them."

Isaac stopped, and Abraham nodded. He looked to Daniel. "Daniel? You're our newest member, so I can excuse you. You probably weren't prepared for this."

"No," said Daniel. "I can go."

"Okay," said Abraham, nodding. Everyone stared at him.

"Not everybody knows all the details about how I moved here. Everyone knows about my father. Or at least, what he's done since we moved. But we had to move because of his job. Because of stuff that happened. And it was hard on me. Leaving everything I knew behind. It's where I grew up. It's where my mom is buried. I—I didn't know what would happen in a new town. I thought this would be a lonely year, and then I would graduate. But things I didn't expect to happen, happened. I met Isaac, and then all of you. And I realized that I can't constantly look to my father for approval, or for a place to belong. I've found that place, and it's right here, with you guys."

"Amen," said Abraham. "We're glad you've found us, Daniel."

They continued around the fire, everyone speaking about their struggles, and then they settled into a sing-a-long, with Abraham playing hymns on his guitar.

Daniel sang along. But an uneasy pit of pain grew in his stomach and lingered even as they laid down to sleep. While they sang, he realized that he had lied to them all, when he spoke about his struggle and triumph.

Because thoughts of his dad had never left him, even for a second. Because his father would have never made him jump off that rock.

19

"I didn't know you were so…dedicated," said Mike.

"Are you making fun of me, Mr. Halloween?" asked Jenny.

He had pulled up to the curb to pick up Jenny for their date. They were going to a renaissance festival. He had been to them before and always had a good time. He could eat turkey legs and donuts while watching knights fight each other. What was there not to like?

But as soon as Jenny stepped out of her house and walked toward the car, he knew she was on a whole different level.

She wore a green dress, medieval style, with white highlights. It featured a corseted midsection that accentuated her curves. Her hair was braided, with emerald ribbons strung off of each braid. She had to bunch up her dress to even get into the passenger seat.

"I'm not making fun of you at all," he said. "You look incredible. I'm the one who looks like a schmuck."

"You look fine," she said, but he didn't feel like it. He wore a t-shirt and jeans, appropriate for a day outside, while still having a thin veneer of fashion applied to it.

"Do you always dress up like this for renfest?" asked Mike.

"Most of the time," she said. "Unless I'm slumming it. Some theme weekends aren't really my jam, so I just dress normally."

"How many times do you usually go?" he asked.

"I mean, they normally run like eight weeks, so probably eight times," she said. "Some people I know will go both weekend days, but I just don't have the energy anymore."

"When you asked me if I wanted to go to renfest, I clearly did not understand your dedication."

"I'm surprised you're not more into it," said Jenny. "You love Halloween. Renfest has all the costumes and play that Halloween does."

"Mmm, not quite," said Mike. "There's not the whole spooky aspect to it. The costumes are only a part of it."

"I get it."

"Maybe you can win me over," said Mike. "You can show me how to really experience renfest."

She smiled. "It's out in the middle of nowhere. Drive west on the highway until you see the big banners flying in the air."

They drove, and soon they were out of Laurel City, with endless fields surrounding them.

"How was your week?" asked Jenny.

"Great, and terrible," said Mike. "We've made a lot of progress on the party. Marion has corralled a bunch of her friends to be a street team. We've got a new dog."

"You got a dog, and you didn't tell me?" she asked.

"Here. We got a new dog. It's a golden retriever puppy. Marion named her Furriosa," said Mike.

"You've got a good daughter," said Jenny.

"I didn't tell you because we rescued her from the pet store massacre," said Mike. "And I didn't want to talk about it any more than necessary."

"Shit, I'm sorry," she said. "I heard about it, but I didn't really piece it together that you were there."

"We were the first ones on the scene. It was horrible," said Mike. "All those animals."

"At least you saved one," she said. "And Marion's making friends. How's your son doing?"

"He seems okay," said Mike. "He's been spending time with new friends. He went camping this weekend."

"Any more word from our buddies at the Holy Church?" asked Jenny.

"No, nothing. They've been completely silent since the dear Reverend's visit. I don't expect that to last. I'm sure he's screaming about my sinful ways at his Sunday sermon, but no one there is going to tell me what he's saying."

"You need a spy," said Jenny.

"I think that might be going overboard," said Mike. "I'll throw my party, and it'll all come out in the wash. How are yooou doing? How's school?"

"Oh, the same," said Jenny. "All the older teachers tell me how to run my classroom while they still teach like it's 1965."

"Sounds like a blast."

"Oh, it's the best," said Jenny. "But the kids make up for it. They're way ahead of where I was when I was their age."

"Speak for yourself," said Mike. "I was ready to take on the world when I was sixteen."

"Really?" asked Jenny. "Because I would have guessed you were a raging ball of hormones that hated everyone, but most of all, yourself."

"You might be right," said Mike. "Maybe."

"Look, there are the flags."

*

"Did the people at the gate know you?"

"You mean Abby?" asked Jenny.

"You seem to know everyone for someone who moved here recently," said Mike.

"I'm a people person," she said. "And I might have had a dual purpose for taking you to the renaissance faire."

"Really?" asked Mike. "What nefarious reason do you have?"

"I have a couple of friends who work the show, and they might help you with your party."

"That's very sweet of you," said Mike. "Who might these friends be?"

They had walked through the opening area of the faire, where all the food stalls were located, along with dozens of picnic tables. The sound of metal clanging against metal had gotten louder and louder as they walked, and Mike found them suddenly right next to a field with two gigantic dudes in armor sword-fighting, each wielding huge longswords in one hand, with a shield in the other. They moved faster than Mike could compute, swinging and parrying, catching the edge of their swords with their shields. One's shield was blue, while the other's was red. Rough helms covered their heads, while chain mail protected the rest of them.

"It's these two," said Jenny.

"Oh," said Mike. "You're friends with knights."

"They don't ride horses, and they dress in more medieval Nordic traditions."

"So not knights?"

"Vikings," said Jenny.

"You *are* friends with everyone," said Mike.

They watched along with the crowd as the two sparred, fighting back and forth, getting more and more aggressive. Red shield slipped as he stepped backward, and blue took advantage, sweeping out red's front leg. Red fell to the ground, and blue pressed his sword to red's neck. Red dropped his weapon in defeat.

Everyone applauded, and then blue helped red up. They both got up and removed their helmets, bowing to the assembled crowd. They started walking the circumference of their sparring area, cordoned off by short straw fences, shaking hands and saying hello and chatting with anyone who stuck around. They eventually found their way to Jenny and Mike.

"Jenny!" shouted the blue warrior. "Bjorn, Jenny is here to visit us again."

"Jenny!" shouted the red warrior, rushing over to her. They both hugged her in turn. She turned to Mike.

"Mike, this is Tomas," she said gesturing to the warrior in blue. He had lustrous black hair, which flowed down his back. His beard was dense, but neatly trimmed. He stood six inches taller than Mike and was twice as thick. Tomas reached out for a handshake. Mike returned it and found his hand engulfed in Tomas' grip.

"Nice to meet you," said Mike.

"I have heard much about you," said Tomas. His voice had a faint European accent, one Mike couldn't place.

"And this is Bjorn," said Jenny. Bjorn said nothing, but extended his hand with a wide, lopsided smile. He was blond, and only perhaps an inch taller than Tomas. His hair was shorter, but wild, curling in every direction. Mike's hand was again engulfed by the second man.

"Nice to meet you," said Mike. "That was impressive."

"Thank you," said Tomas. "Bjorn loses his feet, and then loses the fight."

"Do not take that as a general example. Tomas must resort to trickery to win against me." Bjorn's voice was deep, rumbling from within his barrel chest.

"We were both holding back," said Tomas. "We would both be faster in actual combat."

"That was holding back?" asked Mike. "Have you ever been in a real fight?"

"Not yet," said Bjorn. "Most, most do not want to fight us." He smiled again, and Tomas clapped him on the back, laughing.

"Would you like to try?" asked Tomas.

"Try what? Sword-fighting?" asked Mike.

"No, dancing," he said, keeping a straight face for a solid ten seconds before he laughed again. "Yes, combat."

"I don't know," said Mike. "You guys are serious."

"Jenny tells us you are a police officer," said Bjorn. "You are no stranger to battle."

"I've only fired my gun twice," said Mike. "And I've never faced anyone with a sword."

"I will go easy on you," said Tomas. "No death blows, I promise."

Jenny nudged. "You should try it. It's fun."

"You've fought these two?" asked Mike.

"No, I'm not crazy," she said. "Only one at a time." She smiled.

"Come on," said Tomas, and laid a big mitt on Mike's shoulder, and pulled him over to where there was a break in the fence. Tomas went to prepare himself, and Bjorn dressed Mike. Soon he found chain mail draped over him, and a short sword thrust into his hand. A small circular shield was put into his other.

"Ha! Now, you are a warrior," said Bjorn, from behind him. Tomas danced in place, across from the sparring area.

"I have my doubts," said Mike. "What should I do?"

"Hold your weapon at right angles," said Bjorn. He demonstrated, moving Mike's sword arm. "Thrust your shield, just as if you were swinging a sword. Tomas is strong bastard, and the impact will dislocate your shoulder if you do not swing into the force."

"What? Really?" asked Mike, suddenly worried. He pictured himself being driven away from the renfest in an ambulance. Explaining to Chief Miller that he would be out of the field because he broke his arm sword-fighting.

"Do not worry, Michael," said Bjorn. "You will do fine. Tomas is quick and strong, but he follows similar pattern. Study his movement, and you may land a blow."

"Right," said Mike. "Study his movement."

"Are you ready?" asked Tomas, bellowing from across

the field. A new crowd had gathered. Bjorn pushed a helmet down on Mike's head.

"Yes?" said Mike, and Tomas moved forward, into the middle of the sparring area. He clacked his sword against his shield and Mike did the same, moving closer to him.

Study his movement. You can find a weak spot. He's not invincible. He's just big. And strong. And fast.

They circled each other, and then Tomas swung his sword, and all thought of strategy disappeared from Mike's head as he thrust his shield to meet Tomas' sword. The blade was three feet long, and Mike would have needed two hands to wield what Tomas easily swung with one.

The sword hit Mike's shield, and his legs nearly crumpled from the force. His shoulder rebounded cruelly, and he grunted. Mike looked for the next blow, but Tomas backed off. He was taking it easy. One nearly mortal blow was enough.

"How did that feel?" asked Tomas. Mike swore he could hear his smile.

"I think it collapsed my sternum," said Mike.

"The pain is a reminder you are alive," said Tomas. He walked in, and swung again, the same blow. Mike thought he could predict it, but it came so fast, he had barely the time to get his shield up. He moved the shield differently this time, and it absorbed more of the impact.

"You are learning!" yelled Tomas.

"Study him!" yelled Bjorn from behind him.

"Get him, Mike!" yelled Jenny.

Jesus, this is intense. Tomas circled him like a wolf. *I don't stand a chance. He's so fast.*

"You must attack sometime," said Tomas.

"I feel better behind my shield, to be honest," Mike yelled back.

"Swing the sword at me," said Tomas. "A true warrior does not hide. You are a true warrior. I know you are. Swing your sword!"

Mike watched Tomas' careful footsteps, and while he was in between steps, Mike swung. Tomas hesitated for a moment, but brought up his shield. Mike's sword clattered off of it.

"Aha! That was good," said Tomas. "Not good enough to wound, but good." Tomas then swung again, the lightning strike of his massive blade coming down, but Mike was ready this time, recognizing the same pattern, and he didn't raise his shield this time, instead dropping it next to him and sidestepping, swinging his sword at the same time, aiming for Tomas' mid-section.

Tomas' sword smashed into the ground, and he raised his shield to block Mike's blow, but he was a hair too late, and Mike's sword hit him hard in the side. Mike's arm shook with the blow.

Tomas grunted, but then laughed, and Mike realized he had left himself wide open for a counterattack. Tomas's shield arm tucked Mike's sword and then Tomas' weapon swung down again, right at Mike's open neck. Mike braced for impact, his eyes closed.

The impact never came. He opened his eyes to see the sword laying against the intersection of his neck and shoulder.

"I promised no death blows," said Tomas. He let go of Mike's sword and then plunged his own into the ground. The crowd applauded, and he held Mike's arm high.

"You did well, warrior," said Tomas.

*

They all sat together, the two Vikings on their break. Mike chewed on a turkey leg. He was suddenly voracious.

"You guys want anything?" asked Mike.

"We are vegetarian," said Tomas.

"I'm sure there's something that's vegetarian here," said Mike.

"Even the fried cheese has meat in it," said Bjorn. "It is okay. We bring our own food."

"You guys make your own weapons and armor?" asked Mike.

"Yes," said Tomas. "We forge our own arms. At first, I did not understand. But after using my own sword in battle, I cannot imagine otherwise."

"That's very relatable," said Mike, smiling. "I feel like that all the time, after I fight."

"You're very funny," said Jenny.

"Usually, you don't have to tell people that," said Mike. "Typically, you just laugh."

"It's just delayed," said Jenny.

"Jenny tells us you are planning a Halloween," said Tomas. "Would you like us to help? We can build."

"You guys don't know me. You're willing to help?" asked Mike.

"We want James to live in a Laurel City that is for everyone," said Tomas.

"James?" asked Mike.

"Our son," said Tomas.

"Oh God, I'm a moron," said Mike. "I didn't realize."

"It is okay," said Bjorn, smiling. "You are not the first."

"How old is James?" asked Mike.

"Three," said Tomas. "He is beautiful."

"If you're willing to help, I'll gladly take it. Especially with the work you two do," said Mike.

"You are standing up to the Holy Church. To Laurel. Correct?" asked Bjorn. Bjorn stared at Mike, his lopsided smile gone.

"Yes," said Mike.

"Fuck the Holy Church," said Tomas. "They try to shame us. Fuck them. If you fight them, we are with you."

Bjorn and Tomas got back to work, displaying their arms and armor to the crowds as they sparred. Mike and Jenny explored the grounds, eating faire food and watching the knights joust. It was dark by the time they returned to Laurel City.

Mike pulled up to the curb at Jenny's house.

"I had fun today," he said, looking at her.

"So did I," she said. "We should do this again."

Her eyes glowed in the dim light of the car.

"I don't know if I can do the renfest every weekend, but I definitely—"

She kissed him on the lips, a soft testing kiss at first, and then again, a little more forceful.

"You talk too much," she said, finally, after they broke contact.

"I—"

"I'll call you tomorrow," she said. "Goodnight."

And she was gone, back into her house, her green dress flowing behind her.

20

Norman Palmer woke up to someone shaking him.

"Get up! I told you, you can't sleep here!"

The voice was short and harsh, and Norman cracked his eyes open to see who woke him. The face of David Laurel greeted him.

Goddamnit.

Norman tried to talk, but his tongue wouldn't obey him, and the only noise that came out was a vague moaning grunt. The gallon of wine he'd had for dinner still coursed through his blood. The same numb that had helped him fall asleep kept him from making any damn sense.

David Laurel didn't care. He wanted Norman off his property.

Fuck. He pushed his tongue, made it work. Slowly.

"I'm moving," said Norman. "I'm moving."

"Not fast enough," said Laurel. Others would call him Reverend, but Norman didn't care about that shit. Laurel was a son of a bitch, and that's all he would ever be in Norman's eyes.

He had thought the Holy Church was deserted for the evening. It normally was, on most nights this late. There was a little nook behind the sanctuary, tucked in between buildings, where the heat leaked out and kept it warm year round, even in the dead of winter. Norman had slept there for months before being discovered by Laurel one night in January. Ever since, Laurel had it in for him, and threatened him with arrest every time he saw him, whether or not he slept on Church land.

"Get up and get off my property!" yelled Laurel. Easy for him to say, that son of a bitch.

"I'm moving," said Norman. "Hold your horses."

"I will hold nothing," said Laurel. "You are not allowed to be here. I have told the police multiple times."

The cops didn't care about Norman. He was invisible to them. He struggled to his feet, quickly pulling together his sleeping bag and his camping backpack. He eyed Laurel, making sure he wouldn't try to take either from him. They were both equal to Norman's life, and he would fight for them both, no matter who tried to steal them.

Laurel wasn't trying. He looked like he didn't want to even touch them. He had shaken Norman with his foot, his boot outstretched to kick him in the shoulder.

Norman walked, bundling his sleeping bag as he went. Laurel continued to yell at him, but he didn't follow him. Norman knew he wouldn't. Laurel felt safe at his church, but he feared Norman. Norman had nothing to lose, and Laurel had a lot.

He didn't look back, but he heard Laurel retreat into the church. God knows what he was doing there so late on a random Tuesday night, but what did it matter. It might have been just to fuck with Norman. People like Laurel would lose sleep just to make sure Norman was uncomfortable. It was his lot in life.

He stopped, strapping his sleeping bag to his backpack. He looked around, and saw no one watching, or Laurel's eyes peering at him from the church. He turned down the side street that bordered the Holy Church. The normal spot it was. He walked a block down, and then turned again, into a tightly packed copse of trees that bordered the church.

Norman glanced around one more time and saw nothing. The night was quiet, and no one moved through Laurel City. Norman didn't know what time it was, but the temperature told him it was after midnight. He would take out his watch after he was safe. He didn't trust it out. Too valuable.

Satisfied, he lifted one hanging branch, and then another, ducking and sliding underneath the pine needles, revealing his permanent campsite, hidden inside the small cluster of trees.

Norman had lived here, off and on, for two years. Ever since the concrete factory had gone out of business, and Norman had missed payment after payment of his mortgage, even after he sold his car so he could live in his house for one more month. He should have kept the car. He could have slept there, and turned on the heat when it got cold, or the AC when it got hot. Small luxuries he would kill for, now.

But Laurel didn't know about his campsite. Neither did the cops. The police were kindly enough, knowing Norman wasn't violent, or an addict, only a wino. But they didn't know about this place either, because if they were pushed, they'd move him out. He didn't tell the other Laurel City transients either. They would take it. Like they had taken his old watch.

He didn't know how many of them there were. He'd reckon at least a dozen, but he'd only see the others one at a time, as they passed each other in the street. Laurel City was a small town, but wasn't small enough not to have any homeless. They came and went, and Norman hadn't seen any more than once. It didn't surprise him. They were invisible.

He ducked into his pup tent, big enough just for him, and rolled out his sleeping bag. It was cold, but not chilly enough to risk a small fire. Fires were only when his fingers and toes starting going numb and he couldn't bear it anymore. The chill in mid-October wasn't bad enough yet for that. He bundled up in his sleeping bag and laid down, using his backpack as a pillow.

The effects of the wine were still inside, and he hoped he could get back to sleep. He'd had trouble falling asleep lately. He'd heard noises in the night. Noises he couldn't explain.

Thoughts of the noises were on top now, and he thought about them, but the wine won out in the end.

*

He woke up again, and his mind tricked him, thinking it was Laurel.

"Leave me alone," said Norman, to no one. "Please, just leave me alone. I'm just trying to sleep."

But something brought him out of the semi-sleep, and he remembered where he was. Norman rolled over, to try to fall back asleep, but the something happened again.

A noise. The same sound that he'd been hearing over the past few nights. It was impossible, drifting through the wind, and he'd ignored it. His wine consumption had also increased as the noise first appeared. It wasn't a coincidence. But it was impossible, and he heard it, and both things couldn't be true. So he drank more wine.

But it was there again. The gallon of booze had mostly worn off by now, early in the morning, and there was no ignoring this noise.

Whirrwhirrwhirrwhirrwhirr

The sound of the switch spinning in the air woke him up. He was only seven. He was home alone; they didn't have money for no babysitter, and his step-father had told his mother to get a job, little Normie could take care of himself for a couple hours a day. Little Normie could walk to school, and he could walk back, and he could survive for a few hours without supervision until his step-father got home from work at five. Maybe six, if he stopped to knock a few back at Servino's, it was right on the way, no big deal. That's what he told Norman's mother.

But sometimes it wasn't just a few. Sometimes it was a half dozen, and they weren't beers, but dry vodka tonics, vodka so his breath wouldn't smell. So Norman's mother wouldn't know it was a half dozen.

But Norman had walked home to an empty house, and got himself a snack like he did every day, but there were no cookies in a place he could reach, his mother must have forgotten, she must have, but there were no cookies in a place he could reach. But that didn't mean there were no cookies.

There were some in the cookie jar, there had to be, so he grabbed a stool and climbed himself up so he could reach. And he reaaaached over to grab the lid, but the stool slid and his hand, holding the jar, didn't let go. He should have let go, and nothing would have broken. He'd only have fallen off the stool and hurt his elbow, but instead he dragged the jar off with him, and it broke against the linoleum floor. The jar was cheap, given to them by his grandmother when she got a new one.

But it was broken, and it didn't matter that it was cheap. His step-father would see that Norman had damaged something. And Norman tried to clean it up, but his step-father liked his cookies, just like he liked his vodka, and he would notice, there was no *not* noticing.

Norman tried to clean it up, as best he could, and he started crying as he did, because he already knew what was coming, coming when his step-father came home.

Norman never knew his father. He died before Norman was born, and his mother, anxious to have a male figure in the house for her new baby, married Harold before Norman could walk. Norman never knew his father, so he didn't know if he'd been a good man, but his step-father was a sadistic bastard that lived to hurt others. And he took every chance he could get.

He started crying as he cleaned up the cookie jar, and when he finished he laid in bed, and cried out of fear, and fell asleep before he realized it.

But the sound of the switch swinging in the air woke him

up.

Whirrwhirrwhirrwhirrwhirr

"Nooooorman," said his step-father, in the backyard, up to Norman's window. His droning voice carried, but that didn't wake him up. Harold swung a thin flexible wooden switch in his hand, faster and faster, until the noise started, and then he held it, the sound filling the yard, and then the house.

He droned, and he waited for Norman to report to him. And Norman knew better than to not report. Harold had punched him in the stomach the last time he'd had to drag him out into the backyard.

Norman didn't know if the neighbors heard Harold. He imagined they did. But they had said nothing. And they never would. Norman didn't cry as he got up, and walked downstairs, and into the yard. He saved his tears. Harold wouldn't stop until Norman cried, and even then, Harold would continue if he thought Norman was faking it. So Norman would hold every tear he had until he thought Harold was satisfied, and then he'd let the waterworks loose. Make no mistake, he was still terrified, a fear that wouldn't ever go away, a fear that would linger inside him even as he slept in the small copse of pine trees adjacent to the church.

"Take them off, Norman," said Harold. "For breaking the jar. You know better than that."

Norman didn't argue. Arguing would make it worse. He pulled down his pants, and then his underwear, and he put his hands against the side of the house.

Whirrwhirrwhirrwhirrwhirr
Whirrwhirrwhirrwhirrwhirr
Whirrwhirrwhirrwhirrwhirr

And then the switch swung in, hitting Harold right in the ass, and the pain almost overwhelmed him. The first one was always the worst. He felt blood well up. It would cover his underwear. His mother would wash them out, they always had hydrogen peroxide in the house.

Whirrwhirrwhirrwhirrwhirr
Whirrwhirrwhirrwhirrwhirr
Whirrwhirrwhirrwhirrwhirr

The sound was impossible, but Norman still sat up in his campsite in the early morning. Harold had died thirty years ago, alone and covered in shit in a nursing home. Norman hadn't gone to the funeral. But Norman had never heard that noise again. Sure, he'd heard similar noises, but not that one.

That fear returned, the same terror that had filled him as a child. There was no getting rid of it, it would be there until he died.

But he would find out what made that noise. Norman didn't think himself crazy. Just unlucky. But the emergence of that sound had made him doubt himself. He unzipped himself from his sleeping bag.

The sound got louder.

Whirrwhirrwhirrwhirrwhirrwhirrwhirrwhirrwhirrwhir-
rwhirrwhirrwhirrwhirrwhirrwhirrwhirrwhirrwhirrwhir-
rwhirrwhirrwhirrwhirrwhirrwhirrwhirrwhirrwhirrwhir-
whirrwhirrwhirrwhirrwhirrwhirrwhirrwhirrwhirrwhirr

Norman could hear it outside his tent, knew it was right there, all he had to do was unzip it, push out the flap, and the noise would be there. Harold would be there again, ready to hurt Norman, bloody him until he cried.

A single tear rolled down Norman's face. His heart thudded in his chest, sourness filling his guts.

He pushed it all away. He wouldn't let Harold come and find him. He'd go out and face him. Face him and banish that terror.

Norman reached out and unzipped the tent.

Harold didn't wait for him on the other side. Something else was there, something Norman couldn't recognize.

The noise came from it, provoking sense memory of agony.

Darkness was its face, and it reached inside of Norman.

His only solace was that the pain, unlike Harold's, didn't linger.

21

"Oh God, Norman," said Janine, crouched inside the copse of pine trees. "You didn't deserve this." Norman's head lay at her feet. She covered her mouth and nose with a handkerchief.

"Ever see something like this?" he asked.

"No," she said. "Things like this don't happen in Laurel City."

Gore coated the entire area. Mike looked into what remained of the small pup tent, splashed with blood, with rips and tears through the thin plastic. They had gotten the call this morning, from Ruth, the secretary of Laurel City Holy Church. She had gone out for a cigarette break. She had spotted something on the ground, near the cluster of pine trees. It had been Norman's hand.

Not much remained of Norman. Viscera and organs were strewn throughout the small campsite. Mike felt something graze his head and looked up. A piece of what used to be Norman dangled from a low branch.

"You knew him?" asked Mike.

"Yeah," she said. "Norman Palmer. Homeless. Used to work at the concrete factory until it shut down."

"Did you know he lived here?" asked Mike.

"No," said Janine. "We knew he was in town, and we got calls about him from time to time. Certain places knew him, knew his story, and were more friendly to him. Let him sleep inside on the real cold nights. We tried to help him as much as we could. Even when people told us to get rid of him."

"I didn't realize Laurel City had much of a homeless population," said Mike.

"They come and go," said Janine. "Very few are from here. Most people get out when they see the writing on the wall. But Norman didn't have anywhere to go."

"Surprised it would come to this," said Mike. "With the church right there."

"They don't care," said Janine. "Norman never went there. I talked to him. He was a decent guy. He wanted out of his situation, but he didn't know what to do. He didn't do drugs. He certainly didn't deserve this."

"Same as the pet store?" asked Mike.

"Has to be," said Janine. "What else could it be?"

"I don't think we ever really settled on what's actually doing this," said Mike. "A rabid wolf wouldn't do this. It wouldn't tear apart a full-grown man for the fun of it."

"Sounds like you're thinking it's a person," said Janine.

Mike sighed. The smell of blood caught in his nostrils. He coughed. "I don't know. A wild animal wouldn't have done this."

"Then who? And what's the murder weapon? It looks like he was torn apart, just like the animals. There seemed to be a struggle. Where's the physical evidence? Pieces of clothing? Footprints?"

Mike didn't answer, because there was none. It didn't make sense. The killer had appeared out of thin air, done their grisly work, and then disappeared.

He ducked under the branches and exited the copse, out onto the field adjacent to the church. David Laurel waited for him there.

Goddamnit.

"Officer Dawson," said Laurel. "I hope you're happy."

"Why on Earth would I be happy?" asked Mike. Janine emerged behind him, uncovering her mouth. "A poor man was slaughtered."

"It's your sin that has wrought this," said Laurel, looming over both of them, wearing slacks and a button-up shirt. The early morning fog had melted away, but the autumn chill was still in the air. The last of the summer heat was gone.

"I wasn't aware Halloween decorations caused animal attacks," said Mike.

"Be smart all you want," said Laurel. "But I warned you. I warned everyone. These attacks are not a coincidence."

"Please, can we calm down?" asked Janine. "Can I ask you some questions, Reverend?"

"As long as you're quick about it," he said. "I was in the middle of writing this Sunday's sermon."

Janine stepped in front of Mike.

"Did you notice anything strange last night?" she asked.

"I noticed the victim trying to sleep on Church grounds," said Laurel. "I had to rouse him myself. I don't know why it falls to me. I've called the police multiple times about his trespassing, and you continue to look the other way."

"When was this?" asked Janine.

"I don't know," said Laurel. "Late. I was here alone, working late."

"How late?" asked Janine.

"Why does it matter?" asked Laurel.

"Because, Reverend, you were the last person to see Norman alive, and it'll be useful to figure out his time of death."

He sighed. "It was after midnight. I went home shortly after."

"And you didn't notice anything strange?" asked Janine.

"Other than a man breaking the law?" asked Laurel. "No. I noticed nothing strange."

"A man was ripped apart fifty feet from your church, and you didn't notice anything?" asked Mike, piping in.

"No," said Laurel. "I wasn't aware that the transient was sleeping next to the church. Not camping so close. I wouldn't have allowed it. Are we almost done, Officer? I am not dressed for the cold."

Mike felt fine, and he wasn't wearing any more layers than the Reverend. "I thought reverends were supposed to show mercy on the homeless. There was a guy in the Bible who talked a lot about that…oh yeah, his name was Jesus."

"God helps those who help themselves, Officer Dawson," said Laurel. "Maybe if he'd been more industrious, he wouldn't have been the victim of such a horrible crime."

"He was still a man, Reverend. Maybe during your next sermon you could work in a little bit about helping your fellow man when he's in need. You can go," she said.

"Mark my words," said Laurel. "This won't end. God has marked your sins, and Laurel City will pay the price." He walked away, back into the church.

"What a bastard," said Mike.

"I'm worried that he's right," said Janine.

"What? About God marking my sins?" asked Mike.

"No," said Janine. "That this isn't over. That this is only the beginning."

"I'm going to look around more inside, before we call the clean-up crew," he said.

"I—I don't know if I can," said Janine. "I—"

"Don't worry about it," he said. "Wait out here. I won't be too long." He patted her on the shoulder and ducked back into the copse of trees. The smell hit him again. There was no getting used to it.

He'd handled murders in Plinkett. Usually between people who knew each other. There had been nasty cases, but nothing like this. Stabbings, shootings, violent enough, but no one was ever *butchered*. And ordinarily the killer was contrite afterward. They had been surprised at their own capacity for violence.

As he surveyed the brutality again, he could only see delight in it. Glee. The way the parts were scattered, thrown, it felt almost like a celebration. A celebration of massacre. If Laurel was right, and this was only beginning—Mike didn't want to think about what would happen next.

Briiiiiiiiiiiiiiing. Briiiiiiiiiiiiiiing.

The sound startled him. It was faint, but he knew the

sound, had heard it for years in Plinkett. It was the ringing of their old phone, the black wireless one with red buttons. But it wasn't possible. That noise wasn't possible.

Briiiiiiiiiiiiiiing. Briiiiiiiiiiiiiiing.

He heard it again, fainter this time. Mike followed the noise. It came from the back of the cluster of trees, and Mike had to duck to get through, pushing aside branches, pine needles stabbing into his hands.

The sound was impossible. That phone couldn't be here, couldn't be ringing. Hell, it was impossible at his house. He had gotten rid of it, had replaced it after—

He had replaced it after he got the call about Molly.

Briiiiiiiiiiiii—

The phone rang out again, fainter still, and then ended, abruptly. Mike followed it still, pushing brush aside, and then he found it. Or at least, what seemed like it. He couldn't fathom what else could have caused it, because that impossible sound came from something impossible.

The spot was round, not quite a circle, because it was black, as black as anything Mike had ever seen. There was enough light to see by underneath all those trees in the daytime, but he took out his flashlight, just to be sure. He shone the light down at the dark spot.

It looked like tar at first glance. As he got closer, he could smell it. The stink of sulfur, of gunpowder suddenly overwhelmed him and he coughed, trying to get the foreign scent out of his nostrils. He cupped his mouth and looked again.

It wasn't tar. Tar didn't absorb light. No matter how he angled his flashlight, the illumination went into the substance, and didn't come back out. No reflection.

"Janine!" yelled Mike, to make sure she heard him.

A moment later she pushed aside the brush, back into the campsite. "Where are you?" she asked.

"Over here," he said. "You need to see this."

She walked over, following his voice. Soon she was next to him, bent over, looking where his flashlight pointed. At the spot of black substance, that smelled like gunpowder and oozed into itself.

"What the fuck is that?" she asked.

"I don't know," he said. "But I think I heard a phone ringing from it."

"What?" she asked.

"I'll explain later," he said. "You should get a sample, while you still can."

"What do you mean, while I still can?"

"Because it seems to be disappearing," he said. Mike could swear the spot shrunk as he watched, flowing back into itself and vanishing. And he couldn't prove it, but he'd bet that it wasn't going into the ground. Whatever this stuff was, it didn't belong here.

"Do I have to touch it?" she asked.

"If you can't, I will," he said. He didn't know what it was, but it was the root of the killings. And they needed to know, no matter how hard his guts were telling him to not get close to the substance.

"I can do it," she said, and she pulled out a thin glass tube from the evidence collection kit she carried.

"Don't let it touch you," he said. "I don't think it'll be good."

She slid the tube through the goo. It was thick and resisted being collected. But some still went inside. She capped it, and the substance slowly sunk to the bottom.

"What the hell is it?" she asked.

"I don't know," said Mike.

They watched as the black spot of impossible vanished in front of them. Mike dug below with his heel, but it was gone.

Whatever it was, it had returned to its origin.

22

Daniel sat in the second pew of the Laurel City Holy Church. Isaac sat next to him, along with Abraham and his wife Dorothy, Isaac's mother. He had gone three Sundays in a row now, but the guilt roiling in his stomach hadn't gone away. It had only gotten worse.

He itched his neck, the collar of his dress shirt digging into his skin. It was too tight, but he didn't have the money to buy a new one, and he couldn't ask Dad for it. He still hadn't told him he was going to LCHC, that he was friends with Isaac. Like he cared at all.

Then why do you still feel guilty?

The congregation chattered around him, filling the church with a loud hum. Louder than usual. The homeless man had been killed less than a hundred feet from where he sat, and it had been the topic of conversation wherever you went in town. Not just the murder, which was a rarity in Laurel City, but the way it happened. Daniel had heard his father talking about it on the phone. The man had been ripped apart, and they didn't have any suspects. Everyone at school was scared. There were a few empty spots in the pews, which Daniel hadn't seen before. People were staying home.

"You okay, Daniel?" asked Isaac. Isaac wore his perfectly fitted shirt and tie. He didn't look uncomfortable.

He'd wear the same thing when he became Reverend.

"I'm fine," said Daniel. "There are some empty seats."

"It's scary," said Isaac. "There's a killer out there. Or killers."

"Killers? Plural?" asked Daniel.

Isaac leaned in. "You'll hear more in Grandfather's sermon, but he thinks there's more than one. He thinks—"

The organ started, and Isaac went quiet, as did the rest of the crowd. The service was starting, and everyone waited. The choir stood on the risers behind the pulpit, dressed in white. They glowed underneath the bright lights of the church. The choir director walked up, and everybody rose to sing. Daniel held the hymnal and sang along as best he could. He wasn't a good singer, but no one seemed to care. The Laurels next to him sang loudly, and he joined in.

The service continued, but everyone waited for Reverend Laurel's sermon. The murder had happened right outside their walls. Daniel could feel the anxious tension, waiting for the Reverend to speak his mind on what was happening in their community. *His* community.

Everyone went through the motions for the service, but

then it was time for the sermon. The congregation sat silent. Daniel heard his heartbeat pounding in his ears.

The Reverend walked out, standing tall on the dais, looking out at the crowd. His face was stern and hard. He reached the pulpit, putting down his notes.

"Halloween is not harmless," he said. "That is what I said, two Sundays ago. The holiday has been accepted by the wider Western world and used as advertising. Used as another example of secular fun, with parts of every department store selling costumes and candy. Selling decorations."

"And I heard people scoff at my words. We had folks march out of this very building. They thought my words ludicrous. And I'm almost positive that there are those still remaining in this congregation who think the same thing. I see your faces, and in your faces I see your thoughts. And I could hear them." Reverend Laurel looked out over the people. Locking eyes with everyone he could.

"I could hear them think 'the Reverend is too old-fashioned'. I could hear them think 'it's a holiday for kids to dress up and get candy'. Hear them think 'what's the harm in a couple scares?' But still I said that Halloween is not harmless. That Halloween is evil. That is a gateway to the occult, to sin, to the Devil himself."

"It's hard to deny we are under attack," he said. "Dozens of animals killed at the pet store. A man slaughtered in literally our backyard." He paused. "Attacks by people intent to spread terror in Laurel City. By those emboldened by the celebration of that pagan holiday. By cultists who intend to weaken the Church and this community's relationship with God."

"Because it is also an attack on our faith. Whenever something threatens us, our lives or lifestyle, it is also threatening our belief in the Lord. Our faith that He will protect us and our town. And when agents of Lucifer are so blatantly acting near our homes, it's easy to lose sight of our faith. It's easy to lose it. To cast it aside, to turtle up, or to abandon it entirely, when facing such opposition, that acts so bold, so violently, so cruelly. It's easy to give up, to surrender when encountering something like that."

"Because these are not the attacks of good Christians. They are the strikes of occultists. People without faith, without the one true God. They worship Satan, or even worse, other costumed gods that merely act in Satan's name. They can call them what they will, but Lucifer is his name at the end of the day. And he works every day to undermine and infect our town."

"Now Reverend, you might say, those are strong words. Infect our community? It's just a party. How do you know they're related at all?" Laurel paused again. He shook his head softly. "Because I've sat in prayer. Because I've called upon my faith, and it tells me that of course they're related. That feeling in your gut, deep down, when you hate that something is true, but it's true nonetheless? That's God talking to you. Telling you to do what you know is right. Telling you that deep fear inside is something you have to face. Now, am I saying that the party, or the people holding it, are evil?" He shook his head. "Of course not. It *is* just a party. But that doesn't mean that the lurking affliction in our community didn't see it's announcement, didn't see it's organization, and sprang into action because of it. Because they see it as a sea change. As the perfect time to disrupt our town."

"And as I look out at this gathered congregation, I can only think the opposite. I think of the strength here. Of the moral and ethical power. I think of our gathered faith. And I know that it is strong."

"So I ask all of you to stay strong. Because this is only the beginning. I ask that you speak out against Halloween, and it's spread throughout our town. That you not only do not attend, but you talk to your neighbors. The ones who are too afraid to leave their house. The ones who talk about attending the party. The ones who toil to make Halloween."

Daniel's guts ached. He could feel the eyes of the congregation on him. He'd go home to it. His dad, Marion, friends, working in their garage, making new things every day. The Reverend was talking about them. And he wasn't wrong. They were building Halloween. They had opened the gateway to this horror.

"Let us pray," said the Reverend, and they did, but Daniel couldn't keep his mind on the words to God. He could only think about his father, working hard in the garage, creating symbols to the occult.

*

Daniel didn't need Abraham's prompting to stay after the latest LYE service, held right after the main service let out. He needed to talk to him. The other boys went to change, to play the normal game of touch football. Daniel stayed behind.

"Can we talk?" asked Daniel. Abraham sat at his desk, gathering his notes.

"Of course, Daniel," said Abraham. "How are you doing?

I imagine that sitting through my father's sermon isn't the easiest thing."

"It's not," said Daniel. "But he's not wrong."

"He seldom is," said Abraham. "That was very frustrating to me as a young man, but as I've grown older, I've realized how lucky I was to have him. Believe me, the Reverend, just like me and Isaac, does not blame you for your father's actions."

"I know you don't," said Daniel. "But I still feel responsible. It's happening—it's happening in my house. Every day they're out there, working on stuff. When people drive by, they see the decorations. Everyone in town knows him as the Halloween guy. We've lived here a month, and we already have a reputation. And he doesn't seem to care that it affects me too."

"Have you told him you're attending our services?"

Daniel paused and looked down. He couldn't maintain eye contact. "No," he said. "I'm afraid of how he would respond."

"Would he try and stop you from attending?"

"I don't know," said Daniel. "I don't think he would *do* anything. That's the thing. All he cares about is Halloween. I've tried to tell him it will hurt us in the end, but he doesn't care. He can't compromise."

"You should tell him," said Abraham. "A lie, even in what you think are your best interests, is still a lie. And maybe telling him the truth will make him confront his choices. You can provide him an alternative."

Daniel sighed. "I don't think he'll listen. When he gets like this—all he sees is the path ahead. No matter what happens, he just keeps going. A man is dead. He's investigating it, even, and I don't think that changes anything for him. He'll only try harder."

Abraham nodded and sat silent for a moment. He finally looked to Daniel again, making eye contact.

"Ultimately, Daniel, he is your father, and not the other way around. If you can change his mind, you should. I believe that is what God wants. But if you can't change his mind, and you want to continue to worship the way you want—you must decide. What I said before still holds true. You have a family here. And at a certain point, you must make a choice about which family you truly want."

*

Daniel skipped touch football. His heart wasn't in it. Isaac would understand. Daniel changed back into casual clothes, stuffing his too-small collared shirt into his backpack before driving home. He would talk to Dad when he got home, he would. Daniel would tell him about meeting Isaac, about going to services, about LYE, about the camping trip. He would tell his dad he was hurting the community, and that it was better for everyone to call it off. They would talk about it, and the terrible pain that had been building inside Daniel's chest would finally go away, regardless of how his dad felt about his choices. He wouldn't have to lie anymore.

He wasn't surprised to find his dad working in the garage with Marion. He was a little stunned to find two massive men working in the driveway, a small boy sitting nearby, watching with glee. They had a mobile welding unit set up, and they were putting two pieces of metal framing together. For what, Daniel had no idea.

"Hey Daniel," said his dad, after he noticed him. "You're home early. Everything go okay with your friends?" He didn't really care, he was just pretending to be nice. If he cared, he would have—

Daniel couldn't muster the words. All his courage on the drive home to reveal everything was gone. He couldn't do it now, not in front of these strange men.

"Oh, this is Tomas and Bjorn. They're friends of Jenny's. They're helping with the party."

Daniel only nodded and then went inside saying nothing. There was nothing to say. Dad was only making it bigger and bigger. Why would he listen to him? Why would he care?

23

Mike yanked at the tie, trying to loosen it, just a little. It squeezed at his neck. No matter how much he pulled, it didn't ease up.

"You doing okay over there?" asked Jenny.

"Yeah, I'm fine," said Mike, sliding a finger in between his collar and his skin.

"You look like you're fighting with your tie," said Jenny. "And losing."

"I don't wear them very often," said Mike. And he didn't. The last time he wore it—

It was at Molly's funeral.

He forced his hand away from his throat.

"I promise not to judge you if you took it off," said Jenny.

"It's part of the dress code here," said Mike. "The website

was very insistent on that."

They sat in Tony's Lounge, the fanciest supper club in Laurel City. The only supper club in Laurel City. It was expensive, and the dress code was part of the deal. Mike had worn a suit coat and tie, doing his best to impress Jenny. She wore a rose print dress that hugged her hips and made her look incredible. Her shoes and make-up matched. Mike felt like a schlub sitting across from her.

"What are they going to do?" asked Jenny. "Kick you out?"

Mike looked around. The place was busy, most of the tables occupied by older people. Several of them eyed him as he glanced around. The host looked his way, and Mike's attention turned back to Jenny.

"They just might," said Mike. "I don't feel very welcome here." He kept his vision on Jenny and the menu, but he still felt people's eyes on them.

"I'm sure it's fine," said Jenny. "What are you getting?"

"I was thinking the steak," said Mike. "That's what you order at these places, right?"

Jenny laughed. "I think you can order whatever you want. *I* will be getting the steak, though."

Mike closed the menu. The waiter came with their drinks and took their food orders.

"You seem tense," said Jenny.

"I'm sorry," said Mike. "Work has been weighing on me. Plus all the Halloween stuff. Daniel has seemed distant lately. I can't blame him. I missed his football game."

"Have you gotten any suspects for the murder?" asked Jenny.

"No," said Mike. "And I don't think we'll have any. Seems

to be a wild animal, despite what Laurel says."

"What does Laurel say?" asked Jenny.

"Oh, that demons from hell have invaded our community," said Mike.

Jenny laughed out loud, and then caught herself, a few people from other tables looking their way.

"Sorry," she said. "I know I shouldn't laugh—"

"But it's ridiculous," said Mike. "It is. You better be careful what you say. They're probably watching us right now."

"Who?" asked Jenny. "Laurel?"

"Well, not him directly," said Mike. "But his agents."

"What, these old timers?" asked Jenny.

"Yes," said Mike. "They've been observing us from the moment we came in."

"Well, duh, Mike," said Jenny. "Does that surprise you?"

"Not really," said Mike. "But it's a little unnerving. Does it not bother you?"

"Look at me," said Jenny. Mike did.

"You look great," he said, and she smiled.

"Such a charmer," she said. "What do you see?"

"A beautiful woman," said Mike.

Jenny rolled her eyes. "You see a black woman, Mike."

"Well, yes," said Mike. "I know that."

"What do you think happens when I go anywhere in Laurel City?" asked Jenny.

Mike looked down and then back at her. "People watch you."

"People watch me," said Jenny. "It doesn't matter if I'm dressed well, or who I'm with. They watch me. So when you ask if it bothers me...of course it bothers me. But I can't spend my entire life worrying about it. So, yes, the old couples in this place might eye you because they go to LCHC and they will tell the Reverend about seeing you out. Or they might disapprove of your Halloween decorations, and your plan for a party. Or—" She paused. "Or they don't like the fact that a black woman and a white man are out on a date together."

"I think they're just jealous," said Mike.

"Oh, really?" asked Jenny.

"Yeah," said Mike. "They see the absolute hunk you're at the table with, and they can't help but stare. They're thinking 'that lady is the luckiest woman on Earth. She gets to have dinner with that slice of masculinity, with the shirt that's a size too big and a tie a size too small.'"

Jenny laughed again. "You got me with that one."

"I do my best," said Mike. Their food arrived, both of them ordering steaks. Jenny had another glass of wine.

"The steak is good, at least," said Mike.

"It is," said Jenny. She smiled and extended a hand across the table. Mike held it, sliding his thumb over her palm.

"Sorry for being a bummer," he said.

"It's okay," said Jenny. "It was nice, even if everyone else here is a secret agent for Laurel."

The waiter brought the check, and Mike excused himself and found the restroom. Another man, older, came in shortly after him. Mike used the bathroom and washed his hands. The other man joined him at the sink.

The guy looked to be in his early sixties, with a head full of white hair and dressed in a suit. He washed his hands. Mike didn't recognize him. Mike continued to wash his hands when the man spoke up, never looking up.

"Don't bring her kind back here again," said the man,

who finished and then was gone, out the door, not even glancing at Mike. Mike stood there, stunned, silent, his hands under the water. He felt the rage rise in him, his chest tightening.

He forced himself to turn off the faucet, and dried his hands, carefully. Mike left the bathroom, the man already back at his table, eating his dinner, across from a woman of a similar age. He didn't look to Mike still, even as Mike glared at him. The waiter had returned the check and his debit card, and Mike signed it hastily.

"Thank you for dinner," said Jenny. "I would've—"

"Let's get out of here," said Mike, finishing his last sip of beer.

Jenny looked at him with a raised eyebrow and collected her things. They left without a glance backward.

"You alright?" asked Jenny, again.

"I need to breathe," said Mike, walking down the sidewalk, away from the restaurant, past his car. "Before I do something stupid."

"Something stupid like what?" asked Jenny.

"Before I go punch some elderly man in the face," said Mike, continuing to walk, forcing breath in and out, in through his nose, out through his mouth.

"What happened?" asked Jenny.

Mike told her.

She wrapped her arm in his and slowed him down as they continued to walk. There was a park down the street, and she guided him into it, a square of connected small islands separated by creeks, with wooden bridges.

"Do you know him?" asked Jenny.

"No," said Mike. "Never seen him before. But that doesn't

mean anything. He probably knows me. I'm a cop. I walked out of Laurel's sermon. Or maybe he doesn't, and he's just a racist." Mike sighed. "We should have gotten pizza."

"Maybe next time," said Jenny.

Mike breathed the cool night air, looking out over the dim grass as they walked. His chest had loosened. He could think again.

"Is that what Laurel City is?" asked Mike.

"No, I don't think so," said Jenny. "It's more than the Reverend and his congregation. Even if it's hard to see it sometimes."

"Do you regret moving here?" asked Mike.

"No," said Jenny. "I'm close to my parents. The town is still a good place, with good people. People like you. People like Tomas and Bjorn. They're here, even if you don't see them. Do you regret it?"

Mike exhaled again. "I don't think so," said Mike. "But I just wanted peace. After everything that happened in Plinkett."

"Nowhere is perfect," said Jenny. "Every place has its problems, some places worse than others. Laurel City is no different."

"So what do we do about Mr. Supper Club in there?" asked Mike.

"We ignore him," said Jenny. "Even if we want to beat the shit out of him. We leave them in the dark and show them we're not afraid. It's what you're already doing, right? Isn't that why you're having the party?"

Mike stopped, both of them standing on one of the small bridges. He looked down into the trickling creek below them.

"Yeah, it is," said Mike. "I also like spooky costumes and candy."

"I mean, those are fair points too," said Jenny. "They are fun. Thanks for taking me out to a fancy dinner. The steak *was* good, even if the other patrons are racists."

"Pizza next time," said Mike.

"Sounds like a plan," said Jenny. She leaned back against the wooden banister and pulled him to her. They kissed, softly at first, and then harder, and all his anger was forgotten.

24

"Miss Dawson. Miss Williams. What do you think you're doing?" asked Principal Smith.

They each carried a stack of fliers, each advertising the First Annual Laurel City Halloween Block Party. A large jack-o-lantern dominated the flier. Cara had designed it in her graphic design class, and they had mass photocopied them in the library. The pair stood in front of one of the main bulletin boards, placed strategically throughout the school. They had pinned a couple to each of them in turn, and passing them out to any student who would take them as they walked between them.

"We're posting fliers for a Halloween event, Principal Smith," said Marion, putting on the biggest smile she could. Smith didn't go to Laurel City Holy Church, but Marion had expected pushback, eventually. With the content of Reverend Laurel's sermon spreading through the town, and the worries about the grisly murder of the homeless man, everybody in town was talking about the Halloween party.

And they had done nothing to dispel the rumors. Laurel painted them as Satanists, but all it did was bring attention to the party. Now every flier they posted was a magnet. Everyone wanted to read it, even if they hated the mere thought of Halloween. With the extra help of Jenny, Tomas, Bjorn, and the gaming club, they had gotten more and more confirmations of people attending. Would they all attend? She didn't know, but if the Reverend wanted to fan the flames of hysteria, they wouldn't back down. They'd welcome the inferno.

"May I see it?" he asked. Cara handed him the top sheet from her stack, and Smith looked it over.

"We read the school handbook, and promoting events with fliers, either posted or handed out, is perfectly within the rules," she said.

"I designed the fliers in graphic design," said Cara.

"There's a costume contest?" asked Smith.

"Yes," said Marion. "Winner gets a hundred dollar gift card."

"Hmm," he said. "Very good. Maybe I can talk the wife into doing a couple's costume. Don't let me keep you any longer, girls."

Smith walked off, flier still in hand.

"You think he'll come?" asked Cara.

"We got him hook, line, and sinker," said Marion. As they roamed through the hallways of the school, the teachers they passed mostly frowned, but the other kids seemed excited.

"Is this the Satanist party?" asked a stoner kid named Matt.

"Not officially," said Cara.

"But we can dress up?" he asked. "And it can be gory?"

"Whatever you want," she said.

"Awesome," he said. "I'll bring Loira. She loves horror movies."

Marion hadn't expected the blond preppy girl Tracy to be excited, but she was.

"Oh my God, this is amazing," she said. "I'm invited?"

"Yeah, of course," said Marion.

"That's fantastic," she said, her eyebrows dancing. "It's not like that boring Fall Festival, is it? My mom always drags me to it, and it's always the same dull cardboard box maze."

"Absolutely not," said Cara. "This will be exciting."

"Great! Can I have extras?" she asked.

Marion handed her a handful of fliers, and she was gone.

"One more bulletin board, and we've got the whole campus covered," said Cara. She led the way to the back half of the second floor, and they pinned up a couple next to the notices about the upcoming pep rally.

"We've hit the entire school," said Cara. "The rest of the crew is doing their best to spread it through classes. If no one shows up, it won't be because they didn't hear—"

"Thick as thieves," said a voice, one Marion recognized. It was Issac, his entire clique surrounding him. "Spreading word of their sin as far as the eye can see." He approached them, the group of boys hemming them in. Marion's eyes flitted between them, most of whom she didn't know. But one boy lurked behind them, taller than the rest, bigger than even Isaac. Then Marion saw his face, and she froze.

Daniel.

She hadn't made the connection. But now it all made sense. The football team. Being gone on Sundays. She had been so focused on Cara. On Halloween. Daniel caught her eyes for a bare moment and then looked away. He stood behind the rest. But he stood with them.

Isaac leaned on the bulletin board, his hand on the flier, and then he feigned slipping, ripping it down.

"Oops," he said, with a sinister smile. "Too bad. Looks like I slipped. I'm so sorry."

Marion couldn't take her eyes off of Daniel, even as Isaac glowered at her, over her.

"Destroying one flier won't stop us," said Cara.

"What about two?" asked Isaac, and grabbed the other stuck to the bulletin board, pulling it off.

"We have a lot of extras," said Marion, finally. She could look at him now, but Daniel loomed in her peripheral vision. She'd have to tell Dad. There was no way around it, she'd have to tell him.

"I won't let you drag this town down into Hell," said Isaac. "We won't let you."

"What planet are you from? It's a Halloween party," said Marion. "Lots of places celebrate it, and guess what, life continues as normal."

Isaac got closer to her, and the boys cued off him, surrounding the two girls.

"But that place isn't Laurel City," said Isaac. "We are a town of God. Not of immoral sinners like you and your *girl*-friend. Like your father."

Marion stood tall, her chin up. "You don't control this place. Not this town, or this school. You're just a bully. Like your father and your grandfather."

"You'd do better to follow your brother's footsteps. He's following God's Word. He understands the difference between right and wrong."

Marion ignored him. "Are you done? Shouldn't you be in class? Or kissing your grandfather's ass?"

"How dare you—"

"Oh fuck you," said Marion. "Jesus Christ, you've got a stick up your ass."

"A man died—"

"And what does that have to do with Halloween? Because the only one who's made that connection is your dear Reverend. Not the police—"

"Who coincidentally, just happens to be your dad," said Isaac. "Don't lecture me, sinner." He reached out to grab the stack of fliers from her hand. He was much stronger, but Marion wouldn't let go, the stack of paper contorting in her grip. Both held on, Marion putting her entire body into holding onto the stack. They were everything to her in that moment, and she wouldn't let go, and then Isaac let loose and she fell backwards, and the fliers flew up in the air like feathers. The boys laughed as she hit the ground, her teeth clacking shut on her tongue. She tasted blood, and her vision went to Daniel. He still stood in the back, but he wasn't laughing.

"Why aren't you laughing?" she asked from the ground, staring at him. She was loud now, practically yelling, her voice echoing through the entire building.

"Why aren't you laughing, Daniel?" she asked again. The boys split, letting her see him, but he wouldn't meet her eyes. He stared down, glumly.

"Do you agree with them?" she asked. "Do you think I'm a sinner? Do you think Dad's a sinner? What kind of monster am I, for helping throw a party? Why don't you come over here and push me down, too? I'll get up again, if it'll help. You've always been bigger than everyone else, but you've never been a bully. Until today, I guess."

His eyes finally rose, for a brief moment, and met her fiery gaze, the bottomless sudden anger that she had tapped into, the witch in her coming out. And she saw the sadness in his eyes, the tears, and it froze her. She couldn't yell anymore. It felt like forever, but it was only a moment, and then Daniel looked back down.

"I'm sorry, Marion," he said, his voice a whisper. "But what you're doing…it isn't right."

"Hear that?" asked Isaac. "Sounds like he's decided."

"Fuck you," said Marion, still loud. "And fuck you, Daniel. Not much of a mystery where you're spending your Sundays, huh? Hope you have fun with these goose steppers at Fall Festival."

Daniel said nothing.

"Do we have a problem here, Isaac?" asked Mel, the school's security officer. He was a short, squat man who didn't take shit from anyone. Marion assumed her yelling at drawn him to them.

"No, sir," said Isaac. "We were just leaving. Marion here accidentally fell, and we were just making sure she was okay."

"I'm sure. Get to class," he said, and they left. Marion only watched Daniel as he meekly turned and walked away with them. He didn't look back.

Mel reached a hand down and Marion grabbed it, and he pulled her to her feet.

"Are you alright?" he asked.

"I'm fine," she said. "I bit my tongue, but it'll be okay."

"You sure? I can file a report with discipline," he said.

"Will it make a difference?" she asked.

Mel shrugged. "It's all I can do. With him—" he rolled his eyes. "Nothing sticks."

"Thank you. We'll be okay," she said.

*

Cara drove Marion home. Marion didn't cry until she had to tell Dad, and then all the tears that had built up through the rest of the day all came at once. She told him what happened. She told him what Daniel said.

Dad said he'd talk to him, and then he left Marion and Cara alone in her room.

"I'm sorry," said Cara.

"Sorry for what?" asked Marion.

"Today," said Cara. "For what happened with your brother."

"It's not your fault," said Marion.

"It's not just that," said Cara. "For what went on with my dad. You had to walk home."

"That wasn't your fault either. Is it any better with him?"

"No," said Cara. She hadn't wanted to talk about it, and Marion understood now more than ever. "He doesn't know about us, you know. He doesn't know that, you know, we're together. He thinks we're just friends."

"And he was that angry?"

"He thinks Reverend Laurel was sent here by God. There's no talking to him. And if he knew…"

"You don't have to tell him," said Marion. "It's not worth it."

"I don't have to," said Cara. "But I want to. You're so lucky. With your dad."

Marion hugged her then. They leaned back against Marion's headboard, enjoying being close to each other.

"Will you go to Homecoming with me?" asked Marion. "I don't have a date."

Cara only nodded, and then they kissed.

And then the yelling from downstairs started.

Daniel had gotten home.

25

Daniel would make this right. He would. The pit of anxiety in his stomach had opened a deep furrow inside him, and during the rest of the day after the confrontation with his sister, that seam had ripped further and further apart. By the time football practice was over, his stomach was a great chasm.

He would go home, and he'd apologize to Marion. He'd make it up to her, no matter the cost. Daniel couldn't take that feeling. He couldn't live with that look of betrayal etched on her face floating forever in his mind. Whatever she demanded, he would pay. Whatever it took.

Daniel drove home, avoiding Isaac after practice. He couldn't talk to him right now. It would muddy the waters even more, and Daniel didn't want to widen the gap. He wanted to close it.

He stood next to the front door. He would go in, straight upstairs, apologize, get down on his knees, whatever it took.

Daniel opened it, the stairs in front of him, leading up. He took a deep breath.

Just walk upstairs. Take it like a man.

"What on Earth has gotten into you, young man?" asked his dad. His voice startled Daniel, who turned to see his father rise from the couch. He had been waiting for him. Daniel tried to summon some words, but none came. All his earlier determination vanished.

"Your sister has been crying all afternoon," he said, slowly walking over to Daniel. "She told me you, Isaac Laurel, and a bunch of other boys bullied her and Cara. Knocked her down. Is that true?"

"I—It was an accident," said Daniel, finding his voice. "I didn't mean for it to happen, Isaac had said that we should tear down the fliers, and then—"

"And you don't tell me you're friends with Isaac Laurel?" asked his dad. "You don't tell me you're going to church with him? Going camping with him? I have to call around town to find out my son is spending time with those bigots?"

Daniel felt his face turn red, and his heart shook his chest. His eyes teared up, but he squeezed them shut hard, forcing them down. He couldn't cry. He could barely breathe.

"They're not bigots," said Daniel. "You're just saying that because you have to have Halloween. All you care about is about getting what you want."

"You're not stupid, Daniel. Do you really think any of this is about Halloween? Do you think it's a coincidence that they targeted your sister? Or Cara?"

"They were posting the fliers for your party—"

"I've been doing it too, Daniel. We have plenty of people around town trying to drum up interest, and the Laurels target two gay girls. I didn't *make* them do that. They *chose* who they're targeting. Just like Isaac *chose* you to befriend. To brainwash."

"That's not true. He's my friend," said Daniel.

"I'm sure he is," said his dad. "You're grounded. No more football. No more church. No more leaving the house except for school. You go to class, and you come straight home. You can drive your sister again. Try and make up for what you did to her."

Daniel couldn't breathe. He couldn't leave the team, they needed him; he was *finally* making friends in Laurel City, everyone at the church appreciated him, valued him, *listened to him—*

"You're doing this because I'm going to church there," said Daniel.

"I'm doing it because you bullied your own sister, Daniel," said his father. "What did Marion do to deserve it?"

"Halloween is evil," said Daniel. "That homeless man died—"

"Again, Daniel, what does that have to do with your sister? How you behaved? You're the biggest, strongest kid at the school. If you had defended her, they would have backed off. But instead, you stood by and let them attack her. Even if it was a stranger, I'd be disappointed."

"I was going to—"

"I don't want to hear any more excuses. Go to your room," he said. Daniel tried to breathe, but he couldn't, his face was red, he squeezed his hands into fists, *he doesn't un-*

derstand, I didn't want any of this to happen—

Dad only stared at him and waited. Daniel couldn't meet his eyes. He marched up the stairs, fuming. His loud footsteps shook the house. He turned toward his room, but paused in front of Marion's door. He took a breath.

You could still apologize. You were there, and you did nothing—

No, that's what he wants. Daniel stomped into his bedroom and shut the door. A tear slid down his cheek and he wiped it away, rubbing his finger dry on his jeans.

He didn't understand, couldn't understand. Daniel had found somewhere to belong, and Dad was taking it from him. Taking football and his new friends from him. Every time Daniel found a place to fit in, he took it. He never cared, never stopped to think about Daniel, it was always about him.

You have a family here.

Abraham's words echoed in his mind. Isaac's defense of him. They stood up for him. They cared about him. They listened to him.

He put his backpack down on a chair and then opened his closet. No football? No church? Did he think he could steal everything away again? Daniel refused. He was an adult now. He didn't have to take this. He rummaged through the pile of random stuff in the corner of his closet until he found his crummy black duffel bag. He threw it on the bed and opened it up.

He opened his dresser and began stuffing bundles of clothes into the duffel. He didn't care if it was tidy. He just wanted it all to fit, and he stuffed it tight until it did.

There was other stuff here, half of it still packed in boxes in the basement. He didn't want it, didn't need it. He grabbed his laptop and slid it into his bag. Between it and his phone, he had everything else he needed. He threw on his backpack and then zipped up the duffel and slung it over a shoulder.

He left his room. Marion stood in her open door.

"What are you doing?" she asked.

"I'm leaving," he said. He still couldn't look at her.

It's not too late, you can still apologize.

"Why?" she asked.

He closed his eyes, trying to think of a way to express how he felt, a means to apologize, to preserve their relationship. To tell her how he had felt like an outsider in the family since Mom had died, and how every step along the way had only made it worse and worse, that he didn't blame her, that he loved his sister, that he only wanted to belong *somewhere*, desperately.

But he didn't have them. To say it openly and plainly would expose himself, reveal raw nerves to not just her, but to everyone, and he couldn't. It terrified him, the mere thought of it, and the fear pushed that all away. He said nothing and stomped down the stairs.

Dad waited for him at the bottom. It was impossible not to hear Daniel.

"What do you think you're doing?" asked his father.

"I'm leaving," said Daniel.

Dad stood in front of the door, his arms crossed. "Where will you go?"

"I'm an adult, I can do what I want," said Daniel, avoiding the answer.

"The Laurels don't care about you, Daniel," said his dad. "You're a pawn to them. They want to keep control of Laurel

City, and you're just another piece to them."

Daniel could feel his face turn red again.

"You always do this," said Daniel.

"What?"

"You always make it about you," said Daniel. "Always. Everything is always about you. And if it isn't, you make it become about you. It happened in Plinkett, and it's happening here now. I make friends, I find people who listen to me, and you twist it."

"That's not true—"

"Yes, it is!" yelled Daniel. He towered over his father. "This is all your fault. But you *had* to decorate your yard. You *had* to celebrate Halloween, even though the town doesn't want you to. You could have just moved on, and let us live in peace, but you had to pick a fight. I'm tired of having to fight your battles for you!"

"Daniel—"

"Get out of the way," said Daniel.

"You're not leaving the house," said his dad.

"You can't stop me," said Daniel. His hand balled into a fist.

His father stared at him, his face filled with anger and frustration. He closed his eyes and it all let go, and all that emotion was replaced with sadness. He stepped aside.

"I won't fight you, Daniel. I love you, but this isn't you," he said.

Daniel stepped past him and opened the door. He stood in the open doorway.

"It isn't?" asked Daniel. "How would you know?"

Daniel left, carrying his bags to his truck, and throwing them into the bed.

He drove, and now the tears flowed freely. He didn't want to leave, he had wanted to apologize, he had wanted this all to end, but his father just couldn't let him, he couldn't let him—

Daniel arrived at Laurel City Holy Church, pulling his truck into the nearly empty parking lot. It was a Monday night. There was only one other vehicle there.

He walked into the sanctuary and sat down, his duffel bag and backpack beside him. He hadn't expected it to be unlocked. The lights were on. It felt so strange. The room was usually packed full of people, but now Daniel was alone.

"How are you doing, Daniel?" asked Reverend Laurel. He entered from his normal place, from behind the pulpit. He walked toward Daniel, who sat in a pew a few rows from the front. Laurel wore a dress shirt and slacks.

"I—" he started. "I left my house."

"May I?" asked the Reverend, gesturing next to Daniel. Daniel nodded. Laurel sat down next to him. "What happened?"

"We argued. He tried to ground me. No more football or church. I left, I couldn't, but I don't know—"

"You listen to my sermons," said the Reverend. "I know you do. You returned after he left. You're a good person, Daniel. We all saw it. Isaac saw it. Abraham sees it. I see it. And here you are, coming back again."

"I don't know what to do," said Daniel. He looked at the Reverend, whose face was open and genuine. The Reverend met his eyes. "I have nowhere else to go."

"That's not true," said Laurel. "If you need a home, the Laurels will provide you with one."

26

"So what do we do?" asked Marion. They had waited all night, but Daniel never came back. Marion tried to spot him the next day at school, but she had failed. She heard from the street team that they saw him palling around with Isaac. When she saw Dad that evening and told him, he confirmed it. He had learned Daniel had moved in with David Laurel, only a few blocks from Abraham's house.

He sighed. "I don't know."

"Can't you, you know—do something?" asked Marion.

"Like what? Arrest him?" he asked. They sat in the living room, the television on but muted. Dad was still in his uniform from work. "He's eighteen. I can't hold him against his will, if he doesn't want to be held."

Dad looked down, his elbows on his knees. He leaned

back and stared straight ahead, his gaze lost in the middle distance. Marion hadn't seen him look like that in a long time. Not since Mom died.

Marion felt a vibration from her pocket and pulled out her phone, but it was nothing. Cara had never shown up to pick her up this morning and hadn't answered her texts either. Dad had dropped her off, and she had taken the bus home. Cara hadn't been at school, and her absence compounded all the worry inside Marion. Daniel leaving the house wasn't enough. Her girlfriend also had to disappear. Marion thought to go to Cara's place to check on her, but she was afraid of returning after last time.

"We could, you know, cancel the party," said Marion.

"No," said her dad, immediately.

"Why not? I heard what he said, and he's not wrong, a party isn't worth all of this—"

"It's not about a party, Marion," he said. "It's about control. It's about Laurel keeping this town his. This place is more than a church. And even if we canceled, it would only make things worse. It would prove Laurel right. It wouldn't make Daniel change his mind."

"I don't like him gone," she said. "That's all."

"I know," he said. "Neither do I. And I hate it even more that he's living with Laurel. The Reverend knows what to say, and his damned son and grandson are cut from the same mold."

"So what do we do?" asked Marion.

He sighed and shook his head.

"Daniel's a good kid," he said. "He should know the right thing to do. We have to trust that he will, in the end. That he can figure out what to do. If we push against him, it'll only make it worse. He has to realize himself what the Laurels really are. Is—"

He stopped and glanced down again. Her dad then looked up at her, darting to her eyes, as if testing, and then meeting her vision again.

"Is this my fault?" he asked. "Am I—am I a good enough dad?"

Marion got up and sat next to him.

She took a deep breath, to say something, to try to defend him from himself.

"Because—because it took a long time for me to adjust to being a parent by myself. Your mom always balanced me out. Without her, I couldn't be the same. And they don't have classes for losing your wife and having two kids and trying to make a life at the same time. And you, you were always so easy. You took care of yourself, and we always liked the same things. Daniel...he was hard. He's so competitive, and so social, and always loved sports, and that's not me. I tried to set a good example, to do the right thing, and it just led to us getting exiled from Plinkett. I didn't *want* to leave, we had to, if any of us would lead a normal life again. And here we are, right back into it. Maybe it is my fault. Maybe I should have done more."

"You did fine," said Marion. "You—"

A knock at the front door interrupted them.

"Daniel?" asked her dad out loud. He pushed up to his feet, his eyes wide. Marion watched him go, suddenly full of energy again.

Not energy. Hope.

He opened the door, but Daniel didn't stand there. Cara did. Her eyes were red, her face sallow and tired. She'd been crying. Her backpack was on her shoulders, a carry-on in one arm. Marion rushed over to her and Cara started sobbing as Marion embraced her.

Her dad backed off, giving them some space. Marion pulled her inside the house and shut the door. She gave a quick look to her dad, who motioned that he'd be in the living room. She nodded, holding Cara, whose body shook as she sobbed. Cara was talking into Marion's chest, but Marion couldn't understand a word. She walked her upstairs, into the bedroom. Marion took her bags from her and guided her to the bed.

Words and tears tumbled out of Cara, but Marion couldn't figure out what she was saying. Their fingers were interlaced, and Cara's grip was hard.

"Slow down. Breathe," said Marion. She ran her hand up and down Cara's back. She was burning up. Cara tried to stop and coughed. Marion handed her a tissue and Cara blew her nose.

"They found out," she said, finally, after catching her breath. "Someone told them. Someone told my parents about us."

"When?" asked Marion.

"Last night," said Cara. "Someone called. They wouldn't tell me who. They took away my phone. We fought. For hours and hours. My dad, he just screamed at me. Wouldn't let me go to school. He knew I'd see you. He went to work today, and he was even angrier when he got home. Told me they'd fix me, send me to one of those camps."

"Fuck that," said Marion.

"Something flipped," said Cara. "Inside me. And I screamed and screamed at him. He looked—he looked scared. He told me to get out of his house." Cara faced Marion. "I came here. I didn't know where else to go."

"Do you have any other family?" asked Marion.

"None that think any differently than my dad," she said. "They won't take me in."

"Then you'll stay here," said Marion.

"I—I—"

"You'll stay here," said Marion. "Okay?"

"Okay," said Cara. "What about your dad? And your brother?"

"Christ, you don't know about Daniel," said Marion. "He left the house yesterday. Moved in with Reverend Laurel."

Suddenly, Cara was silent.

"What?" asked Marion.

"Do you think—do you think he told the Reverend about us? And he told my dad?"

A twinge of pain pulled on Marion's heart.

"I don't know," she said. And she didn't. But that there was doubt at all told her how much how she felt about her brother had changed. "He's not here anymore. Let's go talk to my dad."

He waited for them downstairs, blankly watching the silent television, a baseball game playing.

"Cara's parents kicked her out of their house," said Marion. "Because of us." He nodded and looked to Cara.

"How old are you, Cara?" he asked.

"16," said Cara.

"Then it's illegal for them to kick you out. It's abandonment. If you file a report, they'll *have* to take you back in."

Cara nodded, but he continued before she could say anything.

"But I'm betting that you don't want to go back," he said. "That living there was abusive before they knew about your relationship, and now, it would be hellish. Right?"

She nodded again.

"I'm guessing that if you stay here, they won't try and get you?" he asked.

"I don't know," said Cara. "They might."

"Well," he said, "We'll cross that bridge when we come to it. I'm guessing that even if I had you sleep on the couch, you'd end up with Marion after I fell asleep."

"Probably," said Cara, cracking a smile for the first time since she'd come into the house.

He nodded with his own smirk.

"Then stay with Marion. Be quiet after ten. I have to get up early. That work for you?"

Cara smiled widely then and hugged him. He returned it. Marion watched and couldn't help but smile. She wondered how often Cara had been hugged by her parents.

*

Marion and Cara cuddled in the dark, with Marion as little spoon. Furriosa curled up at their feet.

"What will we do if they try and force me to go back?"

"I don't know," said Marion. "I'm sure there's a way out of it. My dad's a cop. I'm sure he knows a way."

"The look on my dad's face—when he told me they would send me away," said Cara. "I'd never seen it before. It scared me so much. I think that's what made me scream at him. He looked like he'd be happy if I died."

"Hey," said Marion, flipping around, facing Cara. "Where

are you?"

"I'm in bed with you," said Cara.

"You're safe," said Marion. "I'll protect you."

"You *are* a witch," said Cara.

"Double, double, toil and trouble, if you fuck with Cara, you'll feel my knuckles," said Marion.

"That was bad," said Cara.

"Shh," said Marion.

They kissed in the dark.

27

"You look beautiful," said her dad. "Both of you."

They had expected someone to do something after Daniel left, and after Cara moved in. They had continued putting the last touches on their Halloween plans, with people helping when they could. Neither of them had heard from Daniel. He had avoided Marion at school. All the LYE boys had. The fliers they posted were still pulled down regularly, but for each one they tore down, the street team would put two up. The town was covered in them at this point. If nobody came to the party, it wouldn't be because they didn't know about it.

The Laurels did nothing, as far as they could tell. And Cara's parents hadn't tried to contact her. They added her to their phone plan and got her a new one off eBay.

But the week had passed without incident, and it was the night of Homecoming. Marion wore a beautiful gray dress, while Cara wore a red one. They had spent hours on their makeup. Marion couldn't help but smile the entire time, even as they poked themselves in the eye trying to apply fake eyelashes.

Marion had never gone to a dance before, had never had a date to go to a dance with before. She had Cara, but underneath the excitement still lurked dread. The war in Laurel City had been quiet. It wasn't like the Laurels to just give up. She knew she and Cara were a target, and Homecoming seemed a convenient and very public place to embarrass them. She had seen Carrie. A bucket of pig's blood kept popping up in her mind, and she didn't have telekinetic powers to fall back on.

They stood in front of the door, and Dad surveyed them before they headed out. He hugged them both.

"You two have fun," he said.

"Dad," said Marion. "What do I do if Daniel is there? If LYE is there? If they, you know, try something?"

He exhaled, and looked her, and then Cara, in the eyes. "Ignore them if you can. If you can't, find a chaperone, and call attention to them. Don't let them operate in the dark. Whatever they're doing, everyone should know about it. But try and avoid them. Try and have a good time. Dance. Try not to think about them. Hell, why would they go to a dance in the first place? Isn't Laurel against dancing too?"

"Is that—is that a joke?" asked Cara.

He smiled. "She's catching on."

"We're gonna go," said Marion. "Have fun with Ms. Gibson."

They left, heading out to Cara's old sedan. They backed out and headed toward the school. The dance was in the gym, cleared out and decorated for the night.

"Are you okay?" asked Cara.

"I'm anxious," said Marion. They held hands, Cara's hand extending into Marion's lap. Cara squeezed in response.

"Me too," said Cara.

They arrived quickly, parking in the crowded lot. As soon as they got out, Marion's eyes scanned the various crowds who loitered on the periphery. Daniel wouldn't be able to hide in this crowd, and especially not in the gym. Both he and Isaac would stand out with their size. She didn't spot any of the LYE boys.

Marion grabbed Cara's hand, and they walked down the covered walkway to the gym, through the flourishes of decorative ribbon and paper draped over everything. They checked in at the registration table and endured the silent judgment of the two older teachers who manned it. But they were past them soon enough, into the low light of the gymnasium, small lights fluttering through the air, a panoply of colors and illumination.

"They did a good job," said Cara, but Marion barely heard her, her eyes scanning over each person, seeing if any of the boys were here, if Isaac was here, if Daniel was here. She didn't spot any of them.

"Marion?" asked Cara.

"Yeah?"

"Are you okay?"

"Yeah, I'm fine," said Marion, but she scanned the crowd again. Still nothing.

"Let's get a drink," said Cara. "We can say hi to Laura and

Ben." They got a drink, served by Mr. Jenkins.

"Hello, girls," he said, handing them two plastic cups. "I'm glad to see you here."

"Hi, Mr. Jenkins," said Marion.

"You let me know if anyone causes any trouble," he said. He winked conspiratorially and then nodded. They both nodded in return. Drinks in hand, they went to one of the tables surrounding the open dance floor, where Ben and Laura sat.

"I didn't know they were dating," said Marion, as they headed over.

"Turns out they both had crushes on each other and neither would admit it," said Cara. "I think Justin tricked both of them into asking the other out."

"Hey guys," said Cara, as they reached the table. No one else sat at it, and they joined Ben and Laura.

"Hey," they said, not quite in unison.

"Having fun so far?" asked Marion.

"We could be playing Descent," said Laura. "Instead we're sitting in here, listening to bad music."

"I mean, it's not so bad," he said. "Okay, it's not great. Descent would be better."

"Have you guys danced at all?" asked Marion.

"No," said Laura. "They've only played boring-ass EDM. I'm not dancing to that."

"What will you dance to?" asked Marion.

"I don't know," said Laura. "Girls Just Want to Have Fun."

"Okay," said Marion, and she marched over to the DJ table, run by a kid who looked like he graduated a year or two ago. He was staring at his phone, the laptop playing whatever playlist he thought appropriate.

"Can you play Cyndi Lauper?" asked Marion.

He looked confused. "Cyndi Lauper? Here?"

"Yes. Girls Just Want to Have Fun. Please and thank you," she said.

"Uhh, sure," he said, clicked a few things on his computer, and then went back to looking at his phone. Marion returned to the table, and after a minute or two the song changed, and the voice of Cyndi Lauper rang through the auditorium. Marion raised her eyebrows to Laura and then pulled Cara to the dance floor. Laura followed her, doing the same to Ben.

They danced, Marion and Cara's hands together. Most of the other kids stayed out there. Most of them didn't care what they danced to. Marion didn't consider herself a good dancer, but she had Cara, and that was enough.

She could feel people's eyes on her from the shadows. The same judgment she felt earlier from the two teachers manning the registration table. Isaac, Daniel, and the other boys were more overt than most, but they weren't the only ones at Laurel City High who disapproved of her and Cara. Her vision flitted through the crowd, even as Cyndi Lauper crooned. She still didn't see Daniel, or Isaac.

"Where are you?" asked Cara, her voice interrupting Marion's search. Marion's eyes snapped to Cara's.

"I'm—I'm dancing with you," said Marion.

"Damn straight," said Cara, and kissed her, holding it for a moment. "Let's dance then."

The music continued, and Marion's eyes stayed on Cara for the rest of the song. They were laughing by the time it was over and retreated when a thick bass line hit for the return to the DJ's normal playlist. The four went back to their drinks, the table still deserted.

"Okay, I'll admit," said Laura. "That was fun."

"It's our Homecoming too," said Marion. "I could request some old school punk songs next."

"I think I'll pass on that," said Laura. "Any sign of you know who?"

"He's not Voldemort, Laura," said Cara. "Isaac is just a kid. His dad and grandfather have warped him. But no, neither of us have seen any of the LYErs."

"Their girlfriends are all sitting over there," said Ben, gesturing toward a table in the far corner of the room with his head. Marion looked. Seven girls, all dressed in various expensive white dresses, nursing plastic cups.

"They look pissed," said Laura.

And they did. Each of them had a slightly different glower on their face, mixed with boredom. They weren't chatting, and each of them would pick up their phone, look at it for a moment, and then put it back down.

"They got blown off," said Marion. "They're not coming tonight. They're doing something else." Marion texted her dad.

Daniel and other boys aren't at dance. Don't know where they are. Just a heads up

He responded with a short thumbs up emoji, and then she put her phone away.

"Weird," said Ben.

They chatted for a while, but none of their other friends had come, and after another half hour of thudding beats, Cara's head ached.

"I think we're gonna leave, guys," said Marion.

"I don't want to go home already," said Cara.

"What about your headache?" asked Marion.

"I just need to get away from the music," said Cara.

"I've got an idea," said Marion. She went over to Mr. Jenkins, still at his station by the punch bowl.

"Mr. Jenkins, can you let us into your room?" she asked.

"Why?"

"We want to play board games," said Marion.

"That sounds like a great idea," he said. "I wish I could join you." He reached into his pocket and handed her his key ring. "I didn't give you these. I'll be by to collect them after the dance is over."

*

"I'll move my guy over here, use a stamina potion, and then open the treasure chest," said Ben. They all sat around the table, still in their dance outfits.

"See, this is much more preferable," said Laura. "How's your head, Cara?"

"Way better already," said Cara. "I don't know how anyone can endure that for longer than an hour or two."

"Some people just have thick skulls," said Marion. "What do you think Isaac is doing tonight? What Daniel is doing?"

"I don't know," said Cara.

"I thought they would be here," said Marion. "It worries me that they're not."

"They're probably sitting in the church, worried about their immortal souls. You were worried that they would ruin the dance, but they didn't, and now you're worried that they're not here."

"It's just strange," said Marion. "Everyone is here, and

they're not. Abandoning their dates?"

"Hey, Dawson, it's your turn," said Laura.

"Sorry," said Marion. She moved her fighter over to the big demon monster. "I attack with my magic sword."

"Are you sure?" asked Ben. "If he hits you next turn, you're donezo."

"I can take it," said Marion. "It's worth the risk."

They played Descent until Mr. Jenkins came to collect his keys and lock up his room.

They loitered in the parking lot, near Cara's car, the four of them talking about nothing. Marion had stopped searching every passing face for her brother, but still thoughts of him lingered in her mind.

What are you doing tonight, Daniel?

She didn't think it could be good, for any of them.

28

The pit of dread in Daniel's stomach hadn't disappeared since he'd left his house and moved in with Reverend Laurel. It had ebbed and flowed, growing and shrinking depending on the time of day, and how busy he was, but it never vanished entirely. The sense of righteousness and justice he had felt driving away from his home had fled, though. The dread was all that remained.

Daniel hadn't had a date for Homecoming, but he had planned to go, nonetheless. Isaac had told him he should, even though Isaac and most of the other boys had dates.

But homecoming night came and then Abraham and Isaac showed up at the Reverend's house, with no girls in sight.

"No dance tonight," said Isaac, a determined look on his

face.

"What? Was it canceled?" asked Daniel. He was about to get dressed.

"No," said Isaac. "But we have more important business to attend to."

"What about Julia?" asked Daniel. Julia was Isaac's date, a beautiful blond that also went to the Holy Church.

"She'll understand," said Isaac. "You can't deny God's will over any woman."

"Can you get ready, Daniel?" asked Abraham, in his customary soft voice. "Dark clothes would be preferable."

"What are we doing?" asked Daniel.

"We're taking back our town," said Abraham. The Reverend stood there in the antechamber silently as Daniel went back upstairs to change. He could hear the Laurels talk quietly among themselves as he walked up the stairs.

He changed into a black t-shirt and dark jeans and returned downstairs. The dread grew. What are they planning?

They're your family now, Daniel. You are a part of this.

The dread inside affirmed that thought. He had made his choice, multiple times now. There was no way back. He couldn't leave the Laurels, not after all they'd done for him. They'd given him a place to belong. They had provided sanctuary from an uncaring father and *made* him a part of their family.

He went back downstairs and followed Abraham and Isaac out to Abraham's SUV. They pulled away.

"Where are we heading, Abraham?" asked Daniel.

"You'll see," said Abraham. "It's another step in taking back our town."

"Is anyone else going with us?" asked Daniel.

"Some of the boys are meeting us there," said Isaac. "But only a few. Only the ones we trust."

It didn't take long to get there. The sun was already down, but Daniel knew immediately where they were. The first thing he saw were the decorations.

"Why are we here?" he asked.

"Sending a message," said Isaac, turning and smiling at Daniel.

"My dad's a cop!" said Daniel. "He's armed."

"He's not home," said Abraham, quietly.

"How do you know?" asked Daniel.

"We have our sources," said Abraham. Daniel remembered the neighbor asking about the Halloween decorations. The eyes looking out from between curtains. It could be anyone.

You're one of them too, now.

The pain in his guts flared higher. His breath burned. He struggled to breathe at all, his heart beating against his chest.

Another car pulled up behind them, parking on the curb.

"That's the boys," said Isaac. "Let's go." They got out, and Daniel followed them, drawn along in their orbit. Isaac carried his backpack, rattling as he stepped.

"Won't somebody call and report us?" asked Daniel. He turned to see both Jason and Mark, both wearing black hoodies.

"Nobody saw anything," said Isaac, still smiling. "No one wants Halloween, Daniel. We're only doing what the town needs. Why would they report us?"

Isaac kicked over a fake tombstone, and then stepped

on it with a heel, cracking it into smaller pieces, the styro-foam breaking. The two other boys joined him, destroying the various decorations, pulling down the corpse from the trees.

"Isaac, give me your backpack," said Abraham. Isaac took it off and gave it to him. "Follow me, Daniel." Daniel did, seeing hours and hours of work by his dad and sister being destroyed in seconds.

Say something. Do something, *Daniel.*

But he did nothing, mutely following Abraham, as he walked up the driveway to the garage door. His dad would have come out by now if he had been home. He was gone. And Daniel kept waiting for the sounds of incoming sirens, or a neighbor to wander over with a flashlight, but none of it happened. Abraham was right. They all wanted this to happen. They wanted them to take back Laurel City.

Abraham put down the bag and unzipped it, pulling out two cans of black spray paint. They rattled in his hands. He passed one to Daniel, shaking the one he kept. It clattered loudly in the night, echoing through the neighborhood. Daniel heard Furriosa barking softly from inside the house.

"Shake it, Daniel," said Abraham. "Have you ever used it before?"

"No," said Daniel. He hadn't. The sound was familiar, his dad and sister using it all the time for various creations of theirs. Like the ones being destroyed right now. Plywood snapped behind him.

"You need to shake it," said Abraham. Daniel shook the can in his hand, the ball bearing rattling around inside, humming through his whole body.

Why are you doing this, Daniel?

He had to. He had made his choice.

"That should be good," said Abraham, his voice still calm and reassuring. "Now spray on the garage door. Let everyone know what he really is."

Daniel stood in front of the giant plain of white, clean and unmarked. The cold metal of the paint can slowly trembled in his hand. He gripped it hard, but he couldn't stop shaking.

Why are you doing this, Daniel? This is your home. You stood by while they bullied your sister, and now you're one of them.

Daniel shook his head. He wasn't hearing his own voice in his head; he was hearing his father's, and no, he didn't understand. Neither his father nor Marion understood. *They* were the ones who didn't listen. *They* had chosen this and set him down this path. This wasn't his fault. The Laurels had accepted him. The Laurels had done more than that; they had embraced him.

"What should I write?" he asked.

"They are sinners, Daniel," said Abraham, quietly. "Let everyone know."

Daniel sprayed.

S I N N E R S

"And you doubted him," said Isaac, nudging Jason. Abraham put a hand on Daniel's back, patting him twice. It felt good, but the moment of confidence while he painted evaporated again.

"Good job, son," said Abraham. "Now let us finish."

The rest of the boys grabbed cans. Daniel watched them

mark up the house. The dread in his gut grew worse as he saw what they wrote.

*

"You proved yourself tonight, Daniel," said Abraham, as they drove back. They had left the front yard destroyed, the house covered in paint.

"I never had any doubt," said Isaac.

"Neither did I," said Abraham. "But there is still value in the test. Just like Jesus and his disciples, he wanted them to earn their place in his inner circle."

Daniel barely heard them. He could only think about the damage they had done to his house.

It's not your home anymore. It's a den of sin, the Reverend said so, his word is God's Word

His stomach burned, burned worse than ever, and he could feel the bile stacking up inside him. He swallowed and took a deep breath, forcing it back down. He couldn't throw up, not here. They'd be back soon, and he could retreat to his bathroom, his own bathroom. The Reverend gave him that, but the SUV didn't turn toward their neighborhood. Abraham continued on.

"Are we not going home?" asked Daniel.

"We're not done yet," said Abraham. "We still have more to do."

They were at the Church soon enough.

"What's there to do here?" asked Daniel. "Where's the other car?"

"They haven't earned this yet," said Abraham. "Isaac has shown his faith. And if you truly want to be a part of the family, this is how you do it."

The anxiety inside him grew again, and he had to swallow down the bile as it surged into his throat.

"You do want to join our family, don't you, Daniel?" asked Abraham.

"Yes," said Daniel, croaking it out, forcing the word.

"Then let's go in. Father is waiting for us," said Abraham.

They went into the church, the sanctuary dark inside. Abraham led them past the pulpit, down hallways, until they came to a door, unmarked and locked. He unlocked it, and then they were in a small brick room, with a massive metal door ahead of them, a strong padlock locking it. Everything in Daniel's mind told him to run, to turn and flee. But he had had already come so far, had invested so much.

"Where are we going?" asked Daniel, but Abraham didn't answer.

He unlocked the padlock and swung the big metal door open. A dimly lit stairwell lay ahead of them.

They walked down into the brick room with dirty, wooden floors. Reverend Laurel waited for them inside, standing at a small table. A book lay in front of him. The book was massive and old. Daniel smelled something, but he didn't know what. A terrible stink, of something unburied.

"Hello, Reverend," said Daniel.

"Daniel," said Reverend Laurel. "I'm glad you're here. That means everything is working out. That you are dedicated in your faith."

"Where are we?" asked Daniel.

"This is where the Church started," said the Reverend. "It started here, and grew up, and out into the city you know. And it's where we will take Laurel City back."

Run Daniel. Something's wrong here, and you know it. Get out now.

But it was too late.

And the Reverend told him about the Book. About winning back the town.

And Daniel touched the Book, and then everything seemed easier.

"We need your blood, Daniel," said Reverend Laurel. They stood around him, in the middle of that dirty, dirty floor. He handed Daniel a dagger, and Daniel took it. It made sense. The Book made it make sense.

NO Daniel, this isn't—

But the overwhelming feeling of dread had finally subsided. Daniel could think again. He realized this is where he belonged. This was his family.

He ran the dagger over his hand, and blood poured out onto that dirty floor, that floor which had seen so much blood.

They pulled Daniel back, back among them, because that's where he was.

And then something emerged. Something black, and sharp, with a formless face.

And it made the noise of his mother dying, and all that dread hit Daniel, all at once.

29

"Aren't you worried about them?" asked Jenny.

Mike and Jenny sat across from each other in Napolitano's, a cozy little Italian joint in Murville, the next town over from Laurel City. It smelled like oregano, and all the tables had checkerboard tablecloths.

"Of course I'm worried," said Mike.

"You should have told me," said Jenny. "I could have volunteered to chaperone. You could have been my date."

"I'm worried about them, but that's parenthood," said Mike. "I've been worried about them since the moment they were born. I worried when Daniel played football for the first time. When Marion started going through her goth phase. I was worried—"

I was worried when Molly died.

But he didn't say that.

"It's a part of it," said Mike. "And if I constantly take care of everything for them, they won't be ready when they're grown up."

"I don't know if I could do it," said Jenny.

"You *don't* know," said Mike. "It's taking a leap of faith, and hoping that you can keep up with all of it."

"That's a big leap," said Jenny.

"Bigger than you can imagine," said Mike. "But if you think about the size of the jump, you're less likely to do it. Do you want kids?"

Jenny stared at him for a moment and then smiled. "That's quite a question for what is technically our third date."

"I'm sorry, I didn't—"

"Didn't think about it, I know. It's okay. I don't know. A part of me desperately wants kids. I'm sure some of it is my biological clock ticking. And I *want* to be a mom. I do. But it terrifies the other half of me. I'm selfish. I like my alone time, and if I'm a parent, that won't happen again for a long time."

"We had kids when we were young," said Mike. "And that's the benefit of youth. We didn't think about any of that stuff. But any fear we had kind of went out the window when Daniel was born. Everyone is selfish, but having him, and the same thing with Marion, it just—it just focused me. There was always something to live for, to work for. Work is always a slog, but the kids, they gave me a drive that I didn't have before. And not just a drive to work hard, or provide for them, you know. I mean, that *was* there, but it's more than that. It made me want to be better. Because everything I did would come back to them. I didn't care about setting examples beforehand. Now, it's all that matters." Jenny looked at him, a slight smile on her face. "I'm sorry. That was a lot."

"You apologize too much," she said.

"The kids, they're not a problem, are they? Between us?" he asked.

She laughed. "We met at parent/teacher night, Mike."

"I know that," he said. "But you know, if we're going to be together long term—I'm sorry—"

"You're apologizing again," she said.

"I'm sorr—"

"See, there it is," she said. "Used to do it myself. Then I stopped saying sorry for things I didn't do. Your kids are not a problem. And is this you asking me if we want to go steady?"

"I mean, do you?"

"You're such a nerd," she said. She reached across the table and grabbed his hand. "I thought we were already official, but here. I hereby decree that you're my boyfriend."

Mike blushed.

"Awww, you're blushing," she said, squeezing his hand. "You're so adorable."

"I'm glad you think so," he said. Their pizza arrived suddenly, smelling like heaven. They ate.

"Any word from Daniel?" asked Jenny.

"Nothing," said Mike.

"I haven't seen him at school," said Jenny. "He's turned into a ghost."

"I don't know what to do," said Mike. "I didn't think it would last this long. I thought he would come to his senses and come back. But he hasn't. He's living with Reverend Laurel. And it makes me more nervous every day."

"Isn't there something you could do, legally?" asked Jenny.

"He's eighteen," said Mike. "I can't control him. Even though he still lived at home, it doesn't matter because technically it was under his wishes. It's no different from someone moving out because they didn't like a roommate." Mike sighed.

"I'm sorry for bringing it up," said Jenny

"I thought you shouldn't apologize," said Mike.

"I'm not perfect," she said.

"I disagree," he said, winking at her.

"Oh lord," she said. "You're terrible."

Mike winked again.

"You're somehow winking with your entire body," said Jenny. "It's very impressive."

"I try my best," said Mike.

"He'll come back," said Jenny. "He seems like a good kid."

"It's not him I'm worried about. It's Laurel. And how far he's willing to go to keep his town in check."

*

They finished their dinner and drove back to Mike's place. He knew something was wrong right away. His headlights revealed broken tombstones and graffiti spray painted all over the house.

"Fuck," he said. As he pulled up his driveway, there were three distinct lines of text in black on his garage door.

SINNER
Dykes burn in hell
NIGGER LOVER

He sat there, his hands squeezing the steering wheel. He could feel the heat rising to his head, threatening to explode. He would drive over to Laurel's house, and he'd pull him out onto the lawn, and beat him—

"Are you okay?" asked Jenny. Jenny's voice interrupted his thoughts. Mike looked over to her, and her eyes were wide and sad.

"No, not really," he said, and sighed, a deep heavy breath, and with it, he pushed out all the anger, all the terrible decisions. "I didn't think it would come to this. But I was wrong. I underestimated him. Or overestimated him, I guess. Thought he was better than this."

"Who? Laurel?"

"Yes."

"Can we do anything?"

"No," said Mike. "I'll look for any conclusive evidence, but I doubt they left anything we could trace to them. The spray paint won't do it. Nothing we can file charges over."

"But who else would it be?"

"It could be anyone in the town, which is what he'll say," said Mike. "If we pushed him. He'll say that it's merely a reflection on how people feel about me."

"What do we do?"

"I'll clean it up," said Mike. "You don't have to stay for that. I'll take you home."

"Fuck that," she said. "If you're cleaning, I'm helping."

"You don't have to—"

"You're my boyfriend, and I'm not a shithead," she said. "But why don't we wait 'til morning?"

"Because, one, it'll be harder the longer we wait. This isn't the first time my house has gotten tagged. And two, I don't want Marion and Cara coming back to see this. I have the right stuff to clean it in the garage. With the two of us working, it shouldn't take more than an hour."

"Then let's work," she said. "Do you have any old clothes I can throw on?"

Mike dug through his old stuff and gave her a pair of ratty workout shorts and a spare t-shirt to wear. He changed as well, and then they cleaned. He threw on every light on the outside of the house, and grabbed some buckets, mixing soap and chemicals to cut through the spray paint. With that and the sponges, the paint came off with a little bit of elbow grease. Jenny came out, his shirt hanging off of her, and his shorts cinched tight around her waist, but still baggy.

"You look great," he said.

"They're your clothes, nerd," she said.

They scrubbed, and the paint started coming off. They worked around the house, crickets chirping in the distance.

"Why did your house get tagged before?" asked Jenny.

"It was in Plinkett, where we moved from," said Mike. "I was a whistleblower about corruption on the force. I was lucky they didn't burn it down."

"Jesus," said Jenny.

"It's why we left Plinkett," he said.

"That's understandable," said Jenny.

"I tell myself that," said Mike. "But I sometimes wonder if the cost to do 'the right thing' is too high."

"It's why I like you," said Jenny. "Because you do the right thing. It just sometimes means that you're out in the middle of the night cleaning off offensive graffiti with your new girlfriend."

"You do make this a lot easier," said Mike.

"I have many talents," said Jenny. "You think anyone is watching us?"

"Oh, probably."

"What a bunch of weirdos."

"They also watched as they tagged the house."

"Why didn't they stop them?"

"Because some of them are with Laurel. The rest are just afraid," said Mike. "Laurel owns the town to them. It's probably not the first time they've stayed silent about something they disagreed with. Easier that way. Doesn't rock the boat."

"Well, if you didn't say anything in Plinkett, that's who you'd be," said Jenny.

Mike didn't answer her, concentrating on scrubbing the paint off the vinyl siding of his house. But she was right, and her words soothed some lingering ache in his guts.

After just over an hour, the house was clean. He tossed the cleaning supplies back into the garage. That *could* wait until morning. He looked through their decorations, and gathered up everything that couldn't be fixed, and threw it in the trash. Everything else he piled up inside. They'd work on it tomorrow.

"I'm out of shape," she said. They went into the house, out of the chill night air.

"I like your shape," said Mike. She elbowed him playfully.

"You know what I mean," said Jenny. "I'm gonna be sore tomorrow. I'm surprised Marion and Cara aren't back yet."

"The dance is going pretty late," said Mike. "Marion will text me when they're on their way back. I'm going to clean myself up." Mike went into his bedroom, throwing his clothes in the hamper and jumping into the shower in his bathroom. He was exhausted, the emotions of the night taking their toll on him, as well as scrubbing the outside of the house for an hour. The hot water felt great, and he closed his eyes as it washed over him.

The cool touch of skin on his shoulder surprised him, and he opened his eyes to see Jenny in the shower with him.

"My grandmother always said," said Jenny. "Don't waste water. Never shower alone." She kissed him on the lips, pressing her body against his.

He suddenly wasn't tired anymore.

30

Mike showed Chief Miller the cell phone photos from the night before, first thing in the morning.

"Christ," said Miller, rubbing his eyes. His cup of coffee still steamed in front of him.

"It was Laurel and his boys," said Mike. "Not a doubt in my mind. Isaac wasn't at the dance last night, or any of the kids in LYE. Awfully big coincidence, don't you think?"

"Coincidences don't make cases," said Miller. "We can't arrest anyone because they didn't go to a dance."

"I know," said Mike. "I never said we should arrest them."

"What do you want me to do?" asked Miller.

"I want you to acknowledge that a member of the community is targeting one of your officers," said Mike.

Miller stared at him, his face blank. Mike stared back,

and then something swung over in Miller's mind, because he closed his eyes, and held them shut, breathing deeply.

"You're right," said Miller, finally. "Hard to argue it was anyone else. Even if it wasn't them, he's the one driving people to do it." He leaned back in his chair and took a sip of his coffee. "Truth be told, Mike, we didn't go to the service last Sunday, and I don't think we'll be heading back anytime soon. The missus said to me in the car on the way home from the service two Sundays ago, she said 'I don't like the way the Reverend is talking so much about Halloween'. That might not mean much to you, Mike, but to me, the fact she said that speaks the world. And then we didn't go this past Sunday, and we begged off being sick, but I don't think we'll do that this Sunday. We're just going to say we're not going."

Silence hung between them. "Has this happened before, Chief?" asked Mike.

"Last year," said Chief Miller. "A woman came around from Topeka. Her name was Susan Hamilton. Reporter, journalist, what have you. She came into town, looking to do a story on the Laurels. I mean, it is an interesting story. How many families found a town and then still end up in it six or seven generations later? Even more, still are important in the town? It's like the American dream, you know?"

"What happened with her?" asked Mike.

"She asked questions. Seems like she interviewed everyone in town. Interviewed me. I gave her the God's honest truth, or at least my best recollection of it. And it seemed fine for a little while. But then she talked to the Reverend, and whatever took place during that conversation, it changed everything. Suddenly half the town was talking about snoopy reporters, and journalists sowing discord. And it wasn't so hard to find the source. I heard it every Sunday. We all did. The Reverend never talked about reporters before that, but then, suddenly, that was every sermon. How this journalist was tearing Laurel City apart."

"And?"

"It kept going for a little while, but she didn't back off. Kept talking to the people that would talk to her. She never reported any harassment, but who knows. She was building some story, whatever it was. She wasn't sticking around for the ambiance. She was staying out at the Motel 6, out by the interstate. But one day, she disappeared. Checked out and never checked back in."

"And nothing else?" asked Mike.

"I don't know," said Miller. "She never filed a story."

"Where did she go?" asked Mike.

"We don't know," said Miller. "No one ever came looking, so I put it aside. Always more to do, you know that. But more and more lately, I worry about Ms. Hamilton."

"You think Laurel had something to do with it?" asked Mike.

"Thought never crossed my mind," said Miller. "He would never do anything like that. But still, it doesn't paint a great portrait of the man. And that stuff adds up. I don't know if he noticed or not, but a few people just stopped coming when all that went down. And I'm not the only one who's quit going lately. If I wanted a man yelling and angry about the world, I could just turn on the TV. It's not worth putting a tie on, that's for sure." He paused, and looked back at Mike. "If anything else happens, you tell me."

"I will," said Mike, getting up. "Thanks, Chief."

"No, thank you," said Chief. "For keeping me honest."

*

They were only out on patrol for an hour before the radio squawked, suddenly.

"We've got a call about a disturbance at the library, emergency 911, but we lost the call, please respond."

Mike grabbed the radio. "We're on our way."

"What the hell? The library?" asked Janine.

"I don't know," said Mike, and Janine sped away, making a left, back toward the center of town. Laurel City's library was big enough, made of four or five sizable rooms. Mike hadn't poked his head in yet, but now he had no choice.

They were there in a few minutes, and the street outside was quiet. It was still early on a Saturday, with only a few cars in the parking lot. They left the lights on as Janine parked at the curb. They hustled inside. The building appeared nondescript, maybe built in the mid-70's.

They found the library empty inside, the front desk unmanned. The inside of the building looked exactly as Mike expected. Cheap brown carpet and old with sturdy looking shelves, rising above his head.

"What's that smell?" asked Janine.

"Rotten eggs," said Mike. But that didn't make sense in a library.

"It's awful," said Janine.

Mike thumbed the catch on his holster and drew his pistol. Janine looked at him.

"Do you know something I don't?" she asked.

"I know that something is wrong," he said. "I'll take point."

"Where do we start?" asked Janine.

"The smell," he said. "It's strongest this way." He nodded toward the reference room, down a cramped hallway. They moved, his gun up, ready. They crept down the corridor, and the stink got sharper, stronger. It was more than sulfur. It smelled like gunpowder.

No, not gunpowder.

Brimstone.

The scent burnt his nostrils, and his eyes watered. He could hear Janine struggle to breathe behind him. He reached the end of the hallway and saw into the reference room. A row of computers lined one wall, tall shelves filled with thick books dominating the middle of the area. Alongside the bitter smells, there was a new one, intermingled. The smell of blood.

Mike started to move forward, to see the source of it all, but the sound stopped him again. The sound of the phone ringing.

Briiiiiiiiiiiiiiing. Briiiiiiiiiiiiiiing.

No, please no—

Briiiiiiiiiiiiiiing. Briiiiiiiiiiiiiiing.

Mike stood in the kitchen of their house in Plinkett.

—I can't do this, I can't do this again—

Mike stood in the kitchen of their house in Plinkett. He had the early shift that day, so he was making dinner. Marion played upstairs in her room. *He'd have to tell her, he'd have to march upstairs and tell his daughter her mother was dead.*

"Of course the phone rings right when I have chicken hands," he said aloud to no one. The chicken thighs lay half chopped in front of him.

Briiiiiiiiiiiiiing. Briiiiiiiiiiiiiing.

He sighed, putting the knife down and washing his hands, soaping them up under the hot water. Hands cleaned and then dried, he walked over to the stand. Mike grabbed the phone off the receiver.

"Hello," answered Mike.

"Hey, Mike, it's Jerry." Jerry worked with him on the force. They had never been partners, but they got along well. Jerry had a little boy named Billy that had play dates with Marion.

"Hey, Jer, what's up?" asked Mike.

"It's bad news," said Jerry. "You should sit down."

"What do you mean?" asked Mike, still standing, his hand braced against the table the phone sat on. A small burst of pain ignited in his chest, and then his stomach. It was nothing compared to what would come.

"It's Molly," said Jerry. "She was in an accident, on the highway. She's gone."

Mike's legs gave up on him then, and he fell to the floor, the plain linoleum hard enough to bruise his ribs and shoulder. He held onto the phone, but he couldn't form words. Tears formed in the corner of his eyes and rolled down his cheeks. He couldn't stop them, no matter how many times he blinked.

"Mike?" asked the voice.

"Where's Daniel?" asked Mike, forcing the sounds out in a croak.

"He's here, at the hospital. He's a little banged up, but he's okay," said Jerry.

Mike swallowed all his sadness and despair. He took every ounce of willpower he had, everything he had ever mustered up, and he pushed his own feelings aside. He stuffed them down and away, to burn away at his guts over the following years, until he finally pulled them out and used them again, long afterward. Here is where it started, and he could do nothing about it.

"Does he know?" asked Mike, as calmly as he could.

"Yeah, he knows," said Jerry.

"I'll be there soon," said Mike, and hung up. If he kept talking to Jerry, no matter how strong Mike was, it wouldn't matter, those feelings would push out of him and he wouldn't be able to stop them, and then he'd be useless, and his kids needed a dad right now, because their mom was never coming back.

He took a deep breath and pushed himself to his feet. He returned the phone to its cradle. He stopped, feeling the churning in his guts. He rushed to the sink and threw up, mostly water and bile. He washed his mouth out and turned off the faucet. He could hear Marion's voice carry down the stairs to him. She was playing with her toys.

He faced the stairs and climbed. It was the hardest thing he ever did, but he did it. But the pain wasn't in the act. The pain was in the climb, in the expectation of delivering the worst injury he ever could to his own daughter, and the sound in the library kept him there, in that moment, until Janine grabbed his shoulder and shook him.

"Mike!" she said in a loud whisper.

"Christ," he said, catching his breath.

"Where were you?" she asked.

"I had to tell my little girl her mom had died," said Mike, without thinking.

"It's impossible," she said. "I couldn't—"

She trailed off, and the look in her eyes told Mike not to follow her statement further in.

"It happened before," he said. "Near Norman's body."

They still stood in the library, and Mike heard the noise of the telephone ringing, ringing, over and over, but he didn't let it in. He erected some kind of defense, a rickety one, but something.

"Whatever it is, it's causing it," he said. Mike said nothing else, but Janine nodded, and she followed as he crept forward, toward the smell of sulfur, of brimstone, of blood.

He looked down each row of shelves as they moved through the room.

The first, empty.

Briiiiiiiiiiiiiiing. Briiiiiiiiiiiiiiing.

The second, empty.

Briiiiiiiiiiiiiiing. Briiiiiiiiiiiiiiing.

The third was a slaughterhouse.

"Oh God," muttered Mike. He couldn't stop himself. He had never seen or smelled anything like it. The stacks of thick books had contained the gore to this row, and this row alone, but Mike had never witnessed violence like this. He was sure that this poor soul was the librarian, had to have been, but he didn't know how they would identify her. He wasn't sure he could even call the pile of guts recognizably human anymore. It challenged his thoughts, and then something moved, and what he thought was a shadow against the shelves was a living thing, and it stared at him, a face that was black and formless, on top of a mass of sharp angles and disjointed limbs.

Briiiiiiiiiiiiiiing. Briiiiiiiiiiiiiiing.

Mike didn't think. He pulled his gun up and advanced,

shooting round after round into what he guessed was its face, the gunfire leaving his ears ringing. But still, he fired into the thing until he was out of rounds.

It absorbed the shots, the bullets popping through its grey-black skin, mottled and pitted. The thing bounced as the rounds hit it. It was not immune to the physics of violence.

Mike stopped when his gun was empty, his feet just shy of the farthest splashes of gore. The sound of ringing ceased, and then the thing collapsed.

"What the hell is that?" asked Janine.

"I don't—" started Mike, and then the thing fell inward. Its shriveled, broken limbs piled in on its dark face. It became smaller and smaller, until it was nothing but a hole of darkness on the floor, nestled between body parts and library books.

They watched it as the hole disappeared, leaving only the corpse of the librarian.

They stared, and they called in the cavalry. It took them hours to collect the body. It had been Mrs. Durbin, a middle-aged woman on duty. She had phoned 911 and then gone to investigate.

Neither Janine nor Mike told anybody what they saw. There was no evidence of it. Mike had picked up his shell casings before anyone else showed up.

They sat in their squad car later. The Chief had given them both the option to go home. Neither had accepted.

"What do we do?" asked Janine.

"I don't know," said Mike. "That thing wasn't from Earth. It smelled like brimstone."

"Are you saying that was a fucking demon?" asked Janine.

"I don't know," said Mike. "But I can't explain it."

Janine was quiet for a while. Mike didn't know what else to say, and he didn't want to tell her to get back on the road.

"My little brother drowned when I was nine," she said, finally. "We were at the beach, down in Florida. Terrible riptide there. We were far out. I think our parents had fallen asleep. I don't blame them. It kept pulling us out, and pulling us out, and pulling us out. And we tried to yell, but no one could hear us. The water was over our heads before long. And I couldn't—" She took a deep, halting breath. "And I couldn't save him."

"I'm sorry," said Mike.

"That's what I heard in there, Mike," said Janine. "I heard the sound of my little brother screaming for me to save him. And I couldn't."

31

Reverend Laurel stood at the pulpit. Halloween was days away, and the Reverend was in rare form, stomping and pounding, speaking with fury and conviction about the evils of Halloween, and the degradation of the town.

Daniel sat in the audience, next to Isaac and Abraham, but he heard none of it. He only thought of the thing born from his blood, and the noise it made of his mother's death.

He had been under a spell after he touched that Book. Everything felt good, felt natural. All the thoughts about Dad rejecting him, ignoring and neglecting him. They all rose to the surface, loud and ponderous and right on top. And the Reverend handed him that dagger, short and sharp. It seemed right, holding it in his hand, an extension of him and his mission.

Because he had a mission now, holding that dagger, and it was to bring the will of God to life, and the Laurels told him to run it across his hand, and he did it. The blood flowed out of him in a torrent, pouring onto that dirty, awful floor. As soon as the blade cut into him he woke up, and the wrongness of it all seized him.

Isaac pulled him back, back away from his own blood, pooled on the boards. But it did not stay blood, as Reverend Laurel read from the Book, uttered words in a language that Daniel had never heard, a language not created for human tongues, but the Reverend made do, the whips and snarls from his throat birthing something from that blood.

The wrongness hit Daniel in the stomach, and the guilt that had piled up inside of him grew and inflated until he thought he would explode. He had fucked up, and there was no forgiveness for this. Marion, his father, they would forgive him. They would let him back into their life and family, because he knew they loved him, that safety net was there, if he got desperate, but there was no forgiveness for this, no return. He knew it, knew it like he knew the color of the sky, except this thing questioned everything else. Its existence alone made Daniel think all and nothing was true.

"I warned them," said Reverend Laurel, in the Holy Church, looking out at his congregation, his eyes passing over Daniel. "I warned them that Evil would be spawned, that Sin would pass over into our world and attack our town, and they thought it was a joke. But it was no joke. And now we see the damage done!"

The crowd shouted back in response. The Reverend had fired up his base, even as Daniel could see more and more empty spots in the pews. It wasn't many, but it was noticeable. It didn't stop the Reverend or change his sermon.

It washed over Daniel. The creature, it had been born from his blood.

No, not a creature. A demon.

There was no other name for what it was. It was a dark thing, spawned from his blood, and the small circle of red on the dark dirty floor turned into a circle of black, and then the thing rose from it, and its face had nothing on it but darkness, and Daniel knew he shouldn't have looked, he should have closed his eyes, but he did nothing of the kind, he looked right into the formless void and then it made the noise, and he suffered, suffered it all over again.

The noise was the sound of his mother choking on her own blood.

He was at football practice, he was twelve, his parents let him play, even though Mom was nervous every time he played. She hated to watch him get hit, even if he already towered over all the other boys. He was the one who mostly did the hitting. But his mom picked him up from practice. It was usually her, she got off work in time, and Dad never could predict his schedule. He still didn't have enough power to choose when he worked. But Daniel didn't know any of that. He knew his mom picked him up from football practice.

She always picked him up from practice, and today was the last time she ever would. She drove a small car, a hatchback, and he sat in the passenger seat. He stared at his phone, playing some game. The game didn't matter, because suddenly there was the sound of honks, squealing breaks, and then the world exploded around him.

He'd had his brain rattled a couple times playing football.

It was a part of the game, but it paled compared to this. He stayed conscious for the entire time, as the world exploded around him, and the multiple airbags popped, his head and body bouncing off the bags, and then trapped between them all, especially with his size.

He had closed his eyes when it happened, and then everything stopped. Looking back, he knew there were other sounds filtering in from outside what remained of their car. Cars, people coming up, trying to make sense of the accident, calling the police. He was sure they were there. Eventually, they would talk to him, even though he was trapped in the wreckage, and it would take them hours to get him out. They would cut the car open to remove him and what used to be his mom out of the wreck.

But then, at that moment, there was nothing else but the inside of the car. He opened his eyes, and he saw the white of the airbag in front of him. He didn't understand it at first, but the sound is what he first recognized. The sound of something wrong, something terribly wrong.

The sound of choking.

It's a primal sound, one that everyone knows, of forced breath, of halting and horrible struggle. And Daniel looked to it, and it was his mother, and the looking made it worse. At that point, he still didn't know what had hit them. He would learn later it was a semi, loaded up with t-shirts. Soft cotton shirts. But the driver hadn't slept and he was late on his delivery and he kept going through a red light and their car and his mom were the first thing the colossal piece of metal struck, and the driver-side airbags didn't have a chance, because the mass of the truck obliterated everything in front of it. The frame bent inward, and the airbags couldn't fire and the metal scraped and splintered along itself and his mother was pinned to her seat, a jagged piece of splintered steel cutting through her cheek, down into her throat, right into the upholstery of the chair. She struggled to move, but her flesh was much weaker than the metal, and she gave up, the blood from her wounded mouth and throat pouring down into her lungs as she struggled to breathe.

Daniel tried to force himself out of the seat, but he couldn't move, the airbags inflated and immobile, the seatbelt tight against his chest. The metal of the car had caved inward around him, a small cage he couldn't escape or bend or move.

His mother tried to inhale, and all she breathed was blood. But she could move her arm, her right arm closest to him, the left smashed and destroyed, hanging useless next to her. Her legs were crushed, but her arm moved, and she slid it over to Daniel, and caressed his cheek, wiping away the tears that were pouring down his face, even as she choked.

She pointed at his eyes and then pointed at her own. She couldn't speak, not through all that blood, but she could tell him to look her in the eyes, and he did, he tried to look her in the eyes, and he could see the love in them. He looked into her eyes, and she put all the love she could in them, and then the choking became too much, the sound filled the car, and she died.

And that's when Daniel screamed.

Reverend Laurel pounded the pulpit again, and Daniel came back to the surface, out of his own mind, the sour burning in his guts, the guilt, still there.

"You all see it," he said. "I know you do. And we can't be foolish. The connection is right there. Halloween has come to Laurel City, and with it, Evil has tagged along. And now we lost poor Mrs. Durbin. It is no longer confined to pets, or to the homeless, but to our citizens. Mrs. Durbin was a long-time member of the congregation, and we have lost her. Lost her in an awful, miserable death, filled with pain."

Daniel could hear the crowd yell behind him now, and that's what they were, standing from their seats, even walking into the aisles, gesturing at the heavens. He was riling them up. They weren't a congregation anymore. They were a rabble, waiting for orders.

"And we will not stand it. I have preached love and understanding, and trying to reach out to your fellow man for weeks now, but it hasn't worked. It has led to more death, and it is clear to me that God wants more from us. God is pushing us for direct action."

The crowd yelled more, cheering. Daniel even heard one voice behind scream to the ceiling, praising God.

Reverend Laurel looked out over his flock, his face red, sweat beading on his forehead. "Fall Festival is canceled. We will march instead, all of us, God's children, and we will protest the Evil that has infiltrated our town. We will stand outside their party, and demonstrate our faith, even in the face of sin."

The congregation screamed all at once, filling the church. Daniel winced, unable to stop himself. The guilt filled him from the inside, and he forced himself to not throw up, swallowing the rising bile back down.

The Reverend took a beat, taking a deep breath himself, and then looked out over the crowd, his voice calm and reserved again. "But now we must prepare. We must muster our strength. Tell your neighbors, and your friends of our plans. We will demonstrate God's power, and our faith in Him. Let us pray."

"Dear Lord, let our faith be true. Let Your Power demonstrate itself on Halloween night. Let Your Light spread throughout this town and push out all the sinners. Amen."

"Amen," the crowd echoed. Daniel said it himself, quietly, but it burned. He should have run, fled from the church, and run back to his dad. His legs ached, trying to pull him up. But he couldn't. He couldn't leave now. He had gone too far to leave. He would see this to the end.

*

The boys of LYE sat around Abraham. Their normal meeting felt like anything but. It didn't feel like a church group. It felt like they planned for a war.

Daniel sat next to Isaac, the other guys slightly behind. They had been pushed into the spotlight, because Abraham needed them there. He wanted them as leaders in what was next.

"All of you listened to Reverend Laurel," said Abraham, his voice quiet as always. "You heard about his plans for Halloween night."

"Where do you need us?" asked Jason. "We want to help. We can lead the march, or the protest. We should be there, at the front."

"No," said Abraham, shaking his head. "We already have volunteers for that. We have more important duties for you boys."

"What could be more important than the protest?" asked Matthew.

"The Reverend and I have other plans, ones we haven't revealed. But we need you all here on Halloween."

"Are you sure?" asked Isaac. "We could take direct action against the party. We could picket line it, surround the community center. They couldn't even go in."

"No," said Abraham. "Come back here on Halloween night. Be here at 7. We will use God."

32

Marion woke up next to Cara. The day felt different.

It was Halloween.

"Cara," said Marion, quietly. Cara slept next to her, her mouth open. She snored.

Marion rolled her eyes and nudged her again. "Cara," she said, a little louder.

"Wha—what?" asked Cara, her eyes slightly open. "Sle-sleep. Let me sleep."

"Cara. It's Halloween. There's no time to sleep," said Marion. Cara opened her eyes suddenly. Furriosa woke too, jumping up and down on them.

"Oh crap, you're right," said Cara, rubbing her eyes, wiping the sleep away from them. "Where's your dad?"

"He's already gone," said Marion, sitting up. "He was at

the community center at daylight, to get things ready."

"Well, what are we waiting for?" asked Cara.

They hadn't redecorated after the Church had destroyed their decorations. Dad had wanted to, but she had talked him out of it. They had focused all of their energy on the community center. That would matter more. A few less tombstones in their front yard wouldn't change anything. A bigger, more successful party would.

Marion made them a quick breakfast, and then they loaded Cara's car with everything Dad had left behind. It was mostly bins of random paper decorations, and smaller stuff that hadn't fit in the SUV. They had been moving material over there for a week, but there was still more. But they made it fit in one trip, loading up Cara's car to the brim.

The community center was only a few minutes away, but halfway there a policeman stopped them, holding up a hand, standing in the middle of Main Street.

"What's going on?" asked Marion.

"A parade?" asked Cara.

"That doesn't make sense," said Marion.

And then they saw the crowd of people, all holding signs. Even the kids, marching in front, held their own.

HALLOWEEN IS EVIL
BAN HALLOWEEN
HALLOWON'T!

They marched down the road perpendicular to them.

"The Church organized a march?" asked Cara.

"They're protesting," said Marion. "They're marching through town, and then they'll protest the community center."

"Jesus," said Cara. "They can't leave well enough alone, can they?"

The marching protesters passed quickly, and then the cop waved them through. They got to the community center a few minutes later. It already swarmed with people.

"Oh my God," said Cara. "And you worried no one would help."

Tomas and Bjorn both worked on the front lawn, erecting some gigantic metal construction. Marion knew it was the frame for a massive draped spectre.

"Hello, Marion, Cara," said Bjorn, waving, wiping sweat off with a brush of his shoulder.

"Do you know where my dad is?" asked Marion. Cara unloaded the car, parking on the curb in front of the center.

"He is inside, herding cats, as they say," said Tomas.

"Thanks," she said. "Just a warning, it looks like the Church is planning to protest us."

"It does not surprise me," said Bjorn. "We will keep our heads down, unless they wish to start something. Then we may draw steel."

Marion stared for a second. "You didn't bring your swords, did you?"

Tomas stared at her, his face stone serious, and then he broke, smiling and laughing. "No, we did not bring our swords." She started inside. "That, of course, is for later."

She walked into the community center, and more people swarmed. She recognized many of them, but some were strangers. Dad stood at the center of it, organizing and conducting traffic.

"Eddie, no, no, the extra blood goes into the second scare

room, we'll need more before the end of the night. Hey, hey! That's the right arm of the clown, that stays here, we'll assemble it as soon as Marion gets here—"

"Dad," she said.

"Oh, thank God you're here," he said. "I think I'm losing my mind."

"Look how many people are here," she said, quietly, between them.

"I know," he said, smiling.

"You'll never guess what Cara and I ran into on the way here," said Marion.

"What? The ghost of Halloween present?"

"No," she said. "A protest march from our friends at Laurel City Holy Church. They were walking through downtown. I'd bet they'll end up here before the day is through. They're going to stand outside and shout at everyone that comes in."

He rolled his eyes. "I was expecting it, but hoped it wouldn't come to that. But I should stop being surprised by the Laurels. He mentioned Mrs. Durbin in his sermon last Sunday."

"How do you know that?" asked Marion. Her dad leaned in close to her, in a false sense of secrecy.

"I have my sources," he said, and winked.

"Dad."

"Can't your old dad have some fun?" he asked.

"I guess," she said. "We have the rest of the stuff from the garage. Odds and ends."

"Great!" he said. "Put it in storage for now. Try and keep it organized. I know it's already a mess back there. We'll probably need some of that stuff before we finish decorating, but it's hard to say what until we actually do it."

"I'll do that and then I'll work on the clown," she said.

"Perfect," he said. "I'm excited to see it built. It will look amazing."

"We'll see," she said. "I still don't know if I can make it come together."

"Are you kidding me? You're the best. It's going to shock everyone. It'll be *the* thing everyone talks about."

"You have to say stuff like that, you're my dad," said Marion.

"Hey, do you know a bigger Halloween a-fic-i-onado than myself?" he asked.

Marion sighed. "No," she said.

"Alright then," he said. "Let me know if you need anything. I can get people to help."

Marion went to help Cara with the boxes, when her dad's voice stopped her. "Marion—"

She turned.

"Did you—did you see Daniel? In the crowd?" he asked, looking up, catching her eyes with his.

"No," she said. He nodded, and looked back down, sorting through the stuff in the open box at his feet.

Marion helped Cara lug the bins and boxes back into the storage area, which, as Dad had said, was already a total mess. Cara sorted it out. Marion returned to the center of the room, where her clown masterpiece would be assembled.

The room continued to move around her, as people set up tables and chairs, and hung lights and paper decorations. Her dad's distant voice echoed around her, but for her, there was only the work. Almost all of her time had been dedicated to the clown, and it had been her most audacious creation yet. She pulled out the pieces and structure of the creature. She called for a ladder, and suddenly one was brought to her. The monster would be ten feet tall, its head brushing up against the ceiling tiles.

She built it, first assembling the skeleton of the thing, made from wood and metal, joints and bolts keeping it standing up. Then she dressed it. The costume was hand-made, because they didn't sell clown costumes for giants in any Halloween store, even the one two towns over. She struggled with a sleeve, continually trying to get the long, extended arm through it, and then Cara was there, pushing the arm through the fabric for her.

Cara smiled up at her, and hugged her leg on the ladder, before continuing on to more work. Every time Marion glanced up, there seemed to be more people helping.

The frame of the clown was done, but that was only the beginning. The true work began by applying the prosthetics. She had made most of them ahead of time, but the assembly would be the hardest part. Blending them all onto the head and torso and making them all stick.

She laid out everything on a small table next to the ladder, but a sound from outside intruded.

She looked to see her father looking toward the door. The sound was cacophonous, hard to identify any one part of it, but then she heard the shouts distinguish from each other, and she realized what it was. The Holy Church mob had arrived. She climbed down and marched outside to see them.

"Marion," said her dad, from behind her, rushing up to her. "You shouldn't go out there."

"Why?" she asked.

"I don't know how far they'll go," he said.

"I'm not afraid of them," she said, and she kept walking. Dad was soon beside her, and they pushed out into the afternoon sunlight. The chill had already set in, and they could see their breath as they stepped outside. The words of the protesters hit them as soon as they opened the door.

"Halloween is murder!" shouted someone.

"Sinners! Sinners!" shouted another.

But mostly, the crowd chanted "EVIL" over and over again.

They got louder as the pair walked outside. The crowd stood in a cancerous mass across the street, lined on the thick sidewalk, bunched up against the community college annex across the way. College kids awkwardly pushed through, trying to get to class, but the protesters refused to move, forcing some students out onto the asphalt.

"E-VIL E-VIL E-VIL," chanted the crowd, the signs among them pumping up and down into the air.

They stared at the crowd. Marion didn't recognize anyone amidst the great mass of people. She looked for Daniel's large frame, but found nothing.

"I thought there'd be more," he said.

"Yeah, it's not actually that many," said Marion. "Hell, we've got more people working."

The protesters continued to chant, but they didn't move, only standing awkwardly in their little space. A police officer stood to the side, next to a flashing patrol car, watching the proceedings. Her dad waved to him, and the officer waved back. He walked over and chatted with him briefly, before returning to Marion.

"Friend of yours?" asked Marion.

"Yeah, that's Bob. Good guy," said her dad. "The Chief sent him over to monitor us, in case anybody lost control."

"I was worried about it," said Marion. "But they just look kind of pathetic."

"Yeah," he said. "But I wouldn't let down your guard. I don't see any of the Laurels. Knowing them, they have something planned for the party itself. We can cross that bridge when we come to it."

"I've got a clown to build," she said, and returned inside.

Marion went to work, the sound of the chanting being covered up by music playing over the PA system. Dad had started the Halloween playlist, and the Misfits and Oingo Boingo were too loud for any of the chants of E-VIL to come through. Everyone moved around her, and Marion built her evil clown.

She flowed as she laid down scars and smiles and hanging intestines. Piece by piece, the beast became more and more complete. She finished all the prosthetics. Satisfied with them, Marion started painting, putting on the finishing touches. She added goop and grease and blood and soon the clown was not a massive statue, but a living thing, looming over all of them, its reaching hands asking for a hug, its giant smile hiding something horrible behind it.

She stepped back and admired it.

"I told you," said her dad, walking up to her. "It looks amazing. Done?"

"Hmm," she said. "Nope, needs one more thing." Marion reached into a bin at her feet, and found a comically oversized flower, a dandelion with a smiley face drawn onto it. She had picked it up on a whim at a craft store, and now she was glad to have it. She grabbed her red pen and added flourishes to the flower's face, transforming its cheesy grin into something terrifying. She stepped up on the ladder and slid it into the clown's small chest pocket. She climbed back down.

"Now it's done," she said.

"Perfect," said her father.

Marion looked around, and was amazed at how they transformed the community center, just within the day. When she had arrived that morning, it was plain and bare, with boring walls. Now the place was bathed in red, black, and orange decorations. They had arranged the tables on one side, with a dance floor on the other. The tables had orange tablecloths, with centerpieces, and party favors at every setting. A buffet of snacks, candy, and drinks were arrayed on a few long tables, and a DJ station stood near the dance floor.

She walked to look at the two scare rooms. They set up one with a scarecrow, looming over a fake cornfield. One or two at a time, someone could wander back into the corn-rows, and would disappear from the rest of the room. It was a great illusion, impressive to make it work in a space that size.

She checked out the other room, the adult's only room. It was an abattoir, with a giant looming butcher standing in one corner, a butcher's knife held upright, about to chop a screaming mannequin in half. Marion had done a few small bits for that, but her dad had handled most of it. The room had body bags, and cutting boards filled with fake meat, and splashes of blood everywhere. Black garbage bags were their friend. It looked impressive.

"I'd say we did good," said her father.

"I'd say that we're ready," said Marion.

"I'd say that we're ready to party," he added.

33

Daniel wanted to ask Reverend Laurel about what he had planned for Halloween night. But he didn't. He was afraid that the Reverend would tell him the truth, and then Daniel would have no excuse for not trying to stop it.

The Reverend drove by the community center on the way there. The protest crowd had thinned, less than half of the original number still standing watch across the street. With the window rolled down, they could hear the music thudding from inside. Multiple people in costumes loitered outside, and every time the door opened, an enormous blast of noise and chatter reached them. A massive hanging specter stood on the front lawn of the center, staring down at them. The Reverend grimaced, but said nothing to Daniel as they sped away.

They were at the church a few minutes early, but all the boys were already there. They all waited inside, spread out among the pews, in pairs and trios. None of them talked. Isaac and Abraham sat next to each other in their normal spot, as if this was an ordinary Sunday sermon. But the gnawing terror in Daniel's gut told him otherwise. Something bad would happen, and he would help.

The Reverend stood in front of the guys, while Daniel took a seat next to Isaac.

"Men," he said. "You're here because you are the backbone of this church. You are the future of it. You are our strong male leaders of the future. All of you. Abraham has taught you well over the past few years, and I believe you are ready to truly join the Church. To commit to God's Will and help us reclaim our city."

Reverend Laurel preached to them, as surely as if it was a full church. His voice was quiet now, but it had the same conviction and hidden fire that he always had when he channeled God's purpose.

There is no part of him invested in God, Daniel. You know it you know it—

Daniel closed his eyes, squeezed his nose. The burning guilt had spread through his body, and now his vision blurred as the soft headache formed inside of him, blasting him with pain.

The Reverend continued. "Are you ready to take that final step? Are you ready for sacrifice?"

Daniel's heart thudded harder and harder in his chest, and he stiffened at the Reverend's last word. He suspected all along, but now he knew. They'd be going back down into that room. With that Book, that was from anything but God.

He could hear the boys around him agree, with scattered yes's. Isaac said nothing, only stared down at his hands. Daniel looked down at his. His hand was unmarked. It should be, by all rights. The dagger had cut deep. The Book had made him cut deep, near down to the bone, but there was no scar. The wound had healed quickly, and it left him with no pain. The absence of hurt scared him more than anything. He should have felt something, some remnant, but there was nothing. There was no scar. At least not on the surface.

"Good," he said, nodding at every boy. "Follow me."

He turned and walked a path that Daniel now knew, all the boys getting up from their pews and stepping into line behind him. Daniel, Issac, and Abraham went last. Daniel felt like a rear guard, but they guarded against nothing. Perhaps only to keep the guys in place, so they wouldn't bolt. To close the heavy metal door firmly behind them once they went into the brick room with the dirty wooden floor.

And that's where they entered. The Reverend opened one door, and then the other, undoing the massive padlock that secured it, walking down into the brick room without looking back. The boys followed, without noise, complaint, or question. Isaac, Daniel, and Abraham went into the room last, and Daniel winced at the sound of the heavy door thudding shut behind them. His headache roared now, and he had to force himself down those steps. His body rejected every movement he made. He felt like he was falling apart. Was it the Book? The room? He didn't know, but he was sure he was dying. He deserved to die, for what he'd done. He had summoned that thing with his blood, and it had killed that poor woman.

Reverend Laurel stood behind the small table, the thick Book laid closed on it. The boys filed into the center of the room, waiting for their orders. The candles were lit, still illuminating the room, giving it more light than it should. Had they stayed lit the entire time? Did they ever burn down at all?

"Men," said the Reverend. "Stand in a circle, around the outside of the room." They formed a circle. "The people of Laurel City have been tricked. They have abandoned God. We have to go further if we will excise their sin."

Abraham stood behind the Reverend, and his face showed confusion at those words. He walked up to his father, close. Daniel could hear him.

"What do you mean? I thought we had agreed—"

"We cannot stand by while they corrupt our city!" said the Reverend, his fury coming to the surface.

"I can't—I can't do that, you know that, it's too great a cost—"

"Are you questioning God's will? Are you questioning *my* will?" asked the Reverend, now staring directly at Abraham.

"No," said Abraham, finally breaking eye contact. "Of course not."

"Good. Then you know what we must do. You must read," said the Reverend. He stood aside, and Abraham took his place, opening the Book, slowly thumbing to it until he got to the right page. The page they needed for this night.

Abraham reached the page and stared at it, the room utterly silent, smoke wicking into the air. The smoke never gathered here.

"Abraham," said the Reverend.

Abraham looked up and broke his silence. "Isaac, enter

the circle."

Isaac stared at his father with a similar look of confusion.

"What?" asked Isaac.

"Enter the circle," said Abraham. "You said you were prepared for sacrifice, did you not?"

"Yes, father," said Isaac.

"Then enter the circle."

Isaac did, stepping into the middle, all of them standing on the dirty floor.

"Now men, hold hands," said Abraham. The boys looked amongst each other and then grabbed each other's hands. Daniel held the two boys' hands next to him, Matthew and Tyler.

"What do I do, Father?" asked Isaac, staring at him. Daniel had never seen the look on Isaac's face before. It was sheer terror.

"Think of God," said Abraham, finally, before looking back down into the Book. Words tumbled out of him, the same dead dialect that Reverend Laurel had spoken before, whips and snarls, gnashing teeth and creaks, noises unnatural to the human tongue. But it didn't sound like Abraham struggled. He had practiced, and he knew the language.

The feeling of inevitable horror filled the room, dread that permeated all skin and surface. Daniel's skin itched, but he didn't dare scratch. If he broke contact with the other boys, God knows what the Reverend would do to him. What the Book would do to him.

As Abraham read, all of them watched Isaac, Daniel included. He looked fine at first, his head down, his eyes shut. But as the words spilled from Abraham, something changed. He didn't move, or fall, or even show any sign of pain, but Isaac wilted as the ritual continued. All color drained from him.

At first, it was his skin. The natural brightness and life of it dimmed, becoming sallow, losing health and life. It wasn't just becoming paler. It was losing all color entirely. He was turning grayscale.

He finally opened his eyes now, realizing that something was happening to him. He moved slowly, in halting motions, struggling against something unseen.

"Father," said Isaac.

"Quiet," said the Reverend, from behind Abraham. "God commands you to be quiet."

"I'm—" started Isaac, but he lost his voice then, the strong tone fading, as if blown away in the wind, even as he tried to put his strength into it. Isaac's eyes went to Daniel, desperate and hopeless. They begged him to help.

They are killing him, Daniel. Do something. You can do something.

The poison burning inside him boiled his guts, and his head screamed with pain. It's too late, I'm already a part of this, there is no way out, everyone will hate me, everyone will blame me for everything—

Daniel. Daniel, look at me.

Daniel looked up. He sat in a small examination room in the ER of the hospital. He was twelve years old. He had bandages on his face and arms, from the minor wounds created by flying glass and crunching metal. He had no broken bones. Not even a concussion.

He had waited there for over an hour, after the doctor and nurse had left him. They said his father would come for him. To not move. To stay there. They had given him a stuffed bear. He held it with one hand, not thinking about it. The only thing he thought of was his mother's eyes, staring at him as she choked to death in front of him.

He had cried and screamed at first, but now he only felt numb. A deep moaning void opened up inside him, so wide he couldn't find the edges. It would close, eventually, but he didn't know it. It would be there forever. A great chasm that had once been his mother.

It was your fault your fault your fault—she went to pick you up you up you up—she's dead because of you because of you because of you—

"Daniel," said a voice, and he looked up to see his dad. Dad rushed to him, falling to his knees in front of him, hugging him as hard as he could. Daniel meekly hugged him back, but he felt a pressure inside that no hug could relieve. His father only held him.

Daniel spoke, because he had to. "We were driving—driving home from practice, and a truck—" He started, but couldn't finish, and he sobbed. Dad squeezed him harder, pushing Daniel's face into his shoulder.

"I know, son," he said. "It's okay, it's okay."

Daniel struggled, but the words finally came from him. "It's my fault. She had to pick me up."

Dad squeezed him, and then let him go, holding him at arm's distance, his hands wrapped around Daniel's upper arms. He saw tears in his father's eyes, something he rarely saw. He looked down, unable to maintain the eye contact. He couldn't take it.

"Daniel. Daniel, look at me," said his dad, and Daniel glanced up again, and stared into his dad's eyes.

"You're sad right now. So am I. And we will be, for a long

time. But above everything else, you know this. This *was not* your fault. Okay?"

Daniel nodded.

"Say it for me," he said. "Say it wasn't my fault."

Daniel swallowed, struggling. "It wasn't my fault."

"It wasn't your fault. You loved your mother, and that will never change. It wasn't your fault. Okay?"

"Okay," said Daniel, and his dad held him. Marion, watching from the doorway, joined them, and hugged them both.

It's not my fault.

Daniel looked at Isaac, and saw him wilt, and knew what to do. He would have to act fast. He let go of the boys' hands, and instantly Isaac changed. But Daniel would have to do more than that. He turned and grabbed the table the great Book sat upon, and upturned it, throwing it into Abraham's focused face. He tumbled backwards, bewildered, the table and Book on top of him. He fell silent, and the dread suddenly left the room.

But Daniel wasn't done. He had one more target before he would return to Isaac.

Reverend Laurel stood stunned, staring at Daniel, face to face, the one person he didn't loom over. Daniel could have hit him, but he'd never been in a fight, and never thrown a punch. Instead, he charged the Reverend, picking him up into the air and driving him into that dirty floor, hitting him with every ounce of force Daniel had. The Reverend grunted and then struggled to breathe, Daniel knocking all the wind out of him.

The rest of the guys only stared. Isaac had fallen to his knees in the meantime, whatever spell being cast on him finally letting go of him. The Reverend moved, and Daniel gave him a hard kick in the ribs, pushing him back down.

He pushed past everyone, grabbed Isaac with all his strength, and threw him up on his shoulder. His chest heaved. None of the boys tried to stop him.

They escaped.

34

The Halloween playlist blasted over the PA system, and the community center buzzed. The place was packed with people. The party was a success.

"Honey, you maybe should relax a little," said Jenny. She slowly squeezed his shoulders, trying to rub some tension out of them. Mike was dressed as Rick Moranis from Ghostbusters, with disheveled clothes and a colander on his head, with weird wires poking in and out of it. Jenny was Sigourney Weaver, in a red silky costume, glittering under the lights.

"I am relaxed," said Mike, staring across the room at the community center, his eyes scanning the guests, looking to see if the food was still stocked, if there were any potential problems.

"Sure you are" said Jenny. "That's why your shoulders feel like rock."

"That's just all my muscle," said Mike, smirking.

"Um…" said Jenny. "Right. All that muscle."

"I am made of iron and stone," said Mike. "As big as Tomas and as strong as Bjorn. Where did they go, by the way?"

"To get in costume," said Jenny. "You know them well enough by now. They go all out on this stuff."

They weren't the only ones. Some of the costumes he saw amazed Mike. The party goers had done incredible work. There was an Ash from the Evil Dead with an actual chainsaw, a couple that came as a gender bent Walt and The Dude from The Big Lebowski, and even a woman with a replica Big Bird costume.

"You should maybe spend some time enjoying your own party, instead of worrying about if everything will go okay," said Jenny. "You've done a lot of work, and endured a bunch of stress, but it's here, and it's succeeding. Maybe let off the pedal for a second."

Mike breathed deep. People snacked and chatted at full tables. An eclectic group of folks filled the dance floor, all in costume. Guests cycled in and out of the scare rooms, and kids kept visiting the candy bar, filling up bags to go home with.

"You're right," he said.

"Of course I am," said Jenny. "Let me get you a drink. Red or green?"

"I'll take a cup of the bat's blood, thank you very much," he said.

"So the red, got it," said Jenny.

"Bat's blood," said Mike, after her. "The green is ectoplasm!"

Jenny didn't respond, just kept walking to the refreshment table.

"I like the costume, Mike," said a voice, and a woman in a chicken costume walked up to him. It took him a moment to recognize Janine, her body draped in feathers, a big red beak cap strapped to her head. Her daughter held her hand, wearing orange and white, holding an oar.

"Janine! You came. Thanks," said Mike. "Are you...a chicken?"

"Well yes, yes I am," she said. "How could you tell?"

"My fine investigative eye notices small, subtle details. Like the fact you're covered in feathers."

"You're a good cop," said Janine. "Fiona is Moana, and I am her chicken sidekick. I'm sure it has a name, but I can't remember it at the moment. I've seen that movie a thousand times, and I still can't remember the chicken's name—"

"Heihei," said Fiona, smiling up at her mom.

"You look great, Fiona," said Mike. "Are you planning on entering the costume contest?"

"Yes!" said Fiona.

"I hope you win," said Mike.

"You guys look great!" said Jenny, walking up with two drinks in hand. She passed one off to Mike and then hugged Janine. "Moana and Heihei?"

"More evidence that you're smarter than Mike," said Janine. "Not that we needed any."

"Hey," said Mike. "I've never disputed that Jenny is smarter than me."

"Smarts aren't everything," said Jenny. "You're my trophy boyfriend."

"Thanks," said Mike. "I'll practice holding my drink next to you in photos."

"Where's Marion and Cara?" asked Janine.

"Getting ready," said Mike. "Marion wouldn't tell me what their costumes were, but knowing her, they'll be crazy awesome."

Janine leaned into Mike, the tip of her beak hat poking him in the forehead.

"Sorry," she said, leaning slightly to move it away. "I saw the protesters outside. Any sign of Laurel?"

"Nope, none at all," said Mike. "I don't like it."

"How about—you know—those things?" asked Janine. Her voice dropped lower when she asked it. It felt wrong to talk about it. To even think about it. After the death of Mrs. Durbin, there had been no further hint of the creatures. No attacks or disturbances. And Mike and Janine had told no one else about it. But it stuck with them. Mike had woken up in cold sweats, the sound of the phone ringing still echoing in his ears. He didn't ask Janine, but if she was asking, he doubted it hadn't affected her.

"Nothing," he said. "Everything seems fine. I've been keeping my eyes open, you know."

"I'll do the same," she said. "Fiona, do you want to go to the scary room?"

"Yes, yes!" shouted Fiona, jumping up and down with her tiny oar. They walked off toward the corn room.

"What were you two muttering about?" asked Jenny.

"Cop stuff."

"You mean, more worrying?

"Well, yes."

"Look around," said Jenny. "Look how happy everyone

is. Sometimes things work out."

"I know that," he said. He took a sip of the bat's blood and blinked.

"Is it okay?" asked Jenny.

"How much sugar is in this? This is sweeter than Mr. Rogers in a candy store," said Mike.

Jenny stared. "Wow."

"I'm a catch, what can I say."

"How do we look, Dad?" asked Marion, walking up with Cara. Mike glanced at the two of them and was astounded.

"You look great," he said. Marion was Lydia from Beetlejuice, in her wedding attire, a red dress with lace and frills. She had a massive wig on, her hair reaching a foot above her head, and her makeup was perfect. But Cara really took the cake. She was Beetlejuice, also in wedding garb, and Marion had gone all out on her makeup.

"Cara, you make a great Beetlejuice," said Jenny.

"Thank you?" said Cara. "Marion did all the work."

"You two look amazing. What did I say? I told you it'd be incredible," said Mike.

"Daaaad," said Marion.

"Unfortunately, you are not eligible to win the hundred dollar gift card," said Mike.

"Aww," said Cara.

"I don't make the rules," said Mike.

"I actually think you do," said Jenny. "It's your party."

"We're not entering the contest," said Marion. "The costumes are for fun. We're going to go find our friends." They quickly vanished into the crowd.

"Let's dance," said Jenny.

"I don't know if you know this about me," said Mike.

"But I am not a good dancer. Believe it or not."

"I would have never guessed," said Jenny. "It's okay. We'll make it work." She pulled him to the dance floor, but half-way there, two massive figures interrupted them.

"Mike and Jenny. We have succeeded with the party!" shouted Tomas, in his trademark accent. "It is going well." Tomas was dressed in heavy armor, a huge sword sheathed at his side. Bjorn stood next to him, similarly clad. A sword hung by his side as well, slightly less massive. A make-up prosthetic covered a third of his face. It looked like a burn scar.

"How does it look?" asked Bjorn.

"It looks good, I told you," said Tomas. "Marion does great work."

"It does look good," said Mike. "Are you guys The Mountain and The Hound from Game of Thrones?"

"Ha! Yes! I told you people would get it," said Tomas.

"Aren't they mortal enemies?" asked Jenny.

"Yes," said Bjorn, with a snarl. But he couldn't keep it up and broke into a smile.

"If you'll excuse us, fellas, we have a date with the dance floor," said Jenny.

"We'll see you there in a few minutes," said Tomas, and the two marched off toward the snacks.

"How are they going to dance in that armor?" asked Mike.

"I don't know, but I'm excited to see," said Jenny.

They reached the dance floor, and Mike tried his best as some spooky EDM thudded through the speakers. Jenny danced next to him, and Mike couldn't take his eyes off of her.

"Am I doing okay?" asked Mike.

"You're doing great," she said, with a smile, and she kissed him. They danced through a few songs, and the weight of everything fell off Mike. The war on Halloween, the feud with the Laurels, missing Daniel, the creature attacks. It all disappeared as he flailed slightly off-beat next to Jenny, who grabbed his hands and kissed him and danced with him. It was all gone for a moment. Mike breathed again for the first time in a long time.

A song ended, and his heart pounded against the inside of his chest.

"I'm out of shape," he said.

"Let's sit down for a bit," said Jenny. They found a mostly empty table. Mike took off his colander helmet and set it down on the table, wiping the sweat away from his eyes with his shirt.

"I feel like I'm melting," said Mike. "It's probably because I have the hottest date here."

"Such a charmer," said Jenny. "That was good. You were almost on-beat by the end."

"There's only one way to Carnegie Hall," he said. "And that's trying really hard and get some pity votes."

Jenny grabbed him. "I had fun, and that's all that matters." Mike squeezed her hand, but all the worries began flooding back in as they sat.

"I'll go get us some more drinks," said Jenny. "You cool down a little bit."

Jenny left him, and he took the moment to soak in the party. It was revving up now, a couple hours in, all the late-comers here, before all the parents took their kids home. The place was packed. Halloween was overdue. The town had wanted it. Laurel either didn't realize it, or was trying to stamp it down. All it had done was make the demand higher.

Mike's eyes watched the dance floor, where Marion and Cara danced. They both smiled and laughed as they moved. Joy rose in his chest. She looked so happy. So much like her mother.

"They're cute together," said Jenny, setting the green drink down in front of him.

"I miss Daniel," said Mike. Jenny grabbed his hand again.

"I'm sorry," said Jenny.

"It's not your fault," said Mike. "I wish I knew what he was doing right now. He's a good kid. He's still so young."

"At some point, you'll have to let go of them anyway," said Jenny.

"That's what's scary," he said. "Letting them go. Halloween isn't scary. Letting your kids loose upon the world is scary."

"The ultimate horror story: PARENTHOOD," said Jenny, in a Count Dracula voice.

"You're not wrong," said Mike.

"You have to trust him," said Jenny. "Trust that in the end, he'll make the right choice."

"I wish he was here."

"Maybe he'll show up."

"What's worrying me is that he might," said Mike. "But that he won't be alone. That he'll have the Laurels with him."

"I know it's hard, but you have to focus on the now," said Jenny. "You can't solve all your problems all at once."

The music started crackling on the PA, and the sounds of Thriller suddenly became a mess of crackles and pops.

Mike got up.

"Someone else will fix it," she said.

"I'll be right back, I promise," he said. "It'll make me feel better, okay? We can dance some more when I get back."

"Okaaaay," she said, and winked.

Mike got up and hurried over to the equipment. The DJ was already there, messing with wires. Mike stood behind him, watching him work. After a couple moments of moving wires around, the sound was fixed, the music playing normally.

"Everything good?" asked Mike.

"Yeah, should be," said the DJ, and he returned to his laptop. Mike took one last glance at the audio equipment, when a sudden noise froze him.

He looked back to the speakers, and then to the DJ, but neither betrayed anything wrong.

The sound happened again, and his heart went cold.

No, not tonight. Not here.

The sound ripped through him, and even though he'd been exposed to it, it hurt him. It would always hurt him.

The sound rang through one more time.

Briiiiiiiiiiiiing. Briiiiiiiiiiiiing.

35

The music thumped, and Marion and Cara danced.

"Let's check out the scare rooms after this song," said Cara.

"Okay," said Marion. She grabbed Cara's hands, and they danced to the jangly bass of an 80s pop tune.

The music paused, and they left the dance floor, Cara pulling Marion to the first scare room, with the scarecrow and the rows of corn.

A few other groups were already inside. The room looked great, with the scarecrow figure attached to the wooden frame, looming over the room, and the rows of fake corn, thick enough to obscure anybody walking farther into it.

Cara watched the scarecrow, and then its head turned to the other side suddenly and she jumped.

"You know it moves," said Marion. "You helped build it."

"Yeah, but that doesn't mean it still can't startle me," said Cara. "Not everyone has nerves of steel like you."

"I'm not that tough," said Marion. "It's just this isn't the stuff that scares me."

"What scares you?" asked Cara.

"Losing people close to me," said Marion.

"Oh," said Cara. "I didn't mean—"

"It's okay," said Marion, waving her off. "Let's go see the butcher." They walked into the adjoining room, through a door, marked with warning signs telling all children to turn away now, that no minors should be allowed entrance without the permission of a parent, blah blah blah.

There were fewer people in the butcher shop. It was bathed in red, with pools of blood and garbage bags strewn around. The ominous figure of the butcher stood in the corner, his cleaver raised to chop up some unsuspecting victim, fake pieces of meat stacked everywhere.

"God, no matter how many times I see him, he still creeps me out," said Cara.

"Then I did my job," said Marion.

"He looks like a pig got up on all fours and became a man," said Cara.

"That's what I was going for," said Marion. "Aren't you glad I'm your girlfriend?"

"Yes," said Cara, hugging Marion sincerely.

A weird smell passed through Marion's nose. She breathed in. It didn't make sense.

"Do you smell that?" asked Marion.

"I only smell the weird fake blood scent," said Cara.

"It's not that," said Marion. "It smells like—it smells like a hospital. It smells like—"

Death. It smells like death.

Marion walked down the hospital corridor. Daniel was right behind her. She hated the smell of hospitals. Ever since Mom had died, she had despised them, and hated their smell.

Where is he? Where is he?

"I think we were supposed to make a right at the last hallway," said Daniel. "I think that sign said intensive care."

"Why didn't you say something?" asked Marion.

"Because I thought you knew where you were going," said Daniel. "Sorry."

"It's alright," said Marion. "I'm—"

"Worried, I know," said Daniel. "Let's just ask somebody. I'm sure someone can help us."

Marion disliked asking for directions, but they quickly found a nurse, and she gave them a floor layout, which would guide them to Dad's room.

The smell was everywhere as they walked, and it flooded her nostrils. She detested it. She hated that she was here again, she hated that she had to be here again, where was Dad?

They finally found the ICU, and they checked in with the nurse at the desk who signed them in and directed them toward the right room. The door was shut. Marion opened it quietly, and the smell was still in there. There was only one bed, and Marion saw her dad, laying there, his eyes closed.

Jesus. There are so many tubes.

He laid back, the bed propped up a little. He had an IV line plugged into his arm, and a breathing tube up his nose. More lines led to his chest, where they monitored his heart rate, and even more on his fingertips. She could barely look at him.

Daniel lightly touched her shoulder, and she realized she hadn't stepped into the room. She forced her legs to move, to walk over to her father, kept alive by tubes and machines.

She stood next to him and grabbed his hand. It was warm, the first warm thing she had felt or seen in this cold, dying place.

His eyes fluttered open.

"Hey, you made it," said her dad, a faint smile on his face. "I was worried the bouncer wouldn't let you into the coolest new nightclub in town."

"Really?" asked Marion.

"A couple bullets can't defeat my great wit," he said.

"What happened?" asked Daniel.

"Not really sure about that. Went on a call and got hit from behind," said her dad. "I don't blame them. I told them one of my jokes."

"Will you be okay?" asked Marion.

"I'll be fine," he said. "I wouldn't mind if you eased up on my hand a little."

"Oh, sorry," said Marion. She had been squeezing him as hard as she could without realizing it.

"Are you guys okay?" he asked.

"We're fine. Just scared out of our minds," said Marion.

"Don't be worried," he said. "Your dad will be A-okay. The doctors are looking after me."

"Do you need anything?" asked Marion.

"I think I'd like to go back to sleep," said her dad. "You can go home. I won't be very exciting for a while."

Marion. Marion!

Cara shook Marion out of her memory. They still stood in the butcher shop. Cara shook her hard.

"Marion, come back!" she said.

"What? I'm here," said Marion.

"You weren't responding," said Cara. Marion looked up, over the other people. They all stood still, with blank stares.

"Everyone's frozen," said Marion.

"Yeah," said Cara. "But that's not it." She pointed toward the far side of the room, behind the ominous butcher, his knife still in the air. "Look."

Marion followed her finger to a shadow, and that's all she saw at first. But then she studied harder, her eyes focusing in on the darkness behind the figure, and she saw definition, fine lines of darkness. And then she saw the dark move slowly.

A thing emerged. It wasn't big, perhaps only four feet tall, but it was all wrong. Nothing that size looked like that. It was black, with intertwined sharp limbs, bent at impossible angles, reaching out slowly, pulling itself out of the shadow. Long limbs, with razor sharp mandibles and protrusions, dozens of deadly arms in every direction. But then she saw its face, its face of nothing.

The legs joined at a small thorax, and from it sprung a malformed uneven plate, its head, but it had no face, no eyes, nothing but a dark formless void that threatened to suck you in, to pull you into its nothingness and keep you there forever.

"What is it?" asked Cara, in a brief whisper.

"I don't know," said Marion. "But it's not friendly. We have to find my dad." Marion thought to Mrs. Durbin. Norman, the homeless man. The pets. The grisly deaths from some unidentifiable animal. It wasn't rocket science. This was it.

"What about the people?" asked Cara.

Marion looked at the other folks, frozen in the room. If the two of them ran, they would kill the rest. They couldn't fight this thing, not without a weapon. She glanced around quickly, the thing still stalking from the shadow, getting ready to strike. She came up with a plan.

"When I run, run with me," said Marion. "Lock the door behind us." Marion moved with a flash, and grabbed a metal sheet pan used to hold some fake meat props. She held it high in the air above her head, and then smashed it into the ground over and over, making a terrible rattle in the room. Everyone around them broke free of the reverie.

She didn't wait any longer. The creature's terrible face had turned, and Marion didn't know how much longer it would stalk.

"Fire!" she screamed. "Fire! Get out!"

Everybody in the room yelled and then ran, not even noticing the thing stalking them in the corner. Marion and Cara were right alongside them, and they didn't stop to see what the creature did. They slammed the door behind them and slid the single lock on it shut. The people kept running through the corn area, and Marion continued to yell fire, shaking anyone still frozen by the enchantment of the demon. They all ran, everyone fleeing into the central hall.

Marion and Cara followed everyone into the main room, closing and locking the second door. The dozen people kept running for the exit, with everybody else staring in confusion.

"Where's Dad?" asked Marion, and then she spotted

him, emerging from a back room. He had slipped on his holster. "Dad!"

They ran over to him. "Dad, there's something in the scare room."

"Dark, weird legs, formless head, inspires visions of dread and fear?" he asked.

"Yes," said Marion. "How?"

"Good question," said her dad. "Is it still in there?"

"We locked the doors," said Cara. "And got the people out."

"Good job," he said. "Find Jenny and help her get everyone out of here, as safely as you can."

Janine walked up, also wearing a holster, carrying Fiona.

"Could you watch over Fiona?" asked Janine. She set her down. "Stay with Miss Cara and Marion, okay?" Fiona grabbed Cara's hand, her face confused and afraid.

"You ready?" her dad asked Janine. Janine nodded. Marion went over to the DJ table and grabbed a microphone.

The same hospital smell came back, stronger than before.

Oh no.

Marion's eyes flitted to the shadows, as the same spindly sharp legs emerged from every source of darkness throughout the community center. One, two, three, four, and she continued to count, and then there were too many. Her heart thudded in her chest. They had to run.

"Everyone run!" she yelled into the microphone. "This is not a drill or a scare! Run now!"

They only stared blankly, their eyes looking into the middle distance.

"They're trapped," said Marion. Dad looked over at

them, desperately, and pulled his gun. He fired into the air, three quick shots.

BANG BANG BANG

The party goers shook their heads, knocked out of their daze. The creatures continued to emerge.

Marion put the microphone to her mouth.

"RUN!" she yelled.

Everyone ran, and the night descended into chaos.

36

Whatever measure that had kept these creatures at bay had fallen. They were pouring into the world, a dripping faucet opened to full blast. Mike raised his gun to shoot, but too many people darted between him and his targets.

The crowd screamed and yelled as they ran outside. The crowd pushed through tables and chairs, anything to get away from the nightmares.

Mike tried to count the number of creatures, but he couldn't. They emerged from the shadows like legion. They came from under tables, from the corners of the room, from the darkness cast by a person behind a light.

As the crowd thinned out, Mike saw a creature emerge from a corner. No one in the way now, and he opened fire, the gun loud inside. Four shots. BANG BANG BANG BANG.

All hit the demon in the amorphous disk that served as a head, and the bullets shook it. It paused, and then toppled over, as if it had to decide if it would die or not. But a single monster dead was nothing. There were so many more.

"Kill any you can," he said to Janine, but she was already drawing down on one, shooting, and then moving onto the next.

"Marion, Cara!" yelled Mike. "Get behind us!"

Marion and Cara, both nearby, moved behind the two, Marion carrying little Fiona. He saw Tomas and Bjorn across the room, both with their swords drawn, Jenny in between them holding James. The creatures slowly stalked them, trying to surround them.

"We move to Tomas and Bjorn," said Mike, and they moved as a unit, shooting any of the monsters that approached. Both Mike and Janine reloaded. They only had so much ammo. They couldn't kill them all.

A creature sleekly crawled within range of Bjorn and with a quick slice it lost its head, viscous oil pouring from its body as it slumped over. Tomas stood his ground as three came from the other direction. He swung through one and then down through another. The third poised to strike, its disjointed legs coiling, but Mike fired three quick shots, and it fell over, dead.

The two groups met.

"What is happening?" asked Tomas. "What are these things?"

"The source of the killings," said Mike. "But other than that, I don't know."

"They are not immune to steel," said Bjorn, and he stepped out and swung through another. "But they do stink.

And they bring bad memory."

"It's how they hunt," said Marion. "They paralyze, and then they strike."

"Whatever they send you, ignore it," said Mike. "Don't get lost in it. They'll rip you apart and you won't even know it."

Briiiiiiiiiiiiiing. Briiiiiiiiiiiiiing.

Mike looked over the community center. It was empty now, except for them, and a legion of the creeping creatures. Everyone else had run to the street, out and away. The place was a wreck. The big clown still stood in the middle of the center, but the stampeding crowd had toppled over and ripped apart all their work. The demons slowly crept toward them, oblivious to everything but their prey.

"We need to get outside," said Mike. "Let's move together. Janine and I will cover our six. Tomas and Bjorn, can you carve a path?"

"Yes," said Tomas simply, and they moved as a unit, with Marion, Cara, and Jenny standing in between, protecting Fiona and James. The grim creatures crept in, slowly but inexorably, and Tomas and Bjorn sliced through them as they advanced toward the door which had swung back shut after the last party-goer fled.

Mike's eyes danced across the room. There were so many. There had only been one at a time before. How could this happen? Some doorway had been ripped open, and these creatures were happy to come pouring through to look for a meal. Because that's all they were. It was clear to him now. They were simple predators, and humans were food.

Briiiiiiiiiiiiiing. Briiiiiiiiiiiiiing.

The phone never stopped ringing, the dread and anxiety

of the worst news of his life there, always there, ready to crush him and send him into despair. He didn't know what everyone was hearing or seeing, but he imagined it was just as bad. The demons served as harvesters of sorrow.

The monsters multiplied as he watched. Mike only fired when they threatened to get too close. Janine shot as well, but for every creature they killed, two more took its place. The shadows teemed with them now, and they slowly crawled out one by one, a multitude waiting for their chance if their brother fell by bullet or blade.

The group moved, the square of weapons keeping the creatures at bay as they reached the door. They had to get outside. The creatures were surrounding them, and if they didn't get out now, they never would.

Briiiiiiiiiiiiiiing. Briiiiiiiiiiiiiiing.

Tomas pushed open the door and Mike went through it, his gun drawn and ready to kill anything on the other side. What he saw took his breath away. He thought they had only spawned inside the community center. The sheer number of them had supported that assumption. But he had been wrong.

The creatures were not confined to the community center.

Blood flooded the gutters.

"Mike. Mike!" yelled Tomas. "Move!"

Mike shook himself out of it and pushed through the door, and the group moved behind him, outside the building now. Everyone was shaken as they took in the horror that awaited them on the street.

The monsters weren't as dense on the road as they were inside, but there were still many of them, and they feasted on what remained of the protesters and party-goers. The demons had caught the protesters in their thrall, the sidewalk across the street coated in gore. The horrible disjointed legs of the creatures had ripped apart men, women, and children, and now they fed.

Mike knew they were predators, but he hadn't known how they ate. They had no mouth, no eyes, seemingly no way to eat what they killed. But now he saw it, saw them feed, and it turned his stomach.

"Oh my God," said Jenny, behind him.

"Close your eyes, Fiona," said Janine. Marion put her hand over Fiona's face, and Jenny did the same for James.

"What are they doing?" asked Cara.

"They're eating," said Mike.

The beasts stood over the varied remains of the townspeople of Laurel City, and one by one, they fed. The oblong plates that made up their head, the formless voids that transmitted fear changed and shifted. They took form, as the flesh slipped inward, spiraling, ribbons of dark flesh morphing into rows of gnashing and gnawing teeth, a dark hole at the center. They submerged this displaced maw into the destroyed skin of the dead, and vacuumed up the remains, pulling in pounds of meat.

"What do we do?" asked Janine.

"Find shelter," said Mike. "Protect our space. Don't let them touch us. Whatever the cost."

"Shelter?" asked Bjorn. "Where is safe from these things?"

"I don't know," said Mike.

The door rattled behind them. "We should barricade them inside," said Mike, and grabbed one side of the specter that decorated the front lawn of the community center. Tomas went to the other side, and they dragged it, laying the metal beams across the exit, wedging it as best they could.

The demons ate, but they devoured the dead at an alarming rate. They would finish soon, leaving the sidewalk and street stained with gore. And they would want new targets.

Mike didn't know what to do, or where to go. Where could they go?

The fiends started looking up, pulling up their heads from the bodies, the mouths closing, the plates turning flat and shapeless again, a dark void inside.

Briiiiiiiiiiiiing. Briiiiiiiiiiiiing.

No, not again.

Mike could feel the combined force of the devils, as they called into the air, pulling the worst sorrow and fear into the minds of anyone still alive.

Briiiiiiiiiiiiiing. Briiiiiiiiiiiiiing.

Mike tried to force out the memories, and push out the fear, but the sound of the telephone ringing was there, taunting him. He knew what it would bring; he knew the destruction behind the call. The terrible knowledge that would crush him, would destroy his life. He looked around. Everyone was frozen. Tomas and Bjorn each stared into the middle distance. Janine was lost. Marion and Cara didn't move, their eyes open, staring. Jenny stared past him, at nothing at all. The combined force of all the creatures, all sending out their siren's call of pain and fear all at once was too much to take. Mike had felt it more than anyone, had learned to recognize it, and still, he could feel himself falling into it. Falling into the pit of despair. Facing the stairs, having to tell his only daughter that she would never see her mother alive again.

Mike tried to step in front of the crowd, but there were too many of the creatures. He fired his gun, hoping it would knock someone out from their stunned condition, but the shots did nothing. One creature fell, but there were a dozen more, all coming toward them, to rip them apart, to feast on them.

They crawled.

Briiiiiiiiiiiiiing. Briiiiiiiiiiiiiiing.

Mike dropped his gun, unable to hold on to it anymore. His hands went to his ears. *Please, please, just stop the ringing. I can't take it anymore. I can't take that moment anymore. The deep pain inside that never left him, it was born then, and he couldn't endure that horrible birth for any longer, the phone the goddamn phone*

It was taking him. He looked out at the creatures as they crossed the street. Over a dozen, and they would kill them and eat them, processing their meat to feed more nightmares for future victims.

Mike closed his eyes and felt his mind lapse back into the worst pain of his life.

M M M M M M M M M R R R R R R R R R R R R R - RPPPPPPPPPP.

Mike's eyes snapped open. The noise shook his psyche loose. That wasn't in his head, was it?

M M M M M M M M M R R R R R R R R R R R R R R - RPPPPPPPPPP.

The sound happened again, and now he knew it wasn't in his head. What was it, though? The noise echoed down the street, and one by one, everyone around him snapped out of their trances.

"What is that?" asked Marion, shaking her head.

"It's a truck," said Mike. But not any truck. Mike picked up his pistol.

The trunk's horn rang out again, and soon it was visible, as it rounded a curve, speeding toward the community center. The honking only got louder, and then Mike saw it.

"That's Daniel's truck," said Marion, and Mike moved backward, they all did, the truck came fast, and none of them wanted to be in the way. The monsters stood in the way as it sped toward them, but Daniel didn't slow down, the demons thudding against the front of the vehicle, and then falling below the tires.

The truck was close now, and Daniel saw the slew of beasts in the road, coming toward Mike and the group. He turned the last curve nearly in front of the center, and the truck went half sideways. Mike was worried he'd flip, but Daniel spun the wheel, drifting through the curve and crushing the creatures in the road, as they dully thudded against the undercarriage of the truck. The brakes squealed as the truck stopped, dented from all the demon's bodies.

"Holy shit," said Janine.

Tomas, back in his own head, swung a sword through one of the straggling monsters, chopping it in half. Bjorn joined him. Janine and Mike both opened fire on the few still in the area. The barricade shook behind them, but it did not budge. Mike's eyes swept out through the area. They were safe, for now.

Daniel jumped out of the truck and circled around to Mike. He stood there. He looked so much older than when Mike last saw him.

"Dad—I—" he started, but then Mike rushed him, and

embraced him, with all his strength. Daniel squeezed him back.

"I'm so glad you're here," said Mike. "I love you."

"I love you too," said Daniel.

They broke their hug, and Mike saw Isaac in the front seat, still weak, his eyes closed.

"What happened to him?" asked Mike.

"All of this," said Daniel. "Reverend Laurel did it. He tried to sacrifice Isaac—there's some old Book—he used it, and he summoned these things—"

"Can we stop it?" asked Mike.

"I don't know," said Daniel. "I saved Isaac. I don't know if we can send them back."

"Where is he?" asked Mike.

"He's at the church," said Daniel.

"Then that's where we're heading," said Mike.

37

"What did you see, Daniel?" asked Mike. He sat in the passenger seat of the truck. They had moved Isaac to the bed, along with everyone else who sat back there. They barely fit, but there was no other way. Splitting up was too dangerous. Daniel had to drive slower, but it was still fast enough to avoid the monsters.

"I saw the Book," said Daniel. "And I saw the brick room with the dirty floor."

"I don't—"

"The room is underneath the church. Older than the church. The Reverend said they built the church on top of it, but it's more complicated than that. It doesn't feel like part of the church. It feels like stepping into a different place altogether."

"What do you mean?" asked Mike.

"It's like a different dimension," said Daniel. "I can't explain it."

"And this book?" asked Mike.

"It was old," said Daniel.

"Older than the church?" asked Mike.

"Older than anything I've ever seen," said Daniel. "The Reverend said it was a family heirloom, but I knew right away he was lying. I've never seen the language in it. Or heard it when the Laurels read it. It's impossibly old. Touching it—"

"You touched it?"

Mike paused, looking out ahead at the road lit by the headlights. *Shouldn't we be at the church by now?*

"The Reverend told me to. And even then, I knew I shouldn't, but then—but then it called to me. It pulled me in. It wanted me to touch it. And I did. I couldn't stop myself. And it made everything that came after easier. I guess it controlled me, but it didn't feel like it, then."

"How did he make the monsters appear?"

"It's my fault," said Daniel.

"Don't say that, Daniel—"

"But it is," said Daniel. "He gave me the dagger, and I cut my hand, and my blood flowed onto the floor, and it turned black and the thing came from it—"

"Calm down," said Mike. "Breathe."

Daniel took a deep breath.

"It came from my blood, and then it killed Mrs. Durbin," said Daniel.

"There's more to it then that," said Mike. "What about the book?"

"Reverend Laurel read from it," said Daniel. "He read something, and the thing came out of my blood."

"It's not your fault," said Mike. "It's his fault."

They both jumped as Janine fired from the bed. Three reports rang out. One of the monsters had gotten too close. Mike looked out of the truck, and the creatures encroached from each side, emerging from the shadows.

"Where are we?" asked Mike.

Daniel blinked. "We're heading to the church."

"But we're not getting any closer," said Mike. "We're still in downtown."

"I headed toward the church," said Daniel.

"Something's wrong," said Mike. Janine tapped on the small rear window of the truck, and Mike slid it open.

"You fellas noticing anything wrong?" asked Jenny.

"Yeah," said Mike. "We're not making any progress."

"The streetlights aren't at full power," said Jenny. "Cara noticed it first."

Mike looked out as they drove, and the streetlights were darker than normal. All the buildings they passed seemed dim, even though the power should be totally fine. More and more of the creatures poked out from the shadows. They *were* the shadows at this point.

"You're right," said Mike.

"But that's not all," said Jenny. "Look up. Into the sky."

Mike stuck his head out the window and looked up into the night sky.

"Notice anything wrong?" asked Jenny.

The sky was dark, but Mike saw nothing strange.

"No moon," said Jenny. "It should be nearly a full moon. But nothing."

Mike scanned the sky, and she was right. There was nothing. What was happening to Laurel City?

"The Reverend said he would take back the town," said Daniel. "He said it when he was trying to kill Isaac."

"Who else was there?" asked Mike.

"Abraham, and the rest of LYE," said Daniel. "They were still there when I escaped with Isaac."

"Christ," said Mike. His mind immediately went to the rest of those boys. About what it took to summon one of those things, a dagger and blood from Daniel. How much would it take to summon an army of them? To do this to Laurel City?

"I don't think he has anything to do with this," said Daniel.

"Daniel," said Mike, suddenly.

"What?"

"Daniel! Stop!" yelled Mike, grabbing Daniel's shoulder. He looked ahead and slammed on the brakes, the truck pinwheeling, everyone in the back grabbing a hold of each other, shielding Fiona and James.

The tires squealed to a halt again, but it wasn't because of the creatures this time. They had run out of road. The headlights beamed ahead of them, and for a few feet, it hit the road, but then it disappeared into nothing. The street had faded into the void. The light itself vanished as soon as it hit the edge of darkness.

"Where's the road?" asked Daniel.

"Where's anything?" asked Mike. He got out and walked up to the edge of the void.

"Be careful," said Marion, from the back of the truck. Mike grabbed a pebble and threw it into the great darkness.

It disappeared without a noise, gone, sucked into the nothingness.

Daniel stood beside him. "It's the same as their face," he said. "Of those creatures. It's nothing. That's where it goes. Into nothing."

Mike stared into it, but the same despair and horror that the demons created wasn't there. There was just nothingness.

"Dad!" said Daniel sharply. "Watch your feet."

Mike looked down, and he saw the void spreading, pushing toward them. If they stayed there, it would eat them up.

"We have to move," said Mike.

"But where? Whatever the Reverend did, it's messing with the town," said Daniel. Janine fired again. Mike glanced behind them, and more of the creatures were creeping in. They would never escape them. There would always be more.

"Hurry, gentlemen," yelled Janine.

"We need to stop him," said Mike. "We need to reverse this."

"What if we can't?" asked Daniel.

"There's a way," said Mike. "There has to be."

"How do we get to the church?" asked Daniel.

"I don't know, but let's move," said Mike.

They hurried back to the truck and Daniel threw it into reverse, wheeling it around and then driving forward, away from the approaching void.

The headlights revealed the road ahead of them, and then suddenly a horde of demons were there. They had been following them. The truck thudded as they ran them over. Creature after creature. Hundreds, if not thousands of them.

"Don't slow down," said Mike. Daniel goosed the accelerator, and the truck's engine used its torque to keep going, even as the front bumper was abused. Tomas and Bjorn knelt on each side of the bed, ready to swing at anything that tried to climb up.

"We have to get away from them," said Mike. "There's too many."

"How?" asked Daniel. "Wherever I drive, it ends up away from the church."

"Whatever Laurel has unleashed, it's trying to keep us away," said Mike. "It doesn't want us there."

"How do we get there?" asked Daniel.

Mike didn't know. The community center was only a couple of miles from the church, and they should have easily gotten there. The void was eating up the town, keeping them driving in circles. The creature's numbers would prove too much at some point. They had to break through.

"Break through," said Mike.

"What?" asked Daniel. "Break through what?"

"Turn around again," said Mike.

"Turn around to where? That darkness is out there," said Daniel. "There's nowhere to go behind us."

"It's trying to drive us into the creatures. We have to fight through the void. The only way out is through."

"I don't mean to be an eavesdropper back here, but were you suggesting we drive into that big pit of darkness?" asked Jenny.

"I think it's the only way," said Mike. "It's trying to scare us away."

"Are you sure, Dad?" asked Cara.

"Yes," said Mike. "Turn around, Daniel."

Daniel whipped the truck into a quick U-turn, taking out more creatures.

"I'm out of rounds," said Janine, she said, firing at a creature that tried to swipe at a tire. Mike handed back his gun.

"It has my last clip in it," he said.

Daniel headed back toward the void, with clear driving ahead of them. Within a minute, they'd hit the nothingness.

"I'm sorry, Dad," said Daniel. "I'm sorry for everything."

"Don't be sorry," said Mike. "It's not your fault."

"I—"

"I don't think you can be held responsible for demons taking over the town, son," said Mike. "I'll place the blame squarely on the shoulders of the old Reverend."

"The creature—it showed me the night Mom died," said Daniel. "Over and over and over again."

"Me too," he said. Mike reached over and grabbed Daniel's shoulder, squeezing it. "It's a raw nerve. It always will be. That's why they attacked it. But your mother loved you. And she always will. And she'd be proud of you."

"I—"

"You saved Isaac," said Mike. "After he helped pull you away from your family. You're a good kid. She helped make you that way."

The void approached, only a few hundred feet away.

"Speed up," said Mike. "Floor it."

Daniel put his foot down, and the motor roared.

"Everyone hold on," yelled Mike, to the people in the bed.

The world grew silent except for the roaring of the truck's engine.

Daniel looked straight ahead and then smiled. One hundred feet.

"What's so funny?" asked Mike.

"How'd your party go?" asked Daniel. Fifty feet.

Mike laughed. "It was great. You should have come." Ten.

"Maybe next year," said Daniel. And the truck hit the void.

38

It smelled like a hospital.

It smelled like death.

No, not again.

The stink flooded Marion's nostrils, and she couldn't get it out. It filled her lungs. She was in the hospital again, trying to find her father's room. It was somewhere, and she looked to Daniel for help, but he wasn't here, not this time. She was alone.

"Hello?" she asked, her voice echoing down the antiseptic hallway, looking for help, looking for guidance, but no one was there. The absent beep of machines filtered down to her, but she couldn't find them. All the doors were closed, all the hallways were identical. The signs pointed to the intensive care, and Marion turned to follow them, but there was nothing but more corridor, her father lost somewhere in this labyrinth, trying to find her way to him.

"Dad?" she asked now, yelling down each identical hallway.

This isn't right, this isn't right

No one answered, and she ran, as fast as her young legs could carry her. Where was everyone? Where was Daniel? Where was her dad?

And then she heard the gasping noise, the terrible sound of lungs desperately craving breath, and she ran toward it, the only sound she had heard, and she knew it was her dad, and she had to save him. He was all she had left, and she couldn't lose him too.

She sprinted toward the noise, down the repeating hallways, never drawing closer, never drawing closer, the doors perpetual, all of them shut, dark inside, all of them full of death, and then she saw the door, the gasping breath coming from inside.

She went in.

Dad was there, laying there, tubes inside him, machines surrounding him. They beeped, and blinked, and every breath that came from him was a desperate gasp, because he was dying right there in front of her, and there was nothing she could do about it. Her mother had been taken from her, and so her father would be as well. She would watch him die. She would be all alone.

Her dad turned to look at her, a terrible sadness in his eyes, and his breath rasped in his throat, the machine sound next to him like an industrial pump, a great wheeze that sounded like the churning air of an enormous beast. He reached to her, and she tried to touch him, to comfort him, to be there, to help him, somehow. But she couldn't touch him, his fingers out of reach, and there was no one there to help. Daniel wasn't there, and her mother was long dead, and now her father would die too, leaving her all alone, helpless.

This isn't right.

A voice inside her mind, somewhere deep down, spoke loudly. The voice spread through her, and through the room, and down the long hallways with a great and loud echo.

Marion blinked, her eyes fluttering from the sound.

This didn't happen. You must not be swallowed by your fear.

Marion shook her head, the rasping breath of her dad still there on the hospital bed, but it wasn't him. It was some creation, something summoned from her memories to drown her in this dark void, but it was artificial. Her father had survived, had survived the shooting, and had taken care of her. And she *had* helped him as he recovered. They all had, all of them picking up the slack after Mom died, all of them doing their best to help each other.

Her father's eyes fluttered open, and it was him again, looking weak, but alive, and he would recover. He smiled at them.

And she wasn't alone. And she wouldn't be alone, no matter what.

She looked back, and Daniel was behind her. He lightly touched her shoulder, and she stepped into the room.

*

Mike was drowning.

A tidal wave had enveloped him, taken out his legs, and had pushed him underneath, grief subsuming him. He couldn't breathe, trying to force his way to the surface, but there was nothing but pain and sorrow filling his lungs.

The call had come, and he had answered, and his wife, his best friend, his love and lover was gone, dead, and now he was alone with waves of despair that hit him hard, over and over again. Tears rolled down his cheeks, but he didn't feel them, couldn't feel anything except overwhelming pain rolling through his body. He would have to climb the stairs, and tell his daughter that her mother was gone, take that agony inside of him and share it with someone that he loved more than anything on Earth.

He couldn't move, his legs full of cement, of the inertia of sadness and torment and grief, and every ounce of him wanted to give up, wanted to collapse there, to give in, to surrender. To let go of his responsibilities, and wallow in that sadness.

Get up. Be a father.

His own voice shook him, the linoleum floor under his hands. He couldn't sit there, no matter the hurt or heartache. Marion needed him. Daniel needed him. He would shoulder that burden, regardless of how much it weighed.

Mike forced himself to his feet, his legs jello beneath him. They wobbled, but he pressed his feet flat, and took a step. His lungs burned, still full of sorrow, but he took leaden steps forward, out of the kitchen.

He would walk up the stairs. He would tell Marion her mother was dead. He would be their father.

The stairway stood in front of him, a dozen steps transformed into a thousand, an impossible journey, an infinite experience of dread, waiting to get to the top, because the pain wasn't in the telling, it was in the anticipation of heartache.

He took a step just the same, forcing his heavy feet up, his hand gripped like iron around the wooden banister. He would crack it with his strength if that's what it would take, pulling himself to the top.

The stairs multiplied, infinite in front of him. He would never reach the end, and there would be no conclusion to his grief, no ending to his sadness. But he took another step, his arm straining as he forced himself up. He pulled and lifted his legs with all his strength, each step impossible, but he did it anyway.

The steps were infinite, and then he reached the top.

Marion's door was down the hallway, and he heard her playing inside with her toys. His breath caught in his throat, but he walked and stopped at her door, and knocked twice softly before pushing the door open. Marion was young, only ten, and she sat on the floor, her toys surrounding her.

"Hi, Dad," she said, glancing at him before continuing with her toys.

He sat down next to her. He told her the news. They cried together.

Marion stopped first.

"We should go get Daniel," said Marion. "He's all alone."

"You're right," said Mike, his heart bursting. "Let's go."

*

The sound of his mother choking to death filled Daniel's ears.

No, not again, please no.

There was no other noise, not now. No sirens, no sounds of clinking glass from the street, no shouts from bystanders. The only sound was his mom trying to breathe through the fountain of blood that filled her lungs.

He knew she was there, next to him, and he could avert his eyes, but that's not what happened. He looked right at her and watched her as she died. And so he did, looking to his left, his body trapped, and he saw her there, the horrific piece of metal skewering her.

And so he watched, and her harried breathing was all that he heard. Of her trying to force breath into her lungs, but finding only blood. And he was trapped, trapped in that moment. And his mom reached out to caress his cheek, and wipe away his tears, her hand dripping blood.

But instead it wrapped around his throat, choking him.

And the wheezing, gasping sound coming from his mother was interrupted by a guttural bellow, dark and angry.

"Your fault," she said, choking him, Daniel trying to move but unable, pinned by the airbags, by the crushed frame of the car. His mother's voice now filled his ears, and all he heard was her, her anger, her rage, her disappointment in him.

"It was your fault, Daniel," she said again, her damaged mouth spitting blood with every dark word. "It was your fault I died. My blood is on your hands. They will stare and know you killed your mother."

Daniel couldn't breathe, his mother's grip tightening around his throat, and he knew it didn't make any sense, she would have died by now, but she persisted, screaming, her words filling the small car, red flying from her mouth onto him, and the terror filled him, trying to breathe, trying to do anything, but he was trapped here—

It's not your fault, Daniel.

His father's voice found him, his memory echoing in his mind.

And he wasn't in the car anymore, his mother's death only a thought again. He sat in the hospital room, waiting for his father to arrive, and then he was there, holding Daniel tightly. And Daniel looked into his eyes.

"It's not my fault," said Daniel.

39

The truck burst through the void, and they were at the church. Daniel slammed on the brakes as they hit the curb and roared up the front steps. Everyone in the bed held on, sliding around violently as they screamed to a stop again.

They looked around, everyone glancing at each other. They all had experienced the void, the bleak place that had taken their worst pain and amplified it. But they all were there now.

The church wasn't the same. The great building was gone now, every piece of wood, the steeple, every piece of stained glass. All gone. Mike jumped out of the truck and climbed the steps. Daniel followed him. What had the Reverend done?

Only one thing remained, in a pit that used to be the

foundation of the church.

A red brick room, with a dirty floor. The Reverend stood in it, the Book in his hands. He read from it.

In front of him was a portal. And something was coming out.

Reverend Laurel read from the Book in the middle of the destruction. Silence filled the air, aside from the snarls and grim noises that emerged from him. A thinning of the air stood next to him. Underneath it laid Abraham, dying. Around him were the remains of the boys from LYE. There had been a price for the army of demons that invaded Laurel City. Daniel had counted them all as friends, and now they were all dead. Isaac would have been among them. Daniel too.

"What are you doing, Reverend?" asked Mike, yelling down into the pit.

He continued speaking in the ancient language that sounded like warfare off his tongue, without looking up. The portal was darkness, filled with the void, just like the barrier to the church, and the faces of the creatures. But something emerged from it, a visceral piece of amorphous flesh, reaching through the portal, trying to grab at this side. It was all shapes and none, and Daniel couldn't categorize it, because it resisted the human eye. But it was there, and it was coming through.

The group stood there, looking down.

Janine raised Mike's pistol. "Stop reading, or I will shoot you," she said.

His strange words continued for a moment more, and then he stopped. He closed his eyes and then opened them, peering up at them. He shut the tome and smiled.

"Please, Officer, I'm sure there's a way we can solve this without violence."

"What are you doing, Reverend?" asked Mike.

"Laurel City was chosen," said Laurel. "Chosen long, long ago. Chosen when Elijah Laurel found this Book, and it led him here, to this very spot. And no matter how much you want to corrupt this town, Mr. Dawson, it still is chosen. And it still belongs to me."

Bjorn and Tomas both looked around, their swords out. Tomas spoke to Mike out of the corner of his mouth. "This seems like a trap," he said. "Where are the demons?" There were no sign of them in what was left of the church. Nothing poked from the shadows. The thing coming through the portal was the only aberration.

"I don't know," said Mike.

"There are no creatures here," said the Reverend, tucking the Book under his arm and walking toward them. He steered clear of the portal, still, and Daniel's eye went to it. He thought he saw it grow slightly wider, a little larger. The thing that wasn't, slowly pushing its way into their world.

"I didn't corrupt your city, Reverend," said Mike. "I didn't unleash those things onto the town. They've killed dozens, if not hundreds. All I did was throw a party."

"You defied God, Mr. Dawson," said Reverend Laurel.

Daniel looked at Reverend Laurel's face, and there was still no doubt in it. There was no question in his mind of his righteousness. Even after all of this. Laurel still thought he served God.

"Why aren't we going down there and kicking his ass?" asked Bjorn.

"He might still have a trick up his sleeve," said Mike. "I

don't want to risk it."

"Whatever's coming through there does not belong," said Tomas. They didn't hide their voice now, and the Reverend only stared up at them. He stared at Daniel.

"Daniel," he called. "Why do you stand with them? Why do you stand with those heathens?"

"You shut your mouth," said Mike, his anger spiking.

Laurel ignored him. "You were with us, and then you betrayed us. We brought you into our family, and this is how you repay me? By taking my grandson from me? By betraying my plans?"

Daniel could feel his cheeks redden again, the same rage that he had felt so long ago when he argued with his dad, and he wanted to think of something, something he could catch the Reverend with. Something clever and brilliant to trap him in his lies.

But he couldn't think of anything. It wouldn't matter, anyway. Laurel would never see his hypocrisy, no matter if Daniel bellowed at him for a thousand years. Daniel looked at Marion, and saw the fear in her eyes, saw the hollow stare. She had endured so much because of him. And Daniel's rage doubled. He had no words, and before anyone could stop him, he charged down into the pit, and tackled Reverend Laurel again, driving him into the ground and then beating him with his fists, the Book under his arm flying.

Laurel fell like a sack of potatoes, all the air driven out of him. Daniel was on top of him, and punched him, repeatedly.

Mike was right behind him, stunned by Daniel's sudden action, but Daniel had already hit Laurel a half dozen times before Mike reached him, and tried to pull him off.

He struggled, and then Tomas and Bjorn were there, helping Mike, and Daniel felt himself lifted off the old man, who lay bloody in front of them.

"You're better than him," said Mike.

"He deserves worse," said Daniel, finally.

"He's done," said Mike. "We've stopped him."

"You've stopped nothing," said Laurel, sitting up, spitting blood out onto the dirty floor. "Do you think I stopped reading because you threatened me? I only had to finish the page, and I did. There is no ending what I've started."

"You're lying," said Marion. "There has to be a way to reverse it."

Laurel pushed himself to his feet. The bodies of the boys surrounded them. Abraham still moved, if but slightly, underneath the portal. He crawled toward the Book.

Reverend Laurel smiled. Blood stained his teeth, running from his busted nose and lips. Daniel had hurt him, but he didn't seem to care.

"You'll never know," said Laurel. "None of you can understand God's glory. Soon you'll realize. Soon you'll grasp His Will."

"Watch yourself, Reverend," said Jenny. The grasping flesh that wasn't reached out from the slowly widening portal. It swept at the air inches away from the Reverend."

"You still don't understand," he said, still smiling. "I don't need to avoid God's grasp. He has chosen me, just as he has chosen my city." He stepped within range of the thing from the portal, and it seized him. It grabbed him and didn't, the non-flesh not quite touching him, but *becoming* him. It took the primordial essence of Reverend Laurel and absorbed him, and he screamed. Whatever the thing did to him, the deep voice of the Reverend was gone, and he screamed and screamed as the thing ate him alive, as they became one, and then the screams turned into nothing as his lungs and throat were a part of it. The twitching creature grew slightly.

They all stared as the not-flesh enveloped him.

"What do we do?" asked Janine.

"I—"

"There has to be a way," said Marion. "This can't be it." She held Cara's hand. Tomas had sheathed his sword and held James. Bjorn did the same and put his arm over Tomas' shoulder. Janine handed Mike his gun and picked up Fiona, bringing her close.

"That was supposed to work," said Daniel, quietly.

"We can't give up," said Mike.

"The Book," said Daniel. Abraham still crawled to it, now out from the orbit of the portal, his chest heaving with exertion. Daniel ran over to it.

"Don't touch it," said Mike. "Remember what you said."

"You must," said Abraham, rolling over and sitting up. "If you want to close that thing, you must touch it."

"What do you mean?" asked Mike. They surrounded Abraham as he sat up against the brick wall, his eyes staring only at the Book.

"The Book. It is now a beacon," he said, every word work. Every breath was halting. He was dying.

"A beacon for what?" asked Marion.

Abraham's eyes finally left the tome and went to the portal. "To that. To whatever lay on the other side. To God."

"That's not God," said Jenny.

"Isn't it?" asked Abraham. "I have spent my entire life studying two holy Books. One of them has led to nothing.

No results. Empty words. The other—it has led to this."

"But this is—unholy. Inhuman," said Jenny.

"Yes," said Abraham. "But it is God, nonetheless."

"You said it was a beacon," said Mike. "What do you mean?"

"As long as the Book is here, it calls to Him," said Abraham.

"Then we destroy it," said Daniel.

"You should know better, son," said Abraham. "You've touched it. It cannot be destroyed. Whenever, however it was created, it is indestructible now. It cannot be burnt, or damaged. It is forever, like He is."

"Then how do we stop it?" asked Mike.

"You must take it to the other side," said Abraham, finally, his eyes back on the Book. "It is the only way. Return it to Him."

"How do we know you're telling the truth?" asked Mike.

"You don't," said Abraham. "But it is the truth. The Book is power, and so is He." He paused, and took a big, halting breath. "I never asked to be a part of this. I didn't ask for this name."

"What's on the other side?" asked Mike.

Abraham still stared at the Book.

"Abraham!" said Mike, but he did not reply. He had died. Whatever ritual the Reverend had inflicted upon him, it had taken its toll.

"Fuck," said Mike. They all looked at the portal, and it grew wider still, and more of the thing, whatever it was, was intruding into their world. Daniel only stared at the Book, his and Abraham's eyes on it.

Jenny reached down and picked it up. She blinked and

held it. She shook her head once. Daniel recognized it as she shook off its influence.

"What are we waiting for?"

"Hey, wait," said Mike.

"Whatever it is," she said, "we don't need it here." She chucked it at the portal, but it floated through the strange flesh of the creature, thudding on the ground across the room.

"It has to be carried through," said Daniel, who walked over to it and picked it up.

"How do you know?" asked Marion.

"I have eyes," said Daniel. "And I watched the Reverend. The thing absorbed him. We have to do the same, while holding the Book. *I* have to do the same."

Everyone stood silent, staring at him. Daniel looked right back, his grip on the Book firm.

"What are you doing, Daniel?" asked his dad, approaching him.

"I'm fixing the problem I helped make," said Daniel, dangerously close to the grasping other.

"This isn't your fault," he said. "I told you—"

"It doesn't change the fact that someone died because of my blood," he said. Daniel felt the tension rise in his chest, but it wasn't guilt. It was righteousness. He would make up for his mistakes. He would fix it this time.

"Please, Daniel," said his father. "I can't lose you."

"Someone has to do it, Dad," said Daniel. "Everyone else here has someone they need to take care of. I'm the odd man out. It's okay. I want to do it."

His father looked at him, his eyes tearing up. He closed them, and a tear trickled down his cheek. Marion walked to him, and he hugged her, kissing her hard on the top of her head. Tomas, Bjorn, Janine, Jenny. They all watched on. They didn't want to be the ones to do it. They would let Mike decide.

"Okay, son," he said, finally. "You can do it. But let me say goodbye. Can I hug you first? Please?"

Daniel looked him in the eye and cried. He nodded, clinging to the Book. He wouldn't let him take it. He would be the one to sacrifice.

His father stepped firmly around the ever-widening portal, the creature getting closer and closer to this side. More and more of it was poking through. It was time, now or never.

His father held his arms wide, and Daniel let him come in close.

THUCK

There was a sudden whip of movement and Daniel couldn't breathe. He gasped for breath, but only a whisper of wind came into his lungs. He couldn't move, he *needed air*. He fell down, and then he realized the Book wasn't in his hands anymore. His dad had punched him in the throat.

His father stood over him. Daniel's hands were at his neck. He couldn't breathe still, except he could, just enough. Dad spoke in his ear.

"I love you," he said. "You have a long life ahead of you. Take care of your sister. And let her take care of you." Daniel reached for him as he turned away, but all his strength was gone.

Mike looked to Marion, to Jenny, to all of them. "I'm sorry." And he stepped into the grasp of the creature. It made no sound, but they all felt it anyway, something pulling and pushing at them, and then the portal, and Mike, were gone.

40

Chief Miller sat behind his desk in his pajamas. It was the middle of the night.

Marion stood next to Janine. The whole group was there. They all still wore their Halloween costumes. Marion felt shell-shocked. Dad had vanished into a hellish portal not even an hour ago. She was more worried about Daniel. He had wanted to sacrifice himself, but Dad wouldn't let him. He hadn't said a word since it had happened. He had only hugged her and cried.

Laurel City returned to normal after the portal closed. The dark void that obfuscated the church was gone, and the demons had disappeared. Marion kept expecting to see more of them emerging from the shadows, but it didn't happen. They had vanished.

The dead didn't return, though. The slew of deceased outside the party were still gone, and who knows how many they killed during the night.

"So. Let me get this straight," said Miller. He looked harried and uncomfortable. She didn't blame him. It wasn't reasonable to expect him to be comfortable with a demon bomb going off in his town. "Demons attacked during the Halloween party and murdered a bunch of people."

"Yes," said Janine.

"And these demons were summoned here by Reverend Laurel, who sacrificed all the youth group boys to do it?"

"Yes."

"And the Laurels come from a long line of demon worshipers, and they had some sort of ancient, powerful book that helped them keep control of the town."

"Yes."

"And the Reverend was trying to summon some other monster here, and give it the city, but Mike sacrificed himself to stop it from happening."

"Yes," said all of them, together.

"Jesus Christ," said Chief Miller. "I think I'm in over my head."

"I think we all are," said Jenny.

"Are you all alright?" he asked.

"Physically? We're all mostly fine," said Janine. "But we watched demons kill a bunch of people, and then saw our friend and/or family member willingly send himself to some hell dimension to save the city."

"So…not good," said Miller, nodding. "But the demons are gone?"

"We think so," said Marion.

"You think so? Or you know so?" asked Miller.

"The Laurels are all dead or absorbed by some monster, Chief," said Janine. "The Book is gone too. We don't know what we're doing."

The Chief shook his head. "Well, we've got a bunch of dead people, and a church that's half disappeared. We can't tell people demons did it, can we?"

"Are you asking *us* what to do about it?" asked Jenny.

Miller shrugged.

Cara piped in. "Can't you call, like, the X-Files or something?"

Miller stared at her, raised his eyebrows, and picked up the phone.

*

Daniel and Marion sat in their living room. Agent Bowman sat across from them. They had arrived en masse on November 1st and had picked apart the town. Bowman was average height, slender, and wore a black suit. He took his sunglasses off when he entered their house.

"You mind if I record this?" asked Bowman.

They both shook their heads. "We're not in trouble, are we?" asked Marion.

"No," said Bowman. "But you have information I need. I was told your father was the one who took the Book back over."

"Yes," said Marion.

"My condolences," said Bowman. "He's a brave man."

"Thanks," said Marion, not knowing what else to say.

"Start from the start," said Bowman. "Tell me everything."

And they did, bouncing back and forth, telling the story as best they knew it. About moving to Laurel City, about Halloween, about the demons. Bowman didn't act shocked about any of the details. He took notes in a small notebook, while his phone recorded it all.

"And that's it?" he asked, when they had wound down the story.

"I think so," said Marion. He reached down and turned off the recording.

"I can't believe that Laurel pulled the trigger just because of Halloween," said Bowman. He started gathering his things.

"Is that it?" asked Marion.

"I think so," said Bowman.

"Wait, wait a second," said Daniel. "Can we ask *you* something?"

Bowman paused and glanced between them. "You two aren't going to call the newspaper, are you?"

"We weren't planning on it," said Marion.

"Then sure. Shoot."

"You weren't surprised by any of this," said Marion.

"No, not really," he said.

"You knew about the Book, didn't you?"

"It had gotten lost a long time ago," said Bowman. "We've been looking for it, but the Laurels have been good at hiding it."

"What exactly was it?" asked Daniel.

"We don't really know," said Bowman. "You probably have a better idea than I do. You touched it. What did it feel like?"

"It felt older than life," said Daniel.

"It's been on our radar," said Bowman. "It's good that it's gone. Fewer things like that, the better."

"There are more of those Books out there?" asked Daniel.

"Not exactly," said Bowman. "But things like it. Things we don't understand."

"Do *you* know what's on the other side of that portal?" asked Marion. "Do you know where our dad went?"

Bowman stared at them for a second. "I don't know. We've had—contact with that place before. It's never gone well."

Marion heard Daniel sigh next to her. He had hoped for a way to get him back.

"Anything else?" asked Bowman.

"Yeah," said Marion. "What's gonna happen?"

"What do you mean?" asked Bowman.

"I mean, what are we going to tell everyone? Nearly a hundred people died. Even more saw those things. Someone will tell the news."

"No, they won't," said Bowman.

"What? Why not?"

"Because we'll pay them," said Bowman. "We'll give them a cover story, and a stipend for keeping it up for the rest of their lives. You two included."

"The FBI pays people to cover things up?" asked Daniel.

Bowman got up and put on his sunglasses.

"I never said I was with the FBI. Have a nice day. Again, condolences for your father."

41

"Dawson, Daniel," said the principal, and Daniel stepped up and shook his hand, and took his diploma. Marion smiled from the crowd. Jenny sat next to her. The audience was a little thin, but everyone applauded all the same. He called up Isaac Laurel later. The applause was a little lighter, then. The town still hadn't gotten over what the Laurels had done.

The town had lost a good portion of its population, and the church was just gone. Isaac had recovered with time, and he had the brick room with the dirty floor bulldozed, and the lot razed. It was just dirt at the moment.

The truth hadn't gotten out yet, and Marion didn't think it ever would. The government stipend was generous, more than enough to live on, and no one wanted to lose it. Nobody mentioned it on the street, and even in closed company they didn't say much. Everyone wished to forget Halloween night. Everybody had faced the worst.

People used the money to buy frivolous things to help salve the wounds. There were a lot more boats in Laurel City.

The cover story was cultists, led by the Laurels. They had used the Church as a shield and had gone crazy and killed a bunch of people. They had burned down their own church and the Reverend with it. There were holes in the story, but no one talked, and with the news cycle the way it was, the insane report about the cult vanished in the wind after a couple weeks. It wasn't too far from the truth, so it was easy for everyone to accept.

Jenny took them out for lunch after the ceremony, with Marion, Daniel, and Cara. They had all been there for each other after Halloween. Jenny, Tomas, Bjorn, Janine…they had all picked up the slack with Mike's absence, as much as they could.

The house was quiet when they got home. Daniel sat down on the couch and leaned back against it, his eyes closed. Marion and Cara exchanged a glance, and Cara understood, going upstairs.

"No more high school," said Marion.

"No more high school," said Daniel. "Now I have to grow up."

"I mean, with the stipend, you really don't have to. We could easily live off of it for the rest of our lives." Marion sat down in the easy chair.

"I can't just sit around," said Daniel.

"Do you know what you want to do?" asked Marion.

"Not yet," he said. "I'll figure it out over the summer."

Silence settled in.

"I miss Dad," said Daniel, his eyes tearing up.

"I miss him too," said Marion. "He'd be proud of you."

"I know," said Daniel. He started crying then, sobbing, and buried his hands in his face. Marion got up and sat next to him, and put her arm around him, as best she could. She grabbed a tissue from the box nearest her and handed it to him. He blew his nose, and she gave him another.

"I wish—I wish we knew what happened to him. I wish we knew what was on the other side," said Daniel. After seeing what was trying to come into our world, Marion wasn't sure she wanted to know. She had made peace with Dad being dead. They had no Book, and no sources that could connect them.

"He loved us," she said. "And we loved him. He did what he did for us. He would want us to live our lives as best we could."

"I know," said Daniel.

The door thudded with three heavy knocks, and they both jumped.

"Jesus," said Marion.

"It's probably the landscaper," said Daniel. "He was supposed to come today."

"I'll get it," said Marion.

The door thumped again.

"I'm coming, I'm coming," said Marion. "Hold your horses."

She opened the door, expecting to see the landscaper, but it wasn't him.

It was a ghost.

It was Dad.

He looked haggard, still wearing the Halloween costume

she had last seen him in. It was covered in blood and sweat and grime. His eyes were sallow and sunken, and a scar marked his right cheek.

"Oh, Marion," he said, and embraced her, squeezing her with all his might. Marion started crying, hugging him back. It was impossible. It was impossible.

Daniel was there, staring, unbelieving.

"Daniel," said their father, and he ran in and hugged him too. Daniel hugged him back, and then Marion joined them.

"How?" asked Marion.

"When is it?" he asked.

"It's May," said Marion. "You've been gone for seven months."

"Seven months?" he said, thinking to himself, nodding, muttering something under his breath. His eyes darted around the house. "Seven months. Okay."

"Dad," said Daniel, suddenly, and Marion looked to him, and saw that he stared at what was in his arms. She looked and saw it. "Why did you bring that back?"

He held the Book.

"I had to," he said. "It's our only weapon against them. They're coming. I have to stop them."

Enjoy War on Halloween?

Sign up here to be notified about Robbie's next novel!

robbiedorman.com/newsletter

Acknowledgements

Thank you to my wife Kim, for her patience and support, and my team of beta readers: Andrew, Matt, Megan, Yousef. Thank you for reading.

About the Author

Robbie Dorman believes in horror. War on Halloween is his fifth novel. When not writing, he's podcasting, playing video games, or petting cats. He lives in Texas with his wife, Kim.

You can follow Robbie on Twitter @robbiedorman

His website is robbiedorman.com

Subscribe to his newsletter at robbiedorman.com/newsletter